When Emiliah Bent meets sexy, powerful CEO Ben Goodall, her world is turned upside down in a whirlwind of passion. Yet, beneath the surface of their blossoming relationship lies a darkness—a danger that threatens to shatter everything Emiliah holds dear.

As their love deepens, so does the peril surrounding her. With each heartbeat, they dance on the edge of danger, their passion igniting a flame that both consumes and exhilarates.

When secrets are unveiled and shadows emerge from the past, Emiliah must confront the truth: the man she loves harbors secrets darker than she ever imagined and her own ghosts threaten to surface, ruining the life she has so carefully constructed.

In a race against time, Emiliah must navigate the treacherous waters of love and deception, where every kiss could be a betrayal and every touch could lead to destruction.

Cover design by Alexis Saez
© 2024 Revelson SAS
www.revelson.com

9 781617 048012

The Story of Emiliah Bent

HANNAH DICKSON

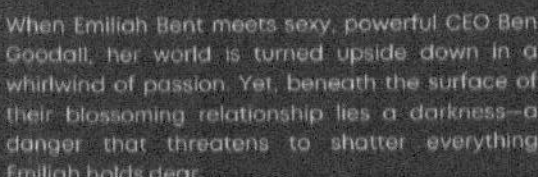

HANNAH DICKSON

With contributions from
Dominic Dickson
Claire Blin

First published by Revelson.

ISBN 9781617048012

Disclaimer:

Although loosely inspired by events that took place in a small village in the Limousin region of France in the 1990s, this book is mainly a work of fiction. Names, characters, places, and incidents are the product of the author's imagination or are used fictitiously. To the author's knowledge, no human trafficking took place in the village, and no British citizens were involved in any way in the abuse of young foster children witnessed by the author at the time.

WARNING: THIS BOOK CONTAINS GRAPHIC PHYSICAL, VERBAL, EMOTIONAL AND SEXUAL ABUSE SCENES THAT SOME READERS MAY FIND DISTURBING.

THE STORY OF EMILIAH BENT

Raised in Winchester, UK, Hannah Dickson moved to a small village in the Limousin Region of France, in 1991, with her family. She attended the local primary school, where she witnessed the abuse of several foster children by the headmaster and mayor. At the age of fourteen, she was sexually assaulted by one of the village's foster fathers, leading her to believe that child abuse in the village was systemic. Hannah went on to study international law and political science at Toulouse University and Sciences-Po Toulouse, and later graduated from Grenoble University with a Master's degree in intellectual property law. After a year working in PR in the UK in 2006, she moved to Paris to join an international PR agency in the technology sector. In 2012, she joined a surgical startup accelerator in Grenoble, before taking on the role of legal director of a surgical robotics company. Hannah lives in Grenoble with her two children and lunatic staffie.

Dominic Dickson also moved to the Limousin village, with Hannah and the rest of their family. He developed friendships with other teenagers in the village, in particular with several of the village's foster children. After high school, he moved away from the area and held various jobs in the South and West of France, working as a waiter, gardener and ratcatcher, and sometimes living on the street. Dominic is now a landscape gardener. He lives in Limoges with his girlfriend, Emmanuelle.

Claire Blin and her older brother Christophe were abandoned by their mother at the ages of two and four. They were then placed in foster care in the Limousin village. Claire and Christophe attended the local primary school, where Christophe and Hannah were in the same class in 1991-92. Christophe was the headmaster's favorite target, and the punishments he was subjected to were, from Hannah's perspective, shockingly sadistic. Christophe tragically died of cancer at the age of thirty-seven. Claire, after having been prevented from pursuing her dream of becoming a truck driver in her youth, eventually became a qualified forty-four-ton lorry driver at the age of twenty-six. She is a single mother of three, and misses her brother every day.

Disclaimer

Although loosely inspired by events that took place in a small French village in the 1990s, this book is mainly a work of fiction. Names, characters, places, and incidents are the product of the author's imagination or are used fictitiously. To the author's knowledge, no human trafficking took place in the village, and no British or Irish citizens were involved

in any way in the abuse of young foster children witnessed by the author or contributors at the time.

Trigger warning

WARNING: THIS BOOK CONTAINS GRAPHIC PHYSICAL, VERBAL, EMOTIONAL AND SEXUAL ABUSE SCENES THAT SOME READERS MAY FIND DISTURBING.

THE STORY OF EMILIAH BENT

By Hannah Dickson

With contributions from Dominic Dickson & Claire Blin

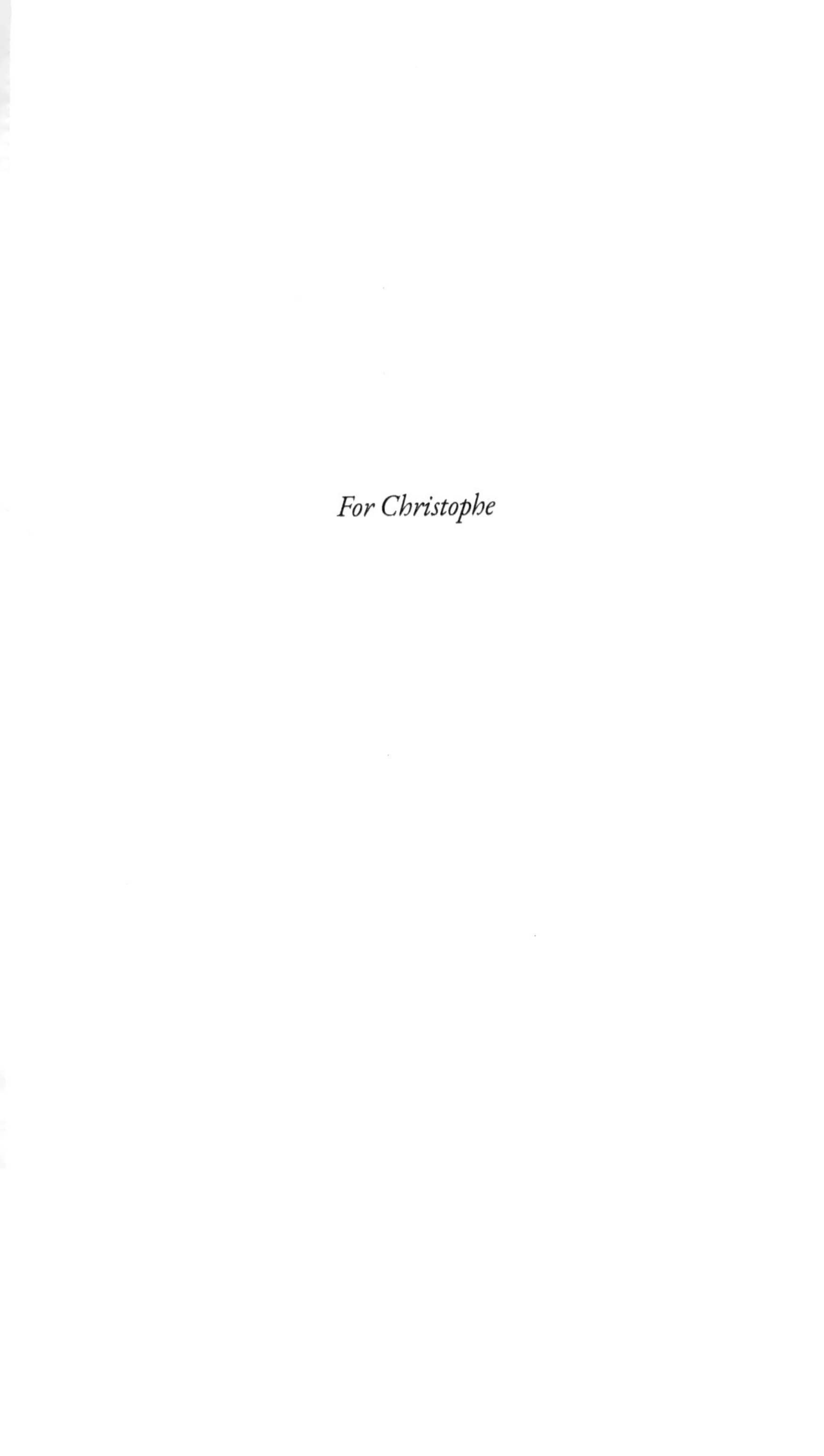

For Christophe

PROLOGUE

Here I am, in Purgatory. A waiting room for sinners.

An ant hauls a lifeless lizard across a lone flagstone, pausing now and then to navigate its massive, tragic burden. Even in this ethereal place, death and the struggle for life persistently echo.

This isn't what I'd envisioned. I'm untethered, floating in an oddly tranquil landscape of ancient stone structures encased by a tapestry of azaleas, tulips, chrysanthemums, and roses. Amidst the floral chaos, weeds stubbornly claim their space while figures draped in white meander between light and shadow under a brooding, cloudy sky. There's someone I'm meant to meet at some point. But in this place, time is a nebulous concept. Have I been here a day or months?

A judgment looms, undetermined, unknown. The inevitability of consequence has been a companion of mine ever since the long, serrated knife, cold and resolute, found a home in my hand. I knew retribution would seek me out. But this? Purgatory, with its strange beauty and stark contrasts?

It's funny, isn't it, how life unravels in the most unexpected ways? I don't think anyone would have expected me to commit murder. It just goes to show, doesn't it? You never really know people, not even yourself.

Even now, the label 'killer' doesn't quite fit. I've tried playing with the word, but it's strange and alien, like running my tongue over the hole left by a missing tooth. I'm numb, removed from any semblance of feeling, still grappling with my darkly lit identity. After all, when you've killed someone, that act becomes you. Whatever else you have done, good or bad, brave or cowardly, is irrelevant. I suppose I've yet to fully embrace my true identity. Part of the reason I'm here is to reflect on my actions. Repent maybe. At the very least, I should ask myself what made me do it. But all I can think of is that very first mistake.

1

For the first time, I saw details I'd never noticed: stacks of ancient press kits on mock-wood shelves, faded framed adverts with clever phrases in out-of-date fonts, plastic plants, dusty magazines. Meloda and I always came to the windowless basement for our 'meetings', but until today I'd been much more focused on our conversations than on the space itself.

She sat, staring at me. "When you say, 'entire press list', do you mean—?"

I nodded.

Meloda gasped. "Jesus. What were you thinking, Em?'

"I don't know." My voice was unnaturally high-pitched. I honestly didn't understand. I'd been swamped. Thaddeus had called. He'd wanted me to rewrite the entire press release. I searched the dusty room for an answer.

Meloda pulled the laptop back towards her. "Let me read it again."

It didn't take long. She looked at me doubtfully. "Maybe

we should tell Vince. Do some damage control, you know?"

Damage control? This damage was beyond control. "No, Meloda. We are not telling Vince. No way."

Once again, I wondered how I could have been so stupid. I'd been in a frenzy. The hotel manager in Shanghai had been so uncooperative, not wanting to accommodate the thirty or so vegan guests. We were still struggling to obtain visas for about half the journalists, and the event messaging was far from finished.

Then, in the middle of it all came the phone call from Thaddeus, consumer technology PR manager at CLOUTech. CLOUTech or 'CLOUT' for short, was our largest client and a major IT manufacturer. Not quite Apple, but still, pretty big. Thaddeus was my main client; not the most senior, nor, by a long shot, the sharpest, but the one responsible for 'managing' the PR agency. I dreaded Thaddeus's calls. Dreaded them. And his call could only have meant one thing: he'd finally gotten around to reading the press release I'd drafted for the new external hard drive launch and had his own ideas on its improvement.

I'd picked up the phone reluctantly. "Yes?"

Why hadn't you just ignored it? Asked my inner critic.

'Hi Emily, I just read your press release on the new hard drive. I have some ideas about how we can improve this together.'

Of *course* he'd got my name wrong. "Hi Thaddeus. You know, now's not the best time. The Shanghai event is next week, and there are so many other priorities right now…'

'Yeah,' he'd interrupted vaguely, "I've been thinking. There's just too much 'sleek' and 'stylish' crap in this release. Send me something more exciting, something sexier. Something along the lines of… hmmm, something like 'Black is back in business' or 'Be in the game with CLOUTech's latest external hard drive'. Hey, I'm just throwing ideas around here; I don't want to write this thing for you. That's what I pay *you* to do." He'd laughed at his own cleverness. "Surprise me. Don't just write down what I said."

"OK, Thaddeus, I'll work on it and get back to you ASAP."

"Yeah. Today would be good."

"OK." It had come out as a squeak. "Bye then."

"Ciao, Emily."

I'd tried to concentrate. Of course, I couldn't deny that describing an external hard drive as 'sleek' and 'stylish' with a 'glossy black piano finish' was ridiculous, but that was the game we played here at work. We had meetings in which we talked about such ludicrous notions as 'sexy products', 'wow factors', seeing things from a 'PR perspective.' That was how this profession worked, but sometimes I had the impression Thaddeus didn't actually understand that the entire setup was a farce that you just had to go along with.

So I had set to work 'tweaking' (another grotesque term I'd learned to use) the press release. Who in their right mind was going to read a press release about an external hard drive? Who? I knew that not one journalist would be interested in this 'news' item, but I'd long since figured out that you never share such certitudes. And at CLOUTech, whose leadership was ironically weak, all the whiney product managers insisted on having a press release for every single product. They couldn't reach their sales targets without a press release, or so they claimed. The result was a constant flow of emails we were forced to send to the press, and which, of course, no-one ever read. Written diarrhoea. Uncomfortable. Incurable. But it paid my bills, so who was I to complain?

I'd been struggling to find a new angle for the damned press release when the strangest thing happened. A limerick popped into my head. It was stupid, but I couldn't dislodge it for the life of me.

Now, I have this thing with limericks. A long, long time ago, when I first read Roald Dahl's *Matilda,* I became obsessed with limericks. I felt like I had so much in common with Matilda, except for her exceptional intelligence, ability to make things fly, and such. Anyway, I must have read the book about two hundred times and spent many an afternoon 'inventing' limericks. After a while, they just popped into my head, and I couldn't shake them off.

I'd be in class with Mr. Gillie, and suddenly, I'd be thinking:

There was a man called Gillie

Who had a very large willy

Attempting to hide it

He walked lopsided

And to all, he looked rather silly

The whole limerick thing got me into all kinds of trouble and didn't help change my parents' belief that there was something 'not quite right up there'.

I just needed to buy time until the event was over; then I'd write something acceptable.

So I'd sent Thaddeus the limerick. I realized he'd probably ridicule my pathetic little poem, but I was beyond caring. He wouldn't be getting back to me for another week at least, so I could focus on more urgent matters.

I'd got straight back to the vegan-intolerant chef, and more problems cropped up. It was a never-ending flow of glitches, flight changes, translator complaints, taxi driver rants, passport issuer protests, and I'd all but forgotten about the limerick when another email from Thaddeus appeared in my inbox.

Damn! He'd never replied to an email the same day. With a sinking feeling, I clicked on the subject line.

From: thaddeus.rivers @clout.com

To: Emiliah.bent@gantandballaster.com

Re: re: External hard drive press release

Love it. Send it out. Include a photo.

My first thought had been: *he can't be serious? He can't.* But he was. He'd asked me to distribute the limerick to the CLOUTech press list, including the *Financial Times How to Spend It* supplement. I suppose I just hadn't had time to think it through. There'd been so much else to deal with.

So be it, I'd told myself. *Thaddeus is the client. It's his decision. Here we go.* And out it had gone. To hundreds of journalists.

I pulled the laptop back from Meloda, who was looking at me sympathetically. My eyes read the five lines for the hundredth time, a sharp pain stabbing my stomach.

There was a hard drive from CLOUT

That no-one gave a crap about

It was basic and black

Flat front and back

But it could store stuff, no fucking doubt

2

G&B was a realm of high-powered creativity and polished professionalism tucked away in the heart of Fitzrovia. The reception area was a study in modern chic, with a sleek, white marble desk standing in its center, in front of wall-to-ceiling walnut paneling, the name Gant & Ballaster standing out in led-highlighted white letters.

To my right, as I walked in, a wall of floor-to-ceiling windows offered a breathtaking view of the iconic London skyline. Natural light flooded the space, illuminating the room's carefully chosen furnishings - minimalist leather chairs, contemporary coffee tables, and tasteful art pieces that hinted at a refined, contemporary taste.

Saskia, the receptionist, gave me a bored "hi" without looking up from her nails as I entered the huge sliding doors.

I exhaled slowly. *Everything seems normal.*

I hadn't dared to check whether there was any coverage before coming into the office. I was a bit of a heads-in-the-sand kind of girl when it came to work glitches, and in most circumstances, that approach worked best.

Moving deeper into the agency, the open-plan workspace unfolded, revealing a bustling hub of activity. Long rows of pristine white desks were neatly aligned, each one occupied by a sleek girl in dangerously high heels or a hipster with all the usual accessories: oversized glasses, goatee, and chunky cardigan. The attire was supposed to reflect the agency's commitment to a polished image of edgy creativity. The air was filled with loud phone conversations, the constant tapping of nails on keyboards, and a general hum of extreme self-importance.

I shifted uncomfortably, feeling awkward, as always.

In the center of the workspace, a sprawling, custom-made conference table dominated the scene. It was a work of art in itself, a gleaming expanse of glass and curved wood, where meetings of great importance took place. Overhead, a constellation of hanging pendant lights shone a warm, flattering glow on the faces of those gathered around it.

The walls were adorned with framed magazine covers and newspaper articles featuring the agency's high-profile clients. Awards and accolades lined the shelves, a testament to G&B's expertise and success in the world of public relations. A glass-walled boardroom offered a glimpse of what looked like an important client meeting in progress, the higher-ups brainstorming campaigns to shape public perception.

I kept my head down as I walked to my desk. Shells and Bells, Caprileander's sidekicks, were huddled in a corner, whispering, and stopped abruptly when they saw me. *They're talking about you. About your stupid limerick.*

My thoughts were interrupted by Vince, my manager, coming out of his office and walking straight towards me, a deep frown on his face

This is it. You've blown it, you idiot. The nightmare has come true. It's all over.

"Hi, Emiliah. I just got in from Barcelona. Rhona wants a word with us. She's skyping from New York." He was unnaturally somber. Vince's management style was usually expressive. The former wrestling coach often had us chant ridiculous motivational phrases just before big events to 'get the endorphin pumping'. It was quite frankly the most cringe-inducing of habits, but it was acceptable for some reason, coming from him.

I felt sick. Rhona Ballaster, known to her underlings as 'the Trunchbull' and to the outside world as the 'Bow Tie Baroness', had summoned me. The six-foot-tall titan of the PR world was the co-founder of Ballaster Enterprises, with her brother, Gary, a rather drab, shorter individual, who rarely surfaced from his office on the top floor. Ballaster had merged with Gant Limited a year earlier.

Rhona's presence always filled every space, radiating a formidable aura that could make even the most confident employee quiver. Her signature style was a black trouser suit and colorful bow tie, with her long raven hair pulled back into a tight, high ponytail. She had an extravagant collection of bow ties, each one a unique creation. She had single-handedly transformed the accessory from a forgotten relic of the past into a symbol of female power and style. Whether in silk, satin, lace, or one time, steel, her bow ties were both a conversation starter and a statement of authority. Rhona was also the genius behind the term 'uber-ungendered', a phrase quickly becoming a buzzword in the fashion industry.

Vince's face was unreadable as he stood behind his desk, gesturing for me to sit opposite him. He would never admit it, but as tall and strong as he was, he was as terrified of Rhona as I was.

Vince nodded at the face filling the screen at the end of his desk. "Rhona, we're here."

"Hello, Rhona," I managed weakly.

Her face was puce. "You sent out a press release in the form of a limerick yesterday."

Oh God.

I could feel my face flaming and my stomach dropping into a pit of despair as Vince looked at me quizzically.

In that moment, I knew with certainty that my career was over. I felt sick. *What were you thinking?*

"You. Sent. Out. A. Limerick." She snarled.

My mouth was so dry I couldn't have replied even if I'd known what to say. Tears began to well in my eyes. Did a reasonable explanation even exist?

Of course there's no explanation, you piece of shit, said my inner voice. *You've done it again, haven't you? You've ruined everything.*

"And your limerick made the headlines."

Her words didn't make sense.

I glanced at Vince, who shrugged.

Rhona's voice cut through our silent exchange. "Julian Lock from the Central Press Agency published your limerick, and everyone picked it up. EV.E.RY.ONE. Well, except for the uber-serious ones like the FT, but who reads them anyway? There's a photo with almost every piece. It's a total hit."

I couldn't quite grasp what she was saying. She inched closer to the screen. I could see the hairs inside her nostrils moving as she snarled at me. "Don't you have anything to say?"

I stared back at her. "I-"

She cut me off. "Don't you think you could have shared your idea with us before going public?" She was practically shouting. "Do you realize we have to prepare clients for this kind of edgy communication tactic? I just got off the phone with Keith Yates, to whom I had to explain our new approach. I had to make it up as I fucking went along. Do you realize what could have happened if I hadn't been there to pick up the pieces?" She inhaled deeply. "Thankfully, there's been a peak in online sales this morning, so they're overlooking the breach of PR guidelines. But believe me, the way you went behind everyone's back with this was way out of line."

"I'm sorry," I whispered.

"What? I can't hear you. Speak up."

I tried to speak louder. "I didn't really think it through. It just sort of popped into my head. Thaddeus approved it, and honestly, I didn't think it would be picked up." As I spoke, I realized I should have kept my mouth shut.

Rhona's face was thunderous. "You're telling me you actually send things to the press, believing they won't be picked up. Are you serious? How do you think that makes us look? Could you remind me what you're paid to do?'

"I'm sorry. That's not what I—"

She pushed her chair back and folded her arms. "Enough! The limerick garnered a lot of coverage. And I mean a LOT. So we are going to build on its success and use the Limerelease as a standard PR tool from now on."

"The what?"

"The Limerelease. We registered the trademark this morning. I want you to teach all our European teams to draft catchy Limereleases™ to promote our client's products."

"Erm... I don't actually think... I mean, the limerick was actually a way of saying that nobody cares about some standard external hard drive." *Which is why I wasn't expecting Thaddeus to approve it,* I added silently.

"Well, as you see, you were wrong. So, your first proper success is an accident, which doesn't surprise me. But now we need to build on its success."

"Yes, but..."

Her face was filling the screen menacingly. "Are you trying to keep this concept to yourself?"

"No, I..."

"I do not take kindly to people who refuse to share their ideas. May I remind you, Miss Bent, that we have a family culture here at G&B. We share creative ideas. Would you care to look for a position in another, more individualistic agency?"

Vince sat down next to me. "Rhona, I don't think this warrants-"

"Silence!" She lifted her six-foot self from the chair and walked away, giving us a glimpse of her New York office. Decorated with dark purple fishscale wallpaper, it had the largest desk I'd ever seen, dim light provided by an enormous black feathery chandelier. *Is that a skull on the mantelpiece?*

Her booming voice interrupted my thoughts, and her face filled the screen again, her green eyes bulging with menace. "I expect to have a Limerelease™ presentation in my inbox by Monday. And you're to start the training sessions next Friday. I'll be sending a summons to all the country managers this afternoon. Understood?"

I nodded slowly as she turned, glaring, towards the door

at the far end of her office, which opened tentatively, a terrified face appearing in the gap.

"The Shanghai event?" I mouthed at Vince, but he shrugged helplessly.

She leaned over, so close to the screen that I was afraid she'd push her way through it into the London office, Japanese horror movie style. "Monday morning, eight o'clock. Without fail." We got a deep view of her enormous bosom, precariously held in place by a lacy décolleté and a large velvet bow tie, before the line went dead.

Vince looked at me awkwardly. "Well. Sounds like the press loved your limerick."

"Vince. I'm so sorry. It was a huge mistake." I tried not to think of the attention I'd brought to the team and to Vince, who did his best to keep a low profile with Rhona.

He smiled. "It's okay. Don't worry about it. What's done is done. But we can't afford to antagonize Rhona. We'll just have to find a way to make this Limerelease thing work."

There was no way it would ever work. The country managers would be up in arms, complaining about yet another ethnocentric initiative from the London office. "Vince, honestly, there's just no way. The whole point of the limerick was to take the piss. Seriously, how are we going to get French PR managers to write limericks?"

"We have no choice. Just do the training session, get it over with, and then we can all forget about it."

But he knew as well as I did that I would be out of a job if it was a failure.

I changed tack. "What about the Shanghai event? I can't not be there."

"It's okay. Take Norah. Attend the first two days to get things rolling, then fly back for the training session."

I returned to my desk, doing my best to give the Shanghai event my full attention. Nora and Helen had worked miracles, booking all the transfers from the airport to the hotel, securing most of the visas, and convincing a nearby American restaurant to deliver vegan food to the hotel.

I kept my head down, ensuring hotel rooms were booked, journalists were given the necessary documentation, and the seventeen CLOUTech Vice Presidents agreed on the overall event messaging.

I did my best to ignore dark thoughts related to the Limerelease™ training, but people kept forwarding me coverage, and all it did was make me feel more exposed than ever.

I cringed when Thaddeus sent a very brash email to all@cloutech.com explaining how his Limerelease had led to an increase in sales. Did he not see how ridiculous the whole thing is?

The office was a battleground, where jealousy and resentment festered like a contagious disease. My strategy had always been to keep a low profile, but now I could feel the eyes of my coworkers on me, assessing my every move.

Vince's team was already vulnerable due to the merger of

Ballaster Enterprises and Gant Ltd, the company I had joined six years earlier. Vince had had CLOUTech as a client for years, and Rhona desperately wanted to take over, hand it over to her minions, and get rid of Vince and his team in the process. We all knew the day would come sooner or later, but we all hung on, determined to see the battle through to the bitter end. Vince, Meloda, Nora and Helen were much more than colleagues; they were friends, and I couldn't bear the thought of losing them, even if it meant working in a hostile environment. The antagonism brought our little team closer, and we knew that any misstep would give the enemy ammunition. But my limerick initiative was more than a misstep, and there was no way to cover it up. It was out in the cold, bleak open, defenseless, waiting to be attacked. I kept my head down, fully aware of the attention I'd brought to our tight-knit little team.

My fingers tapped away at the keyboard, attempting to regain some sense of control over the chaos I'd created. But just as I was once again fully immersed in event preparation, I sensed a presence behind me.

Caprileander, known as 'Capri', flanked by her sidekicks 'Shells' and 'Bells', towered over me like a Scandinavian model, smiling her white, saccharine smile. She wore her Dolce & Gabbana pencil dress like armor, a badge of superiority in a cutthroat environment. "Emiliah, dahling," she purred, her voice syrupy sweet, "I couldn't help but read the Limerick you sent out." Her perfectly manicured fingernails tapped the top of the shelves beside my desk.

My heart sank. Even under normal circumstances, she had a talent for identifying and magnifying the tiniest flaws, so you'd feel utterly incompetent. My limerick initiative was a gift of naked humiliation handed to her on a silver platter. She continued, her large blue eyes fixed on me, blinking innocently. "I'm not sure if it's really in line with CLOUT's PR guidelines. Do you?"

I felt heat rise in my cheeks. Capri's words were like venom, injecting the sting of insecurity into my veins. I mustered a weak smile, doing my best to play along with her little charade. "Oh, I must have misread the guidelines, Capri. Thank you for the reminder, though."

Her lips curled into a predatory grin, and she leaned in closer, her YSL scent overwhelming. "Of course. We're all here to help each other, aren't we?" Her singsong tone was laced with condescension.

Shells, with her perpetually raised eyebrows, added in a mockingly innocent tone, "You know how important it is to get these things right. Capri just wants to uphold the agency's reputation, doesn't she?"

Bells, twirling a strand of her glossy black hair, giggled. "Yeah, we wouldn't want anyone to, like, get the impression that our agency was like some kind of, like, joke, would we?"

Their laughter, like a chorus of judgmental birds, rang in my ears. I could feel the walls closing in, their presence oppressive and unyielding. I nodded, forcing another smile, though inside, I was crumbling.

As they finally drifted away, I was mostly angry with myself for letting them bully me like that. *Why can you never stick up for yourself, Emiliah?*

I turned back to the event messaging. In the harsh light of this section of the office, my words looked stark and exposed, every potential misstep glaringly obvious. I sighed, knowing I'd have to rewrite it, scrutinizing every line to avoid Capri's criticism.

Across the room, I noticed Meloda, giving me a sympathetic look. She mouthed, "You okay?"

I nodded, not trusting myself to speak.

But as I started to type, I could feel the embers of defiance beginning to smolder. I knew I couldn't confront Capri directly – that would be career suicide in this environment – but I could start finding small ways to assert myself, to push back against her petty tyranny.

As I closed my PC at nine, I felt trapped. *It's all your own fault for trying to be clever. Who do you think you are? Stupid, stupid girl.*

3

By midday on Saturday, I was more than ready for a break. I'd spent the morning checking one-to-one schedules and editing press releases. I hadn't even started the ridiculous Limerelease™ training presentation. I'd have to put something together at the end of the day. I decided to head out to Spitalfields.

The street, still slick from the morning drizzle, mirrored the hesitant mid-day light, casting haphazard reflections across the pavement. The aroma of freshly baked bread wafted through the crisp, damp air as I strolled past an old bakery, its windows fogged up by the heat of ovens battling the chill of the English spring.

As I approached Spitalfields Market, the distant murmur of lively chatter and sporadic laughter began to percolate through the atmosphere. The sky, a tapestry of ashen greys, contemplated the prospect of rain, its cold, muted light bathing the streets in a gentle pallor. As I drew nearer, the distinctive cacophony of the market — traders announcing their wares with rhythmic certainty, the trill of a busker's violin weaving through the dialogues of bargaining and banter — began to sculpt itself from the

East End's ambient hum.

Stalls, adorned with kaleidoscopic arrays of fruit, textile and trinkets, invited glances from the crowd. The rich tapestry of aromas — sweet, tangy, spicy — made me ravenous.

I found a free table at my favorite stall. Sitting at a rickety bar stool at the tiny high table, I slowly chewed baked potato stuffed with beans, cheddar, sour cream and chives, with lettuce drizzled in olive oil and lemon. After some hesitation, I resisted the temptation of caramel-drenched banoffee pie with my coffee. I wandered around for a while, taking in the colors and smells of the market.

On autopilot, I headed east, against the flow of people, apologizing absent-mindedly as I brushed past strangers. Turning into a side street, I was finally free from the herd. I stared at the building for a while, then pulled out my keys and unlocked the padlock, pushing the door open with a loud creak.

What my ex-boyfriend Peter and the other artists called 'the studio' was a decrepit industrial workshop with no insulation, all heating provided by an ancient Godin stove in the center of the room. The smell of linseed oil, cold tobacco, and stale coffee greeted me as I entered. They had no idea I had kept a key. There was little chance of them coming in on a Saturday. Every surface was covered in yellowing newspapers, tins of brushes, old, dried-out tubes of paint, dirty rags, and overflowing ashtrays. The ancient metal-framed windows threw huge squares of light into the room, illuminating the paint-specked floor. Hundreds of canvases in all shapes and sizes were stacked against the walls and although they all looked very similar, all very dramatic and somber, when you knew the artists, you learned to recognize each of their individual styles.

I stepped forward, breathing in the musty air. I let my fingers trail on the windows and furniture, leaving trenches in the dust and greasy lines in the grub.

Lying down on the tired sofa, I stared at the ceiling. This was as close as I could get to my old life. The life in which I'd had a group of people outside of work.

You always ruin everything. What is wrong with you?

In the early days of our relationship, I would rush off to the studio as soon as I got out of work. I'd be full of awe and wonder as he excitedly showed me his latest paintings. When we were alone, we'd make love on the sofa and later in the evening, he'd rush out to the Moroccan restaurant next door and bring back piping hot couscous with lots of harissa, and we'd eat it wrapped up together in a blanket. Or we'd have lamb tajine at the palette table in the courtyard behind the studio, the light of a large candle flickering across our faces, washing the food down with *Côtes du Rhône* from the stash they kept, the smell of caramelized onions, cumin, and coriander mingling with that of paint and tobacco. We'd head off home, hand in hand, and make love again later before falling into a deep, contented sleep. If Liam, Yann, Targon, or Nick were there, we'd all settle down together with bread and cheese, cucumber and tapenade, and talk animatedly about politics. But things had gradually changed. The heated arguments had turned into a feud between Peter and Liam. They had begun working in silence, and no one ordered from Mohamed next door when he stopped extending credit. Peter became less and less interested in my opinion, so I found myself avoiding both the studio and the subject of his art. He grew to hate my suburban taste, my ignorance. I did everything I could to understand what I'd done to make him hate me. So much so that by the time he left me, it was as much a relief as it was painful. I'd run out of energy. Only recently had I started coming here on the weekends to relive the memories of the early days. I was pulled here by an invisible force, but every time, I experienced the dull pain of seeing that everything was as it had always been, as if I'd never existed.

Snap out of it, Emiliah. You've got work to do.

4

As I dressed after a quick shower, having decided to postpone the rest of my weekend work until Sunday, I looked around my quirky, tiny flat with satisfaction. I marveled again at the prettiness of the space I had begun working on six years earlier. I never tired of the beams and ancient hardwood floors, formerly covered in a dirty burgundy carpet. I took in the fluffy carpets scattering the floor, the linen curtains I'd spent several evenings sewing, the vintage photographs and set of mismatched, chipped mugs. At the time, I'd pointedly ignored Peter's suggestions that maybe I should go for a darker, more industrial look. You definitely wouldn't call the space stylish, but it was warm and welcoming, and I loved it.

I glanced at the clock as I ran my hand over the uneven cement countertop. *Shit.* I was late for my evening with Meloda. I pulled on heeled boots and a loose black jumper, left my wild mass of red curls loose, locked the door, and ran-jumped down the old stairs, hurtling into the street, and sprinted to our local wine bar, Assemblage, miraculously not tripping on the cobbles.

Meloda was sitting at a corner table, drinking a cocktail. I rushed over to her, knocking into a table as I went.

"Hey, watch out!"

"I'm so sorry." I looked at the couple glaring up at me, and a wave of shame flooded me. "I'm really sorry."

"Sorry, Mel," I said, sitting down.

Meloda patted my hand. "Don't worry, Sweetie, I just got here. So how are you? I understand your Limerick mishap turned into quite the opportunity."

"I don't know If I'd say that," I replied with a snort. "It's painful. I'm dreading the training session on Friday. I don't even know what to say."

"Can't you just wing it? I mean, Rhona's bound to realize it's a stupid idea. And if *she* doesn't, everyone'll realize it's just another one of her ludicrous initiatives."

If only everyone at work had as much common sense as Meloda. Then again, she's exceptionally bright. When her parents died in Haiti, she lived with various relatives and friends until she was offered a place at Imperial College London by a program helping gifted children from developing countries. She studied engineering and graduated with a first-class degree. After working in the semiconductor industry for a year, she realized it wasn't the best environment for a black woman and switched to PR, where her technical knowledge enabled G&B to bring in numerous clients in the very lucrative semiconductor industry.

I caught Fabrice, our usual waiter's eye. "Comme

d'habitude?" I mouthed. He nodded and rolled his eyes in mock desperation. I turned back to Meloda, now able to give her my full attention. "Yes, it is a stupid idea. But I'm the one who came up with the limerick in the first place. Urgh, I just can't bear to think about it. Anyway, enough about work. How are you?"

Meloda beamed at me just as Fabrice arrived with a large glass of red wine.

Leaning back against the distressed brick wall, swirling the glass of *Tain L'Hermitage*, I realized how much I'd missed these girls' nights out. It had been a while since we'd last met up.

"Emiliah! Hello? Are you there?"

My eyes flicked open to see Meloda looking at me accusingly.

"What, er... sorry. I was just soaking it all in, enjoying the atmosphere."

Meloda rolled her eyes. "You're impossible, Em! I was talking to you. I have something to tell you."

I pulled myself up, fully alert. "What? What is it?"

She gave me a dazzling smile.

I knew that look. "You've met someone!"

"Yes, I have."

"Who is it? Do I know him?"

She looked at her cocktail, playing with the little umbrella. "No, no, you don't."

"What? What is it? Is there something wrong? Is he married or something?"

She gave me a sharp look. "No, no, nothing like that."

I stared at her suspiciously. "Meloda, there's something you don't want to tell me. What is it? It's not a client, is it?"

"No." She seemed more annoyed than embarrassed now.

"Well, what is it? What's wrong?"

"Nothing's wrong, it's just..."

She was obviously struggling with something, and the wine told me the best way was to tease it out of her. "Does he live with his mother?"

She threw her head back in typical Meloda fashion and laughed. "No!"

"Does he wear leather trousers?"

"No!"

"Does he wear a wig?"

"No!" she giggled.

"Does he carry a manbag? Does he have gold teeth?"

"I don't think so," she replied doubtfully, grinning.

I could have gone on all night, but Meloda became subdued.

I leaned over and put my hand on hers. "Hey, Sweetie, what's wrong?"

"Em, it's not a he. It's a she."

I stared at her, not understanding. Then understanding.

"But… I thought…"

"So did I."

I reached over and hugged her. "Meloda, I love you so much. I'm very happy for you. Tell me about this mystery woman."

So she did. And the more I learned, the more I realized how much of a threat Meloda's new love interest could be to me.

5

I was finally at the office. The flight back from Shanghai had been horrendous. The plane had been delayed by four hours. The man next to me, a very large Dutchman, had managed to smuggle pâté onto the plane. The smell had been so bad that I'd had to put my earplugs in my nose.

I ran straight to Bells' desk. "Hi, Bells," I said, trying to catch my breath. "Er, where are the training presentations?"

She looked up at me with doe eyes. "Oh, I'm sorry, Emiliah. I just haven't, like, had time to do them. It's just been, like, crazy this morning." She started typing, a ghost of a smile on her lips.

I felt my insides crumbling. "But Rhona told me you'd have them ready this morning. I just got in from the airport."

"I'm sorry. I just haven't had time," she said in her sing-song voice. "But you should really be better prepared, and, like, rely on your own team to assist you."

My cheeks flushed in anger. "My team is in Shanghai."

"Sorry, can't help you," she shrugged, this time not even looking up from her PC.

"Okay," I squeaked. "I'll print them out now. I should have just about enough time."

"Oh no, sorry." That doe-eyed expression again. "The printer's not working. Capri needed me to print out twenty copies of the CLOUTech PR Guidelines, and the system got clogged up. And, of course, I can't get hold of IT. They're supposedly all on a course."

"But my Limerelease training session starts in..." I checked my watch hysterically. "Thirty minutes."

She looked up at me with the most insincere look of sympathy I'd ever seen. "Sorry, Emiliah."

I looked out of the window behind her desk. It was pouring. I hesitated for half a second before dashing down the stairs and out of the building.

I pulled out my phone, tapping frantically to locate the nearest Printfast. It was on Percy Street. Nine minutes on foot, according to Google Maps. I ran as fast as my four-inch heels would allow, pushing past people on the street and running across roads.

Where the hell is it? I checked my phone again, swiping the screen with sweaty fingers and praying I'd run in the right direction. The screen didn't respond – it was never very reliable in the rain. Tears welled in my eyes as I grabbed a man walking a dog. "Er, excuse me. Can you tell me where Printfast is?"

He stared at me as if I'd just asked if he knew where Neptune was. "D'you mean the shop right behind you?"

"What?" I swirled around. "Oh yes!" I shrieked. "Thank you!"

He rolled his eyes and walked away, pulling the dog away from me.

I hopped around while the presentations were being printed, even though I knew I should be calming myself down and mopping up the sweat under my armpits.

By the time the manuals were printed, I had six minutes before the session was due to start. Sprinting back, one of my heels got caught on the ancient paving on Colville Place, twisting my ankle. "Ow!" I cried out. "Oh my God, that hurt." I tried to put my foot down, but a sharp pain shot up my right leg, making me lose my balance. I dropped the pile of freshly printed presentations in a puddle.

I wanted to cry. *Why am I still doing this crap? I'm almost thirty, for God's sake. Why do I keep agreeing to all this shit?* Then I did something really stupid; I kicked a lamp post really hard. "Ow!" I cried out in pain for the second time in minutes. *Oh God, I think I've broken my toe.*

Limping and doing my best to carry the pile of soggy training manuals back to the office, I felt despair take over me.

By the time I entered the packed conference room eighteen minutes later than scheduled, my hair and clothes soaking, my makeup patchy, I knew that however hard I tried, this whole experience would be a disaster.

6

Breathe in. Hold it. Now, breathe out slowly, as if through a tiny straw.

I cleared my throat and tried to look convincing. "Erm. Hello everyone. For those who don't know me, my name is Emiliah Bent, and I'm an Account Director at Gant & Ballaster, managing the CLOUTech B2C account." I paused, heart thumping. "I'm here today to present Gant & Ballaster's new concept, the Limerelease™." I looked around, forcing myself to smile enthusiastically. Click. The first page of the presentation came up. "According to *Wikipedia*, a limerick is a form of poetry, specifically one in five lines with a strict rhyme scheme (AABBA), which is often humorous. The first, second, and fifth lines are usually longer than the third and fourth."

I could see eyes glazing over.

I turned away from the presentation. "The aim of a limerick is to tell a funny story in a few shortlines, which is why using them for press releases makes so much sense. For as you all know, journalists receive numerous press releases every day, and a limerick is a way of getting their attention and giving them the jist of the story." *Wow, how stupid can you sound? Can you hear yourself?*

Five minutes in, the presentation part was over. It had been too hard to explain the history of the limerick to all these busy, hard-working European country managers. *How the hell am I going to make this last half a day?*

"Um, I'll give you all fifteen minutes to come up with a limerick describing a technological product of your choice. It doesn't have to be a CLOUTech product; pick anything you like. This is just an internal exercise. When you've finished, please help yourself to coffee; then we'll go over your work."

I limped out of the room and hurled myself at the coffee machine. Sipping quickly, I looked around before lifting my arms to check my body odor. *Mighty God. If it smells that bad to* me, *what does it smell like to everyone else?* I picked up a second capsule and looked around the stylish hall. Everything, from the shiny resin sideboards to the artwork hanging from the walls to the enormous flat-screen TV on the far side of the room, screamed money. If we had this much to spend on interiors, why couldn't we afford a couple more people on the team?

My eye caught three plates of glistening pastries on the sideboard to my left. Cinnamon rolls. They looked soft and crispy. Before I could stop myself, I grabbed four, looking around to check that I was still alone. Wrapping them in paper napkins, I headed for the loos. Safe in my cubicle, I ate the first one in three bites, breathing heavily through my nose. The second, I ate more slowly, savoring the doughy, sugary taste. I couldn't stop at two. With the third came the slow, filling pleasure. Every bite was heavenly. The sticky crunchiness, the creamy pastry, the sweetness of the icing. *Hmmmm.* I looked at the fourth roll. *You don't have to.* I didn't. I really didn't. I was full, satisfied. But what the hell? What difference did one more make? I forced it down in a hurry before I could change my mind. Then, checking the coast was clear, I hobbled out to the sinks and grabbed a load of paper towels, holding half the wad under the tap. Back inside the cubicle, I pulled off my top, wiped my underarms dry, washed them with the wet paper towels, and patted them dry again. I pulled out the mini deodorant I always kept in my back pocket and lathered my skin, hoping it would mask the acrid smell. I'd have to nip out and change later.

The bathroom door creaked open and slammed shut. I froze. You never wanted to come face to face with someone else in the loos. I bent over and rested, head between my knees. *You're such a loser, Emiliah. Get a grip.*

When I arrived back in the hall, a crowd had gathered around the coffee stand; not just the Italian, German, French, and Swedish teams, but what looked like the entire London office. And, of course, there was the statuesque blonde head who made my life miserable, Caprileander Justin-Wells.

When the coffee break had gone on for as long as was acceptable, I cleared my throat. "Okay, everyone. Time for the next part of the session."

Nobody moved.

Be assertive, be assertive, goddammit. "Okay," I shouted, clapping my hands. This time, everyone looked at me. I blushed. "Um, let's, er, let's continue, shall we?" And I walked back into the conference room, praying they'd follow.

Thankfully, the group moved slowly back into the room. Not just my Limerelease™ trainees but everyone in the hall. *OK. Just stay focused. Imagine them all on the loo. Who am I kidding? When has that technique ever worked?* I stood awkwardly at the front of the packed room. "So, now that you've all had time to compose your own limericks, each group will read theirs out. Gunter, would you like to begin?"

Gunter stood up obediently. "Zertainly, Emiliah. Hu-hum, here vee go:

> **Zere voz a PC vrom Apple,**
>
> **Zats price voz very reasonable,**
>
> **Wiz Nvidia GeForce GTX graphics,**
>
> **And a RAM of thirty-two Gigabits,**
>
> **It offered efficiency to many people."**

Giggles rippled across the back of the room. Capri and her clique were whispering, all mocking smiles and raised eyebrows. *Boy, do I hate her.* I had to control the room. "Er. Excuse me. If anyone wants to attend the training session, that's fine, but... um... please be quiet while we're working."

For a second, everyone stopped talking. Then they just resumed the chatting and snickering. Hot with humiliation, I cleared my throat, preparing to ask Capri and her clique to leave, when the room went quiet. The door was thrown open, and there stood Rhona, six feet tall, hands on hips. The Trunchbull. We all quivered. She thundered in, followed by the senior directors: Walter, head of the healthcare unit; Jessica, fashion and beauty director; and, of course, Vince, technology director.

Rhona looked around the room with mild distaste. "Okay, everyone, I want you all to pay attention. The Limerelease™ is the latest tool in the Gant & Ballaster three-sixty-degree spherical PR toolbox."

Some of the country managers sitting in the front turned around to glimpse the formidable woman. I knew for a fact that none of them used the bloody toolbox. I mean, how practical does a 360-degree spherical PR toolbox sound? It was basically a booklet of communication tools to address anything from messaging to social media and advertising, all encapsulated in a glossy book that cost over a hundred thousand pounds to produce, to 'help' the country managers. The thing was just too damn complicated. The country PR teams mostly went with their gut, and it usually worked.

I snapped back to the present to hear Rhona hammering home the importance of the toolbox: "Need I remind you all why our toolbox is spherical; why it is different from our competitors' toolboxes?" Everyone in the room avoided eye contact. "Because," she bellowed, "*we* offer three-hundred-and-sixty-degree communication."

She paused for effect. "The newest element, the Limerelease™, which shall be included in an additional booklet, is a return to authentic communication. We're playing on nostalgia here." She was really on a roll. She glared at the country managers, daring them to challenge her. "Old-fashioned communication will become the new way forward. Think faxes, think telegrams, think switchboards. We'll reinvent them all. But we have to move fast. Our competit—"

Rhona's tirade was interrupted when a tall man in faded jeans and a black t-shirt pushed the door open. He looked vaguely familiar, but I couldn't place him. *Who the hell is he?*

A ripple of excitement crossed the room. Every woman, as well as a few men, looked at the newcomer lustily. He was incredibly good-looking, tall and muscular, with an intense aura and a crew cut that gave him a vaguely military demeanor. Hands went to throats, mouths pouted, and papers fanned the air. With all the fluttering going on, I was half expecting Etta James to turn up and start crooning in her gravelly voice. I was actually surprised the man didn't pull out a can of Diet Coke and pour it slowly down his ridiculously sexy throat.

Was this the new advertising guy people had been talking about? He seemed a bit too traditional. No beard, no oversized glasses, no hair gel, no fan. No, he was too *outdoorsy* for the world of advertising. He looked more like the type of person who'd break into an enemy's lair and single-handedly retrieve a deadly vial of Ebola stolen from a clandestine laboratory, walking forward tenaciously and firing in all directions. Then he'd run out of weapons, shrug, and resort to complicated Aikido moves to fight off eight enemies at once.

Rhona snapped us all out of our reverie. "Mr. Goodwall." Then to the rest of us: "Ben Goodwall is the CEO of PeakSleek. I suggested he attend this training session to better understand our disruptive approach to communications."

Oh my god. That's why he looked familiar. PeakSleek was big deal. Once a rather bland sportswear company, PeakSleek had become the most popular activewear company in the UK over the past two years. The company's founder had been ousted by the investors, and Ben Goodwall had been brought in to turn the business around. He had shut down all the stores, focused on e-commerce, and reinvented the company's image by plastering black and white billboards of muscular, topless men in every city. The products weren't even visible in the adverts, which centered on hot, topless men with the line 'PeakSleek Me'.

Mr. Goodwall smiled a dazzlingly white smile and said "Call me Ben", before turning to me and nodding. "Please. Go ahead."

Oh God, make me disappear.

I felt weak. *I don't think I can do this. Stay calm.* "Okay, everyone, let's remember that limericks are light and funny. Try and imagine that we're not really trying to sell a product. It's more about the poem than the product. Yes, Gabriella?"

"I do not understand-a what is the point of writing such a ridiculous-a poem-a."

Boy, this is hard. "We're using limericks as marketing tools. Instead of writing press releases about our clients' new products, we are telling the press a funny story."

"But-a why-a?"

"Because that's what we've decided to do," came a booming voice from the back of the room. Rhona didn't actually add 'you bunch of uncivilized idiots', but she thought it so loudly that you couldn't miss the implication.The room descended into fearful silence. "Carry on," she said in a menacingly low voice.

I shot a look at Ben Goodwall, who stared back intently.

"So," I wobbled, "remember that in a Limerelease™, the product is just an excuse. The aim is to be funny." I looked around the room. Everyone had their heads down. They were all petrified of being fired on the spot, all except 'Call me Ben', who just seemed intrigued. Blushing, I turned back to the Italian team. "Gabriella, is your team ready to present your limerick?"

"Yes-a, Emiliah. Danilo will present-a the poem-a."

Danilo stood up, looking confidently at his colleagues Roberto, Romeo, Fabio, Julio and Elio.

"Okay-ya. Here-a wego-a:

There was a printer from Toshiba

That-a had-a incredible stam-eena

Its colours were exciting

Its-a blacks-a penetrating

And its ink-a seemed to last-a for-eva.”

I stared at them for a second. “Erm, thank you guys. That was very ... erm... catchy. We’re definitely getting there. Let’s try and focus on humor rather than the... um... er, the steamy side of things.”

Muffled giggles erupted from the back of the room.

I’d like to see you up here, bitches.

Next up were Sorensen and the rest of the Swedish team. They were usually quite creative, so I hoped they wouldn’t disappoint. I tried to act upbeat. “Sorensen, please, go ahead.” Sorensen, Abjorn, Johann, and Ingegard stood in unison. Two men, two women; all blond and tanned, all looking terribly enthusiastic and Swedish. They filed silently to the front of the room, and Sorenson cleared his throat. “We were very inspired by the limerick and the AABBA structure. Of course, in AABBA, one cannot miss that you have ABBA, so we wrote our Limerelease™ as a song.’ And without further warning, they launched into a humming intro, clicking the rhythm with their fingers, before singing:

Gimme, gimme, gimme a hard drive from HP

Can’t somebody find at least a USB key?

Gimme, gimme, gimme something for my data

Help me make my files so much sa-a-a-fer."

Then they all hummed another line of "Gimme, Gimme, Gimme", before dramatically ending with:

"Gimme a taste of your techno-ho-logy."

The four of them looked around the room, beaming. Rhona bent her head, covering her eyes with one of her ham-sized hands. I clapped enthusiastically, unable to bear the sight of them waiting for a round of applause. Unfortunately, only a few people followed my lead, and Sorensen and the other team members' faces dropped.

I had to help them. "That was wonderful, guys! Great work. Thank you!"

I turned to the French team, needing to get the focus off the Swedes. "Claude, ready?"

Claude, the French technology director, stood ceremoniously. "Yes, Emeeleeah. I am:

Zis Asus dongle his so so so beautifool

Zat wiz eet you will be very 'appy and cool

It is much much much more zan just a tool

Wiz zis dongle, you 'ave power, you will rrrule."

"Er, thank you, Claude. That was... nice. Your poem doesn't exactly fit the structure of the limerick, though, which is A A B B A."

Clause stared at me defiantly and shot a quick kamikaze glance at Rhona. "Yes, but in France, we prefer ze *Alexandrin* poem. We do not'ave zis *Limerrrrick*. Ze French press will not want zis *Limerrrrick* press release."

"Yes, Claude, I understand, but we have to be consistent throughout Europe." I looked over at Rhona, who nodded almost imperceptibly, giving me the strength to go on. "Whether or not your country's journalists understand the idea of Limericks is irrelevant." Even as I was saying this, I realized how little sense it made. I wondered if this was what it felt like to work for the Records Department in Orwell's 1984. But Rhona wanted me to push on, so I did. "Okay, Claude, let's try and tweak your poem to sound more like a Limerick."

I was now, as Meloda had put it, 'winging it.'

I cleared my throat. "How about this:

There was once a dongle from Asus

A fun, nifty tool that amazed us,

That's the AA. Now for BB. You could say something like:

It streamed to routers and nodes
Sent files and uploaded codes

Then all you need is the final A. Let's say:

A compact gadget that fits in any..."

Fits any what? What rhymes with 'Asus'? There was a long pause. Everyone was waiting. I could feel the tension building, the anticipation. They were all wondering if I could come up with a word that rhymed with 'Asus' and 'bonus'. I just couldn't think. 'Purse' wouldn't work, but that was the idea. I was sweating again. I needed to think of something that really rhymed. *What could I say? WHAT?*

"ANUS!" I shrieked.

Shocked silence. *Did I really say that? Did I really shriek?* The room was silent. *Maybe I didn't say it out loud; maybe I just thought it very, very hard.* But then I heard a strangled sound coming from the back of the room, and my heart sank.

It started with a snort disguised as a cough, but I could see the laughter bubbling up inside him. He was snorting and crying and obviously trying to stop himself, but he couldn't control it. Ben Goodwall was laughing so hard that he seemed to be in pain. I could see him looking wildly for an exit, but the crowd around him had him blocked in. He was shaking, and tears were running down his face. Nervous laughter erupted here and there. I wanted to disappear. It was the worst moment of my life. Pure, unalloyed mortification. I had never wanted to disappear as much as I did then. *Please, God, please make me die. Please, world, forget I ever existed.*

Weakly, I tried to change the subject by returning to the history of the limerick and its satirical function. "The term Limerick comes from county Limerick, and it..." my voice trailed away as his laughter got worse. He was bending over in peals of hysterics. More people started laughing. No one was listening to my presentation anymore.

"May... maybe," I stuttered," maybe we could take a break," and with that, I ran out of the room. And I kept going, tears of humiliation blinding me as I ran down the stairs, floor after floor, and exited the building before walking down Eldon Street as fast as I could, putting as much distance as I could between me and them. I stopped in front of Hugo Boss and pretended to focus on the clothes on sale in the window, willing my tears not to overflow.

Get a grip, get a fucking grip.

Someone tapped my shoulder. "Hey."

I span around defensively.

There he was. Ben Goodwall, CEO of PeakSleek. He took a step back, taking in my alarm. "I'm sorry. I didn't mean to scare you. I just wanted to check you were okay." His eyes were full of concern. "Listen. I'm really, really sorry I laughed." He smiled, obviously remembering the scene. "Look, let me make it up to you. We'll go back inside, and I'll personally make sure everyone listens while you finish."

He held out his arm to guide me back to the office.

I started back, moving away from his arm. "It's okay. I just... I'm not very good at speaking in public." I quickly brushed away my tears.

We walked back to the office in awkward silence.

He stood to one side, letting me enter the building first.

I shot him a furtive glance. "I need... I'll be there in a

minute."

He was still waiting in the lobby as I emerged from the loos, having washed my face. He walked me back to the lifts, and then into the conference room, his hand on the small of my back.

I was in a daze, but I managed to get through to the end of my presentation, and to my great surprise, everyone clapped when it was over. From relief, probably. But whatever. It was over. Ben Goodwall was the most enthusiastic, clapping and catcalling as if I'd just beaten the pole jumping world record.

As everyone filed out of the room and Rhonda led Ben Goodwall to the next meeting, he looked back at me over his shoulder, a quizzical look on his face.

7

As my sneakers pounded the Southwark Park footpath, cold rain slapping my face, I went through my mental checklist. *Get hold of Lester Hamilton at the Financial Times. Schedule Nora and Helena's annual reviews. Make everyone forget about the disastrous training session.*

When the Ada Salter Rose Garden came into view, I slowed to a walk and took in my surroundings. I never tired of the Wisteria-covered awnings, even in this weather.

I lifted each foot, one after the other, onto the top of a bench and bent over, enjoying the pain of stretched calf muscles.

Set up a conference call for CLOUTech's latest product introduction.

It was early, six maybe, and so far I'd only met three people, early morning dog walkers. Exhaling icy cold air and buzzing from the run, I set off home. I had less than an hour before catching the tube.

I rushed up the steps and let myself in. My blueberry overnight oats were swallowed in a hurry as I leaned against the counter. After carefully placing the bowl and spoon in the sink, I headed for the shower.

I sighed with pleasure as shards of hot water hit my body. When I was done, I straightened my wild curls into a sharp, shoulder-length bob, applied a hint of bronze eye shadow and lip gloss, and pulled on the pin-stripe trouser suit and starch white blouse I'd laid out the night before. I clasped a chunky crystal necklace around my neck and pulled on my work sneakers, slipping my heels into my handbag.

Before leaving, as usual, I looked around my flat lovingly.

As soon as I'd landed my first job, I'd focused on buying a flat. Going out and enjoying London life had held absolutely no interest for me. Creating a home for myself was an urgent priority, even if it meant a thirty-year mortgage. The money I'd gathered in my old life covered part of the cost, but it was not enough to buy a flat in London. I spent weekend after weekend visiting tiny studios and one-bedroom flats I couldn't afford everywhere from Streatham to Woolwich. Every space I had looked at was characterless, small, dark, gloomy and over budget. By month five, I was beginning to lose hope. Then, one day, Amanda, the only estate agent who hadn't tired of me, had taken me to a 1930s house in Shoreditch, divided into three flats. She had walked me up to the top floor and opened the door to a one-bedroom flat. On the right side of the main room were two doors: one leading into a dark, grimy bathroom, the other into a minuscule bedroom. On the left side of the flat was a fat-encrusted steel and melamine kitchenette. The space in between, under the eaves, was covered in a burgundy carpet from floor to ceiling. "Of course, it does need a bit of work, but I thought that, given your budget, you might like to take a look," Amanda had said doubtfully.

"How long has it been on the market?" I'd asked, trying not to show my excitement.

"A few weeks, I think." Amanda had struggled to open the windows, and I discreetly pulled up a corner of the carpet from the floor, glimpsing the rough wooden floorboards underneath. *This is it. This is my home.*

"Do you think there's room for negotiation?" I'd asked vaguely. When Amanda had smiled at me and I'd beamed back, I'd known it was a done deal.

When I finally received the keys, I danced around the dirty, empty space, squealing with joy.

That first day was spent pulling what I could of the carpet off the floor and walls until the early hours of the morning. I eventually curled up on my coat on the floor and fell into a deep sleep.

The following morning, I showered in the ancient bath, carefully avoiding the filthy grey walls, and measured each room. Meloda had turned up at noon to see the flat for herself.

"Oh my God, Emiliah. Are you mad?" She looked at me, aghast, as she took it all in. "I had no idea you'd bought something like this. I hope you have a huge renovation budget."

I shrugged, not wanting to admit my budget was tiny.

I was stung by her opinion but determined to prove her wrong. "Don't worry, Mel, you'll see. I'm going to transform it. You just wait and see what nights and weekends of work will do to this place."

"Well, not tonight, Em. There's no way I'm letting you work this evening. Hovel or no hovel, you're coming out with me."

And so out we'd gone to an art exhibition. Meloda had marched right up to the group of artists, determined to meet new people. They were all over her in minutes, chatting, teasing and flirting. How wouldn't they be? Meloda was easily the most stunning woman I'd ever seen. She had it all, with her warm eyes, model body and contagious laugh. At the time, she'd had an amazing afro haircut. She seemed not so much oblivious to her beauty as indifferent about it. She was fully aware of the effect she had on men, but didn't really seem to care that much, and definitely never made me feel inferior in any way.

I'd waited on the sidelines, never at ease with new people, and knowing that next to my gorgeous, sparkly friend, I'd be invisible anyway. I'd decided to move away from the banter and take another look around. All the paintings could have been by the same artist, they were so similar. Tortured, dark, a little... murky.

"What do you think?" A tall, serious-looking man with spectacles had appeared beside me.

"Who, me?" I'd blushed. "I don't really know anything about art. I'm just here with a friend." I'd nodded in Meloda's direction. She was surrounded by four men, talking loudly and laughing, her head thrown back.

The dark-haired stranger had looked at me with interest. "But you must have an impression, if not an opinion?"

"Erm, I'm not really sure. What do you think?"

He'd stared at me in silence, then, "This one is Yann's. I painted those over there. Peter Decourt. Nice to meet you." He'd half-smiled.

I'd blushed. "Oh." I'd taken another look at the series of three paintings of what looked vaguely like an anorexic prisoner. "I really like those. They're very... um... thought-provoking."

He'd looked at me for a long time until, unnerved, I'd suggested we join Meloda and the other artists. We'd spent the evening at their studio, with a large group of people, drinking prosecco to celebrate their first exhibition, the first in what they'd hoped would be a long series. We'd talked animatedly through the night.

"You were a definite hit," I'd told Meloda with a wry smile as we walked home in the early hours of the morning.

"Hmmm. It was fun," she'd said. "*You're* the one who's landed a boyfriend, though."

"No way, Meloda. I don't have time for a boyfriend. I have a flat to renovate, remember?"

After dropping Meloda off at her place, I'd headed back to my beloved flat and set about removing carpet from the walls again.

A few hours later, there had been a knock at the door.

Expecting Meloda, I'd been surprised when a dark-haired man had stood before me, holding up a bag of croissants and a thermos. He'd half-smiled. "Thought you might enjoy a bit of breakfast... and maybe some help?"

"Er, okay, hi, um, Peter. Come on in. But you don't need to do any work. I don't want you wasting your Sunday."

"I have no other plans," he'd said, settling down on the floor and ripping open the bag of croissants.

"Mmmm," I hadn't even thought about eating, but biting into the buttery croissant, I'd realized I was ravenous.

From that day on, Peter would turn up every day after work and every Saturday and Sunday. It was obvious he wanted our budding friendship to develop into something more, and he had become more insistent. He claimed he'd never met anyone like me and was certain we were meant to be together. I began to doubt my resolve. He put such effort into courting me that I eventually succumbed. I came home from work one evening to find red roses on every surface of the flat: all over the floor, but also on the countertop, in every cupboard and drawer, in the bath, on the loo seat, everywhere. Even though I found it all a teeny bit cliché, I was been touched and amazed that anyone would go to such lengths for me.

So when I found him in the bedroom, holding out a single red rose and looking at me with forlorn puppy eyes, I caved. I walked over and kissed him, and he kissed me back. He maneuvered me towards the bed and lay me down on the prickly roses. Not wanting to break the mood, I did my best to ignore the sharp pinpricks of pain on my back as we had sex.

Very naturally, Peter had moved in, and we'd developed a routine, with me leaving early in the morning and meeting him at the studio in the evening.

But ever so gradually, things had changed. I'd somehow managed to make him hate me. I'd had to face the truth: I was just not cut out for romantic relationships. I was too self-centered, too traditional, too suburban, always wanting my place to be clean and tidy. And I'd bugged him to start earning a living, not feeling strong enough to carry the financial burden alone. So what if he hadn't been as focused on working as I was? I'd been so intent on creating a safe place for myself that I'd gradually destroyed our relationship.

In the end, he hadn't been able to keep the disgust off his face. So I hadn't really been all that surprised when he announced he'd met someone else.

We were in crisis mode at the office.

Three weeks earlier, Nora, one of my account managers, had set up an exclusive one-to-one interview between *The Economist* technology editor Stephen Holbrook and Keith Yates, EMEA VP at CLOUT. It was an amazing coup: no one got interviews with *The Economist*. No-one. But somehow, Nora had pulled it off. We'd danced around the office, overjoyed, shouting, high-fiving, and, at the end of the day, headed down to the local bar, Paris-Seychelles, for cocktails.

But the demons of PR had intervened, deciding that if an interview with the Economist were to be had, it would not be without complications. First, Thaddeus asked us to change the date so that he could attend both the Economist interview and a meeting with Katia Jablonski, a Slovakian model who'd recently become a CLOUTech brand ambassador.

We'd fought back to ensure Thaddeus didn't change the date and managed to get him to back down, which he did rather sulkily. Then Keith Yates' assistant had sent us a list of topics he agreed to cover and questions he didn't want to be asked. We had ignored the list, as you do, but Thaddeus, who was on copy, forwarded the email to Stephen Holbrook. Then the cancellation email had come.

You'd think you could blame this kind of thing on the client, but you can't. When you were the agency, you were responsible. This is something Vince hammered into us on a daily basis. "The client is king, guys, and we're just meaningless, replaceable lackies. Remember: shit rolls downhill, and we're right at the bottom."

We were trying to talk to anyone at *The Economist* to do whatever we could to salvage the interview, when Rhona called.

Vince signaled us all to shut up as he answered his phone. "Hi, Rhona."

We froze.

"Yes. Yes. Yes, of course. Yes, I'll pass you over."

There was a brief moment of silent collective panic before Vince handed me the phone, and everyone else breathed a sigh of relief.

"He-hello?"

"Bent?"

"Yes Rhona, yes, this is Emiliah Bent."

"I want you to stop working on the CLOUTech account immediately."

My heart began thumping. *This is it. You're being fired.* "I'm sorry?"

"Are you deaf? You're to stop working on the CLOUTech account immediately. We can find someone else. Ben Goodwall has asked that you pitch for the PeakSleek account."

"What?"

I heard her take a sharp intake of breath. "I said. Ben. Goodall. Wants. You. To. Pitch. For. The. Breathe. Account." She enunciated slowly.

"But, erm, I, er-"

"Oh, for God's sake, stop dithering. This is a great opportunity, which Capri would manage far better than you, but Ben Goodwall specifically asked for you. He wants to meet you later today. He's going to call you. Don't mess this up." And she hung up.

My face was burning when I handed Vince his phone.

He stared at me suspiciously. "Why are you blushing?"

"Nothing. I, erm, I just have to go." And I rushed to the bathroom with a huge smile on my face.

9

Sitting at my desk, I stared at the ceiling. PeakSleek. What an amazing company to work for. How the hell was I going to come up with an original, engaging PR campaign to pitch? And with no resources? Nora, Helen and Vince were swamped with CLOUTech, and Rhona had tasked me alone to come up with a pitch.

I began by researching the company. I skimmed over the branding articles, which I knew about, and did some digging on the company. I discovered that PeakSleek, despite its previously dusty image, had a really interesting history.

During World War II, in a humble workshop in Sheffield, a man called George Anderson, a skilled and innovative textile craftsman, had designed equipment for parachute rigs used by soldiers behind enemy lines. His meticulous attention to detail and commitment to quality had quickly earned him a reputation for crafting some of the country's safest and most reliable parachute equipment.

George had faced an uncertain future as the war drew to a close. The demand for military equipment had dwindled, leaving him with a surplus of parachute gear. It was during this time that George had decided to focus on an emerging trend: the development of leisure parachuting. With unwavering determination, George had rebranded his workshop "PinnacleGear" and begun marketing surplus parachute equipment for leisure parachuting. His venture had garnered attention from adrenaline junkies and adventurers hungry for the exhilarating experience of skydiving.

PinnacleGear's reputation had grown, and George had expanded the product line to include high-quality mountaineering gear. With the growing fascination for exploration and conquering of new heights, mountaineers had flocked to PinnacleGear for its durable and reliable equipment. Climbers, equipped with PinnacleGear ropes, harnesses and carabiners, had tackled some of the world's most treacherous peaks.

But George's innovative spirit hadn't stopped there. He'd recognized another niche market in need of safety and quality: the world of high-rise construction. Window cleaners who scaled the towering skyscrapers of rapidly growing post-war cities needed reliable harnesses to ensure their safety. PinnacleGear had adapted once again, designing and manufacturing specialized harnesses that had become the industry standard for high-altitude work.

The brand's iconic logo, a mountain peak, had become, over time, a symbol of trust and reliability in the world of sportswear. As the decades passed, PinnacleGear had continued to innovate and extend its product range. From outdoor apparel for hikers and climbers to state-of-the-art gear for extreme sports enthusiasts, the brand's commitment to excellence had never wavered.

Anderson's son, Geoffrey, had taken over the company's management in the 1980s, branding PinnacleGear as a testament to the enduring spirit of innovation and adaptability. He had transformed the company into a global sportswear powerhouse, providing adventurers and athletes with the tools they needed to reach their own personal summits. But over the past ten years, with the emergence of strong competitors, the company's sales had gradually declined, and Geoffrey Anderson had decided to raise money to avoid lay-offs.

No sooner had the investors taken over seventy percent of the stock than Geoffrey had been pushed out, and Ben Goodall, CEO of PinnacleGear's number one competitor, had been brought in to run the company.

An article in the Financial Times, describing Ben Goodwall as 'the man with the magic touch' described the methodology he had used to turn companies around. The sexy Mr. Goodwall believed in focusing on customer preferences to determine the transformation of a business. *Original.* He explained in the article that his first step was to take a scientific look at customer feedback, market trends, and competition to define the business and financial strategy. He'd then take a close look at the company's people. Who were the forces driving the company forward? Who had a different agenda? What were people's motivations? He would spend time with each manager, listening carefully to their vision for the company, their personal objectives, and any problems they faced. Then he would cut costs aggressively. He knew there were always ways to cut out extra weight, become leaner. He tested people's adaptability and willingness to change. And he believed every company could be turned around with the right approach. The core of his approach was to ensure the entire team embraced change and quickly adapted to evolving market conditions. He then implemented the necessary changes, slashing business units and focusing on the core business that generated profits. And every step of the way, each measure was methodically assessed with numbers, statistics, and customer feedback.

I checked Glassdoor. The employee feedback was mixed: sometimes complimentary, more often critical. The more I read, the more intrigued I was. I'd never had opinions about the way businesses should be run. To me, work was a bit of a pretense, a game in which you had to take part to survive. It was important to act as if everything was really important when in reality, none of it mattered. I mean, I understood, of course, that doctors' and nurses' careers were important, but marketing? Business? What was it all for? I wondered what it was like to have such clarity, so little doubt about how things should be done. The various articles I read explained how Ben Goodwall had turned three companies around using the same ruthless methods, driving sales, gaining visibility, and exponentially increasing profits.

The guy was serious. If anyone was to uncover me as the fraud that I was, it would be him. Why had he asked for me, of all people, to pitch for his account? Was it to expose me to the world?

I needed my proposal to be good. My life depended on it. PeakSleek was launching several new product lines: moisture-wicking fabric products made from recycled plastic, new rock-climbing harnesses, shoes, jackets, gloves, and more. What did PeakSleek customers want most? Was it simply great outdoor experiences? Reliable products? To look cool? I started reading rock-climbing forums, looking into hiking groups on Facebook, and checking out fitness influencers on Instagram. What type of brand image would attract new customers? How could we build on the PeakSleek Me campaign?

I jotted down some ideas, acutely aware of how rubbish they were but needing to plough on. I didn't have much time left to prepare the pitch, as I would be in Paris the following week.

My phone rang. Unknown number. "Hello?"

"Emiliah." The deep voice was familiar. "Ben Goodwall here."

Shit!

He paused for a second. "Are you free for dinner tonight? I need your thoughts on our new product lines and how to market them."

"I, erm-"

"Shall we say eight? I'll pick you up."

"Okay," I squeaked. Hands trembling, I put my phone on the desk.

What am I going to wear?

10

"Here we are." Ben patted my hand, sending a jolt through my body.

The car stopped and the driver walked around to my side to open the door. Nestled in the heart of Bermondsey, the tall, unpretentious building stood as a quiet sentinel against the busy city. Its unremarkable yellow brick façade revealed nothing of the life within. The windows, framed in peeling grey paint, were either dark or covered in curtains. Narrow black balconies, accessible from each floor, jutted out like afterthoughts.

I looked up inquisitively. "This?"

He smiled and led me through the front door.

Is he a psychopath? Is this the end?

The dimly-lit entrance, housing a wall of letterboxes, revealed nothing more. A faded welcome mat, its fibers worn thin, lay in front of a simple grey lift. I followed him and he pressed the button.

Whatever.

We alighted on the top floor, facing closed doors. He smiled down at me. "This way." He opened a door into a stairwell.

"Where are we going?" I asked suspiciously.

"Don't worry." He smiled as he took the first few steps upwards. "This isn't a trap, Emiliah. It's just a bit of an unusual place."

My heart started beating. The stairs ended at what looked like a fire door. Ben pushed it open, and we found ourselves in a rooftop restaurant with glass windows and a glass roof. I looked around in awe. It was like a tropical garden overlooking London, with tiny fairy lights hanging from small palm trees, huge oleanders in pots, and candles flickering on every table. A garlicky smell hit me as I took in the Mediterranean atmosphere. "It's beautiful."

A man with a huge belly wearing a tracksuit came rambling over to us. "Ben!" he exclaimed before rattling on in a language I couldn't identify. He made a gesture for us to follow him, still speaking his strange dialect, and showed us to a table in the corner with a stunning view of the city.

Ben gave the older man a friendly tap on the back. "Thanks, Stavros." Stavros grunted and sauntered off.

As we sat down, I looked around in awe. "What was that language?"

"It's a Cretan dialect. Stavros doesn't speak English or even Greek. Just his dialect."

"And you speak this Cretan dialect?"

"Oh no. Nobody actually understands him. You'll get used to it. You don't actually need to understand what he's saying. He and his wife are the most amazing cooks, and cooking is an international language." He looked at me darkly. "A bit like love."

Did he really say that?

I looked around. "Are there no menus?"

He smiled. "Nope."

I was trying to think of a witty way of asking him to be more explicit when Stavros returned, banging a bottle of rosé on the table and placing tiny rolls of stuffed vine leaves drenched in olive oil between us.

"I take it there's no vegan option?" I smiled.

Ben's dazzling grey eyes widened in horror. "You're *vegan?*"

"No." I laughed, glad I had managed to unsettle him. I popped one of the rolls into my mouth. It was heavenly.

A few minutes later, Stavros reappeared, banging more plates on the table, chipped ceramic dishes containing the most delicious food: peeled bell peppers in olive oil, lamb meatballs, tomato, cucumber and feta salad, warm pitta bread slathered in butter and garlic, marinated calamari and warm, soft slices of grilled aubergine.

I tore off a piece of warm pitta and dipped it in the tzatziki.

"This is delicious, Ben. What's the restaurant called?"

He shrugged. "I don't even know if it has a name. We wouldn't understand it anyway. My boxing friends and I call it the Roof Taverna."

"Your boxing friends?"

He wiped the corner of his mouth with a worn linen napkin. "Yes. Boxing is one of the many sports I practice."

Where does he find the time? I wondered.

I remained silent for a few moments, not sure if I would be able to ask an intelligent question.

He leaned forward. "So Emiliah, what made you take up a career in PR?"

I paused, unsure how to explain that my career had so far been built on a series of coincidences. "Well, I studied political science and I love writing. When I was in my final year, I found a leaflet advertising Gant Ltd's graduate programme, and I applied." I shrugged. "They needed a French speaker, so I was hired."

He nodded. "And where did you learn French? Did you study abroad?"

I flushed. "No, I erm, I lived in France for a few years as a child."

"Oh," he said. "Where was that?"

I swiveled the stem of my wine glass between my thumb and forefinger. "Mainly in the South-West, near Agen."

He frowned. "What did your parents do?"

"Oh, er, well, my father was a visiting professor at Toulouse university," I lied. "We lived quite a long way outside of Toulouse; my parents wanted to live in the countryside," I added hurriedly.

I swallowed. "Anyway, it was a long time ago and I don't remember a lot about it."

Ben looked at me in silence, his expression quizzical.

Say something! Change the subject! "So, erm, where did you grow up?"

He shrugged. "Hong Kong."

"Hong Kong? Wow! What was it like growing up there?"

"It was awful." He looked into the distance, and I could see the pain in his eyes.

"How so?" I asked softly.

"Well, I was at a very exclusive boarding school with lots of wealthy expats, but it was a cruel, cruel place. I had braces and glasses at the time. I suppose I was an easy target for bullies."

I felt a pang of compassion for this gorgeous man, who was clearly more vulnerable than he seemed.

I leaned forward. "I'm so sorry. It must have been very hard."

He stared at me, frowning. "I never tell anyone this stuff, you know. What's your secret, Emiliah? Here I am, confiding in you as if we've known each other for years."

Saying I blushed would be an understatement. My face burnt. *How could this, this... man, this gorgeous, successful CEO, be talking to me like this?*

I took another piece of pitta. "Well, I must say, I'm glad you brought me here. It's beautiful. It's as if we're not even in London."

He was staring into my eyes again. "If you could go anywhere, Emiliah, where would you go?"

Think of somewhere original. "Erm, I don't know, erm... Kazakhstan?" I'd actually seen beautiful photos of the country in National Geographic.

He leaned back and crossed his arms. "Really?"

I smiled. "Well yes, but there are other places too. For example, I've always wanted to go to Gordes, in Provence. It sounds beautiful."

His eyes crinkled. "I love Provence. It's very special." He stared at me in silence for a moment.

It turned into a magical evening, thanks, in part, to the wine, which helped me relax. I learned all about Ben's harsh upbringing in Hong Kong, his need to escape outdoors, and his love of not just boxing, but rock-climbing, kayaking and skiing. How he discovered boxing in his twenties when one of his friends had challenged him to a fight, and he'd trained for three months nonstop. How he used similar techniques he'd acquired practicing sports to manage companies.

He's so driven, I mused, fascinated.

I told him about my love of the countryside and of curling up with a good book in front of a roaring fire. And about my first ambition, to be a farmer's wife, which made him laugh uproariously.

"You wanted to be *what*?"

So I explained how, as a child, I'd been obsessed with James Herriot's books, how I'd dreamed of running away to a farm, milking cows, collecting eggs, bottle-feeding lambs, and warming abandoned kittens in an old range. "I was young," I said defensively. "I had a romantic vision of farm life. But I grew out of it in my teen years."

He gave me another intense stare, making it impossible for me to escape the mesmerizing grey of his eyes. "And you ended up in international PR, little miss farmer's wife."

He's so hot, I found myself thinking as he poured me yet another glass of wine. *And really sweet.*

Ben's driver was waiting outside the building when we left the restaurant. The perfect gentleman, Ben walked me to my front door. He bent down and gave me a kiss on the cheek that lingered a second too long. "Night night, Miss Bent," he murmured.

"Goodnight," I whispered before running inside.

As soon as I closed my front door, I leaned against it and sighed. *Ohmygodohmygodohmygod.*

11

The Friday night before my trip to Paris, I met up with Meloda for dinner and she introduced me to Felicity.

Raki Room, a Turkish restaurant near Shoreditch, glowed with warm, golden light, casting intricate patterns on the crimson walls. The scent of spices and sizzling meats wafted through the air, painting an exotic tapestry that transported us far from the bustling streets of London.

Seated at a corner table, I observed the two women—Meloda and her new love interest, the enigmatic Flit, originally from New York, but who'd lived all over the world.

Meloda's eyes sparkled with affection. "Flit, this is Emiliah Bent," Meloda said with a smile. "Em, meet Felicity - Flit, the woman who's captured my heart."

I extended my hand to the woman of quiet confidence. She was taller than Meloda, which was quite a feat, and about ten years older. Whereas Meloda was always fabulously dressed, Flit had a much simpler style: jeans, sneakers, chunky cardigan. Her handshake was firm, her gaze piercing. "It's a pleasure to meet you, Emiliah. Meloda's told me so much about you."

As I settled into my seat, the menu arrived: a treasure trove of exotic flavors and tantalizing choices of kebabs adorned with fragrant herbs, vegetable stews, mounds of aromatic rice, and baskets of warm, freshly baked bread.

"So, Emiliah," Flit gave me her full attention. "You also work at Gant & Ballaster?"

"Yes, although I'm not as specialized as Mel," I replied with a smile. "And it's certainly not as exciting as your work, but PR does pay the bills."

Flit nodded, her curiosity lingering in the air. "And you have a new client, I hear? Breathe? That must be interesting."

I blushed violently. "He's not a client, not yet anyway. We have to pitch for the account."

Flit looked at me with curiosity. Meloda chimed in, her voice filled with affectionate teasing. "Oh, you have no idea. Emiliah's really caught the eye of their CEO."

"Mel!" I chastised.

Flit leaned back in her chair, her gaze never leaving mine. "There's nothing wrong with leveraging your influence, you know."

"Why don't we order?" I asked, quickly changing the subject.

When the food arrived, the conversation flowed to safer shores. Flit, it turned out, had a gift for storytelling, her words weaving vivid tales of her journalistic adventures. The restaurant seemed to hum with the laughter and camaraderie of our gathering.

When we were wiping our plates clean with flatbread, Flit turned her attention to me again, her gaze sharpening in a way that made the room seem suddenly colder. "So, Emiliah," her voice casual but carrying a weight that hinted at her journalistic instincts, "Meloda's told me quite a bit about your work together, but I'd love to hear about your childhood. What was it like growing up in France?"

I smiled tightly. "Oh, you know, it was pretty standard. School, friends, the usual ups and downs of the early teens." My answer was as bland as I could make it.

Her eyes locked onto mine, as if she sensed my childhood in France was a topic I wanted to avoid at all costs.

"It was only two years," I added hurriedly. "Not exactly a significant part of my childhood. It's all very hazy now. Lots of fields, cows, sheep, you know. Really not that interesting, unlike Meloda's." I glanced at my closest friend. Meloda had grown up in Jacmel, Haiti. Her parents had been doctors, and her father had been shot at work by a gang of Chimères when Meloda was six. Her mother had later died of breast cancer, and although she didn't end up homeless, Meloda was very much left to fend for herself for a number of years.

Meloda's hand found mine under the table, a subtle show of support. She instinctively understood the intricacies of my past without knowing them. Flit, however, continued to tread where few had ventured before. She leaned in, her voice lowering. "Yes, Meloda's childhood is fascinating. But I imagine yours must have been interesting too."

I could see I had awakened the investigative journalist in her. She sensed I was hiding something. There was no way a couple of years in France was as interesting as living it rough in Haiti.

I shrugged. "Not really, not that I can remember."

Her gaze lingered on me for a moment longer, a silent acknowledgment of the dance we were performing around the truth. Then, mercifully, she turned her attention back to the waiter, who brought us the dessert menus.

As the evening wore on, and Flit told us of her missions overseas, even in war zones, I found myself drawn into her enigmatic world, her charisma and passion undeniable. She spoke of the bustling streets of Cairo, the serenity of Japanese temples, the vibrant chaos of Istanbul's Grand Bazaar, and the utter devastation of Yemen.

As we bid farewell to our enchanting evening, I couldn't help but wonder how long I could maintain this delicate equilibrium and keep my past hidden in the shadows while embracing the unfolding complexities of the present. The seed of unease was planted. Flit's questions, innocent as they might have seemed to anyone else, felt like the gentle prodding of a lockpick at the edges of my past.

12

The elegant 16th arrondissement of Paris was a neighborhood that exuded sophistication, with its stately Haussmanian buildings and meticulously manicured gardens.

My elder sister, Davina, emerged from her imposing entrance, her expression guarded as she approached me. Her straight dark hair was neatly pulled back, and her tan, tailored coat spoke of a successful life.

She gave me a perfunctory nod, her lips forming a tight smile. "Emiliah," she said, her voice cool. "It's been a while."

"Davina," I replied, trying to infuse warmth into my tone. "Yes, it has."

The unspoken weight of our shared history hung between us. A breeze rustled the leaves of the chestnut trees that lined the quiet Parisian Street, but it did little to dispel the chill that enveloped our encounter.

I glanced past her to the imposing entrance of the building. "Is Katie ready?" I asked, shifting the focus to my niece, our one fragile connection.

Davina's eyes softened just a fraction as she nodded. "Yes, she's been looking forward to seeing you." Her gaze flitted to the ornate wrought-iron gate, as if seeking refuge in its intricate design. "Come inside."

As we entered the building, the marble-floored foyer echoed with the sound of our footsteps. The silence was palpable, broken only by the distant hum of an elevator. It was as though the very walls held their breath, bearing witness to a strained reunion.

We climbed the polished stone staircase to Davina's apartment on the third floor. The air was scented with lavender, a fragrance she had always loved as a child. It felt oddly comforting amidst the tension.

Katie, my nerdy niece, was waiting in the living room. Her face lit up when she saw me, and she rushed over to hug me tightly.

"Auntie Em!" she exclaimed, her voice filled with excitement. "I've missed you!"

Tears welled in my eyes as I hugged her back, a surge of love and longing washing over me. "I've missed you too, sweetheart." I savored the hug for as long as I could, lingering on the faint thread of family ties.

I was taking Katie to the Louvre, something I'd promised to do the previous year. Why a twelve-year-old girl would want to visit the Louvre was beyond me, but Katie was one of those kids with an insatiable curiosity that spread into every field, from biology to history to electronic music.

Davina watched the reunion with a measured gaze, her emotions hidden beneath a façade of composure. As Katie and I settled into a conversation about her latest school adventures, I couldn't help but steal glances at my sister. The pain of our shared past, the wounds that had never fully healed, hovered just below the surface. Davina had allowed me into Katie's life, but she couldn't bring herself to forgive me for what I had done all those years ago.

I stood up, eager to leave my sister's stiff presence. I glanced at Katie. "Okay, let's go."

She widened her eyes. "Now?"

"Yes, now. We'll grab something to eat at the Restaurants du Monde in the Louvre mall."

She looked at me with a sly smile. "Do we have time to dress up?"

I stole a look at Davina. She gave me a barely perceptible nod.

"Oh, go on then."

And just for the heck of it, I let Katie dress me in one of her outfits. As we were of similar height and build, we looked like sisters by the time we left. Davina did not comment or show any kind of emotion. We were both clad in black pixie boots, red tights, me a short black velour skirt, red top, and black, sleeveless furry jacket, she in black shorts and an oversized woolly red jumper. She'd braided our hair in the same half-up, half-down fashion, and we wore identical loopy red and silver earrings. I looked and felt fourteen, minus the acne. I looked a bit silly, but who cared? It wasn't as if I was going to see anyone I knew.

I shut the front door, brilliant winter sunshine warming our faces. We walked all the way from the 16th arrondissement to the Pont de l'Alma, then along the Seine to the Alexandre III bridge, across the river between the Grand and Petit Palais, and out onto the Champs Elysées. Water glistened on the pave stones as we crossed the Place de la Concorde, chatting about Maître Gims, Harry Potter and school, and I gradually relaxed.

When we reached the Louvre Gardens, I was relieved to see there were only two people waiting at the entrance. "Excellent. We won't have to queue."

I walked up to the tall man and much shorter girl and tapped the man on the shoulder. "Excusez-moi ?"'

As he turned around, I stepped back in shock. "Mr. Goodall! What are you doing here?"

He looked at me strangely, as if he couldn't quite place me. Then recognition dawned, and he smiled, eyes twinkling. "Miss Bent!" He turned to Katie. "Hello. You must be Emiliah's older sister?"

Katie giggled. I was devastated. To talk to this...*man*, I needed to be elegant and sophisticated, not fitted out in furry jackets and pixie boots. I felt ridiculous and childlike.

"This is Fiona, my sister.' Ben gestured at the pretty, pale girl standing beside him. 'I only see her about once a year.

My parents live in Singapore."

Fiona looked at Katie and me in awe. "Wow, I love your hair. How did you do it?" And Katie, beaming, explaining how she had learned to braid with YouTube tutorials. "You can learn so much with Youtube. You should check out the marble runs and trotbot tutorials. They're really cool."

Surprisingly, Fiona didn't seem put off by Katie's geekiness, and in no time, they were talking dystopian novels, computer games and preferred Greek mythology. Ben rolled his eyes. "Well, I guess we'll have trouble interrupting then now. Shall we get some lunch?"

I bit my thumbnail. "Actually, we're on a bit of a tight schedule. After the Louvre, we're going to to the Champs Elysée for a bit of shopping, before heading to the Plaza Athénée for tea. We're having a special Aunt-Niece day."

He nodded slowly. "You know the Louvre's closed today, right?"

"Really. I was really looking forward to... to...erm...."

He raised an eyebrow inquisitively. "The Mona Lisa? The Raft of the Medusa?"

"Mmm, yeh," I replied, looking away.

"Were you just looking forward to the Restaurants du Monde?" The smile reached his eyes before his mouth, which twitched just a fraction. "They are open today, you know?"

I relaxed a little. "Now that we're here, I suppose we *could* have lunch here."

He nodded. "Sounds good to me. Come on, girls."

As we passed the inverted pyramid, which was being skillfully washed by window cleaners, Katie and Fiona were still nattering away. "I *know*, right? I mean... Katniss.... Tobias .....Four...' 'Yes, *yes*! I *know*!" They were both squealing with delight at having found a kindred spirit. Still, I needed to make it clear we wouldn't be hanging around for long. "Girls. To be clear, Katie and I will leave in exactly one hour."

Two hours later, the girls were still at it. "Right? I mean Hogwarts...Snape.... Hufflepuff?"

Ben and I still hadn't broached the subject of PeakSleek. He was asking me questions about myself, which I did my best to deflect. As we talked, I became increasingly aware of his stubble, grey eyes and muscular forearms.

The usually busy Carrousel mall, now empty but for a few people enjoying a leisurely lunch, had an abandoned atmosphere. As we talked, my mind wandered back to the people cleaning the inverted Louvre pyramid. The window cleaners, attached with harnesses, had been prancing around from one area of the pyramid to the other, slathering the glass with soap before scraping it off and wiping it down. The movements, the jumps, the sweeps of scraper against window were so graceful that while I chatted idly with Ben, it was as if I was recalling an improvised, contemporary ballet.

Then I saw it, the idea that had been missing from the pitch.

Ben was staring at me intently. "Did you hear what I just said?"

I snapped back to the present. "Oh God. I'm sorry. I just thought of something for the PeakSleek campaign."

He leaned back and put his hands behind his head. "Tell me."

Why did you mention it? How can you be so stupid? "I can't. I really need to work on it. It may not be such a good idea."

"Try me." He was no longer smiling. There was a directiveness in his voice that I couldn't disobey. So I explained my idea.

"I like it," he said, nodding. "I can really see that working, actually. What about if you-" he hesitated for a second before making some suggestions of his own. My heart thumped with adrenaline as I saw the scene coming together. "Yes! Of course. Yes." And the more we talked, the more ideas blossomed. I could hardly wait to get this thing started.

Fiona and Katie were staring at us. I blushed, making them giggle.

I checked my watch and blanched. "Okay, let's go. We have shopping to do." I picked up my black furry handbag.

Katie and Fiona shared a glance and then Katie gazed up at me with puppy eyes. "Oh Em, puh-leaaaase can Fiona and

Ben come with us? Maybe we can all go to Plaza Athénée for tea together as well? Please, please, please, please?"

Fiona looked regretfully at Katie. "We're going to the Sia concert tonight. I'm not sure we'll have time for shopping *and* tea."

'O.M.G,' Katie said in a dramatically low voice. "You. Have. To. Be. Kidding. Me. How did you get tickets?"

Ben excused himself and headed for the loos as Fiona explained that Ben had bought the tickets for her birthday months earlier. "It was such an amazing surprise. I guess he must have bought them as soon as they became available."

She was still telling us about every detail of the surprise when Ben returned. "Okay, girls, time to go."

We set off for the Champs Élysées and visited every girly shop on the avenue. Katie and Fiona tried on numerous clothes and accessories, giggling and shrieking, while Ben and I fetched, exchanged, and advised. I couldn't help thinking that Peter would never have agreed to go along with all this silly, girly stuff.

"Why don't you try this?" We were in the changing rooms at Zadig & Voltaire, and Katie was holding out a little black number.

I looked at the dress with the low backline and raised my eyebrows. "Really, Katie?" I frowned.

"Yes," she nodded eagerly. "Hang on." She ran off, to find more items and returned a few minutes later with lacy black tights, petrol-blue shiny heels, and a matching blue clutch.

"Hmm," I conceded as I headed towards the changing room. I could sense Ben, standing near the cabins, holding clothes, watching me.

I pulled my clothes off, aware we were separated only by a piece of fabric. When I emerged gingerly from behind the thick, cream curtain, Katie and Fiona were showing him their finds, and he was giving them his full attention, oohing and aahing. They eventually turned around when I pretended to cough.

Fiona's mouth dropped open. "Wow."

Katie was gaping, too. "Auntie Em! You *have* to buy that outfit. I've never seen you look so sexy."

I give her a stern look. "You're too young to be using that kind of language, Katie.'"

Ben didn't take his eyes off me as he spoke to Katie. "Young lady, I agree with your aunt. That said, I agree with you, too."

I blushed. I couldn't believe he was flirting with me like this. What would Rhona think?

They were all waiting for me outside when I exited the shop. Katie hugged me fiercely. "Guess what, Auntie Em? Ben has found extra tickets for the Sia concert. Please say we can go? Pleeeease?"

I stared at him, a combination of feelings washing over me. "What about the Plaza Athénée?" I asked without much conviction.

Katie and Fiona were jumping up and down, desperate for me to agree to the new plan. "We can go there any time. Please, please, please, please, Em. Pretty please." She gave me another sad puppy look.

"Okay," I smiled. I was actually quite excited. "But I'll have to call your Mum and make sure it's okay with her."

Both Katie and Fiona hugged me fiercely, and Ben gave me a discreet wink.

13

The taxi raced through Paris as the sun was setting. Despite having been here many times, I was always amazed by the beauty of the illuminated monuments and boulevards at dusk.

While Katie pointed out her favorite sights to Fiona, Ben studied my face. "Are you okay, Emiliah?"

"Fine. Thanks, yes, no problem," I managed. Surprisingly, Davina had been okay with my whisking Katie off to an unplanned concert, but I was nervous. What did he expect in return? I'd flirted with the man, and now we were going to a concert together. I should probably have called Vince to make sure it was okay.

Ben chatted with the girls until we arrived at the concert. It was so cool. We were guided backstage by a guy who looked very much like a CIA spy. The air was electric, charged with the energy of countless fans. Katie and Fiona, wide-eyed and buzzing with youthful excitement, clung to our hands, their smiles mirroring our own. It was their first concert, and the joy in their eyes was infectious. Ben smiled down at me, and I felt a strong urge to hug him. I didn't, though, which I felt demonstrated great professionalism on my part.

The atmosphere backstage shifted. It was a world apart from the frenzied energy of the crowd. Here, the air hummed with a focused intensity, a collective breath held in anticipation of the magic unfolding.

Suddenly, a light shone on what looked like a llama walking onto the stage. Then she appeared, the iconic bow on her head.

'I grew up in a thunderstorm,' Sia sang. The llama started undulating, then separated into four dancers, revealing a fifth in a tan leotard. "Maddie," I breathed. The dancer crouched, kicked, and pirouetted, accompanying Sia's voice perfectly.

Sia's voice engulfed the stage, and the world seemed to pause. Her presence was magnetic, her voice a powerful force that resonated deep within our souls. The girls stood between us, their hands gripped tightly in ours as the first notes of 'Chandelier' filled the air. The stage was a spectacle of color and light, each song accompanied by dancers who brought the music to life in a visual feast that was nothing short of mesmerizing.

A tangible energy pulsed through the crowd and connected us all. In this moment, surrounded by music and light, I felt a shift. The man beside me was more than a prospect. His fingers brushed mine, sending a jolt of electricity through my body.

Katie and Fiona were standing in front of us, hands clasped

and gazing at the stage, as Ben moved closer to me and took my hand in his, softly stroking my palm with his thumb. It was thrilling, exciting, clandestine.

The stage of the Olympia bathed in ethereal light as Sia's voice soared, once again. The crowd swayed, lost in the magic of her performance. He moved closer still, putting a strong arm around my shoulder. I stood perfectly still, unsure what was expected of me, but reveling in the moment.

Every song was magical. The atmosphere was electric. The crowd sang in a way I'd never experienced.

When the final notes of 'Breathe me' faded into the night, we lingered, not quite ready to leave the magic behind. But as Katie and Fiona turned towards us, Ben and I both quickly moved away from each other. The walk back to the car was quiet, Ben stealing glances at me while the girls described every second of the concert.

In no time at all, we were back in a cab, on our back to Davina's, singing at the tops of our voices.

We came to a stop in front of Davina's building. We all piled out and before I could stop them, Fiona and Katie had disappeared inside. I turned to see Ben paying the driver and the car driving off. I stared at him. "Hang on, didn't you want him to wait? How're you going to get home?"

He took my hands in his. "He's just driving around the block. He'll be back soon. So will Fiona."

Under the soft glow of the Paris streetlamps, the air was thick with anticipation.

Ben took my hand in his and I felt that familiar jolt. The city seemed to hold it breath, as if aware of the magic unfolding.

I swallowed, my heart thumping violently. He looked leaned towards me, stopping inches from my lips. "I had a wonderful time tonight, Miss Bent." He paused. "I like you very much."

I blushed fiercely.

He leaned in and kissed me on the cheek, close to my lips but not quite touching them. "Really very much," he murmured, leaning down again, kissing me lightly on the lips. My chest was about to explode.

I do, too. I really, really like you.

He kissed me a third time, a teeny bit more insistently, and suddenly, his arms were wrapped around me, and my lips were parting, and we were melting into each other.

The taxi pulled up behind us and Ben pulled away gently. Then Fiona re-appeared, and Ben smiled at me. "See you at the campaign presentation."

14

Back in the office, we were all holding our breath, unable to move. Rhona was sitting at the head of the conference table, dwarfing everyone around her. To her right was Capri, the favorite. To her left, Shells and Bells. "Mmmm. I suppose that could work."

I breathed a sigh of relief.

Rhona glared at me. "It'll need tweaking, though." She turned to Capri. "I'd like you to work on it." She paused, obviously struggling to remember my name, before nodding in my direction. "She'll provide any background information you need, Capri. Then, hopefully, we'll have something presentable for the pitch tomorrow."

Capri gave me a smug smile. "Of course, Rhona. No problem." She snapped her laptop closed and, perching on her shiny Louboutins, walked confidently out of the room, giving us all a glimpse of thigh escaping the slit in her immaculate pencil dress.

Boy, do I hate her.

"Right." Rhona thumped the table with one of her

massive hands, making us all jump, and turned to Vince. "CLOUT. Gimme the shit." She pulled a piece of wood from her massive bag and started chewing it while Vince gave her the lowdown on the current activities and recent accomplishments. Her manners were appalling. *How did she get away with it?*

Vince was pacing the floor, going through each item on the agenda, subtly underlining the successes, and avoiding the glitches. She had to be impressed with all the results we'd achieved. Even though Keith Yates's interview with *The Economist* had fallen through, the team had secured several big features on CLOUT's European leadership in the past few weeks, including a very flattering portrait of Yates in the Financial Times.

"Cut the crap, Vince." Rhona's voice sliced through Vince's like a razor. "I want figures.' You show me that your team's efforts have increased CLOUT's sales, and I'll give you the pat on the back that you're obviously craving. Until then,' she lifted her muscular frame from the tiny chair beneath her. 'Until then, I really don't have time for your self-congratulation."

She strode out of the room, Bells and Shells in tow.

Meloda stood up. "Geez, that was intense."

Helen leaned over to Vince. "Shall I check and see if the lunchboxes have arrived?"

Vince flexed his muscles. "Sure. I need a break. I'll be back in fifteen."

I stared into space, wondering what Capri would do to the campaign I'd presented. I hoped she'd keep Ben's ideas at least.

"Where is everyone?" Capri was back, peering around the door and staring at me accusingly as if I'd made everyone disappear.

"They're just having a break. Helen's gone to get the lunchboxes."

She raised her eyebrows, and we sat in silence.

When Helen reappeared with the pile of boxes, I stood up to open the door. Bells didn't even look up from her smartphone.

Suddenly, everyone was back in the room, helping themselves to the lunch boxes. Before I could grab a calamari one, they'd all been snatched, and I was left with *pigeon à la crème*. Not my favorite choice. Capri, Bells, and Shells picked at their meals as though the food had been chewed and spat back into the elegant, corrugated cardboard boxes.

Rhona scoffed through two Pigeon boxes, seemingly oblivious to our shock at her snorting and wiping her face on her forearm in the manner of Henry the Eighth. She stifled a belch before clearing her throat. "Okay, Capri. Can you take us through the revised campaign?"

Capri gave us all a fake smile before launching into her presentation. "Here we go. So, I thought there were some interesting ideas in Emiliah's presentation, but the whole thing obviously lacked a professional eye."

How dare she?

She clicked through each slide, explaining how the PeakSleek pitch would benefit from a much more fashion-oriented approach. Gone was the Louvre stunt. Gone was the dedicated website with videos of rescue workers, sky-scraper window cleaners, and famous climbers; gone was the fundraising campaign in Nepal. It was all gone. Replaced by traditional PR, comprising a product launch, celebrities, and a design competition. My heart sank. I'd put so many hours into this. The market research, the barriers to entry, the creative ideas. I had been so looking forward to presenting it to the PeakSleek team. I couldn't help thinking they wouldn't like her version as much as they would have mine. It didn't feel like she was showing much interest in the markets PeakSleek was trying to capture.

"And so this is how," Capri paused for effect, "we're going to make climbing cool again. For everyone, from window cleaners to Olympic medallists." She looked at Rhona expectantly.

Rhona finished her notes, screwed the lid onto her fountain pen, and looked up at Capri. "Sit down."

Capri slid into her chair, looking slightly less confident.

Rhona looked straight ahead and inhaled. "I must say, that was a particularly pathetic effort."

Capri's face fell, but Rhona hadn't finished. "That was

actually the worst piece of work ever pitched to me."

Even to me, it seemed a bit harsh. We all kept our heads down. Rhona was at her nastiest, and avoiding eye contact was advisable. "I'm beginning to wonder whether you have the brain power to hold a position such as yours." Capri's face was a combination of shock and pain.

"Was what I asked you to do so difficult?" Rhona glared at Capri, expecting an answer. We all sat uncomfortably through the excruciating silence.

A piece of food flew out of Rhona's mouth as she shouted. "Well, was it?"

"No." Tears were running down Capri's cheeks.

"Get out of my sight." Rhona didn't even look at her as she said this, and Capri ran out of the room.

"We'll go with your version." She didn't even bother looking at me as she said this. "I have a call now until six. Let's wrap up."

As I headed to the loos, I felt my shoulders relaxing. *Thank God that's over.* When I opened the door, I heard sobbing in one of the cubicles. I hurried to reach another cubicle before Capri exited, but she pushed her door open violently. "Come here to gloat, have you?"

"No, I-"

"Just so you know," she walked towards me, her face inches from mine. "Once Ben Goodwall has approved the campaign, Rhona will take it away from you. She hates

Vince, and she hates your whole team. And anyone can see *you* are just not up to the job. You may be okay on paper but look at you, all hesitant and clumsy. What client is going to put you in charge?" She stared at me, disgust contorting her face.

So she knew. They all knew I was a fraud.

15

"Emiliah?" It was Vince. His voice sounded strained, barely above a whisper. "Listen, Emiliah, we all have food poisoning."

"What?" I gripped the phone tighter, my knuckles turning white.

"Nora, Helen, Bells, Shells, and me, we all have food poisoning. From the calamari in the lunchboxes, I think."

My stomach dropped. "But the pitch is today, Vince."

"I know, I know, I'm sorry. You and Rhona will just have to manage alone."

The news hit me like a punch to the gut. As Vince's strained voice relayed the devastating information, a cold wave of dread washed over me, leaving me momentarily paralyzed. The room span as I grappled with the enormity of the situation. The pitch was today, the culmination of weeks of late-night work, and now most of the team was incapacitated. My heart pounded in my chest, a frantic drumbeat underscoring the panic rising within me. I envisioned expectant faces of the PeakSleek marketing team, not to mention the charismatic CEO, and the monumental task that lay ahead. Rhona and me, alone. How could Rhona and I possibly pull this off without Vince's leadership, without the cohesive support of our team? The weight of responsibility threatened to crush me, my confidence evaporating like mist in the harsh light of reality. I felt a lump in my throat, the urge to scream or cry or run building with each passing second. But there was no time for that. I had to act, to somehow find a way to salvage this, even as the ground seemed to crumble beneath my feet.

"But Vince—" The line went dead before I could finish. I stared at my phone in disbelief. This could not be happening. The pitch was our biggest opportunity yet, and now half the team was out.

Why didn't I insist on having the calamari? Why am I so nice? I checked my watch. Forty-five minutes to go. I'd have to drive myself there. The plan had been for Vince to pick us all up, and we'd planned to rehearse again in the car. I ran downstairs and into the street, my mind racing through the presentation points I'd need to cover on my own.

Where's my car? I zoned out for a minute while trying to remember where I'd last parked it. The world seemed to blur as my thoughts swirled, a cacophony of panic and half-formed plans.

"Watch out, bitch!" shouted a cyclist as he swerved to avoid me. I jumped back, pulse racing.

Shit, that was close. I stepped backward onto the pavement, shaking slightly. *Oh yes, I remember*. I turned right and headed towards the underground car park. The weight of the situation bore down on me with each step, urgency electrifying my every movement.

I bolted to my car, almost tripping over my own feet. I threw open the door and slid into the driver's seat, my mind a whirlwind of fear and determination. The engine roared to life, and I reversed out of the parking spot, my heart thundering in my ears.

Crunch. *Fuck*. I'd scraped the car against a pillar. I drove forward, making the crunching sound worse. I didn't dare check the clock.

I arrived at the barrier. *Jesus, where's my badge?* I fumbled in my bag, sweating profusely, but it wasn't there. I felt a lump forming in my throat. My hands trembled as I rummaged through papers, makeup, and receipts. My pulse quickened as precious seconds ticked away.

I pressed the emergency assistance button repeatedly, each beep amplifying my sense of dread. Finally, a disembodied voice crackled through the speaker. "How can I assist you?"

"I've lost my badge," I stammered, glancing at my watch again. "I need to get out, urgently."

"Please write out a cheque for the lost badge fee and hold it up against the screen."

A surge of frustration and disbelief hit me. Who uses cheques anymore? But I complied, scribbling furiously, the pen slipping from my sweaty grip. I held the cheque up to the screen, hoping the attendant could read my frantic scrawl.

"Hurry, please," I begged, my voice cracking.

After what felt like an eternity, the barrier lifted.

By the time I arrived in front of the long, low building bearing a huge PeakSleek sign, I was six minutes late and desperately needed to pee. There they were, Ben, a group of his colleagues, and Rhona, taller even than Ben, in a red suit and purple bowtie. One look at her told me everything I needed to know: there would be no time for a bathroom break.

My bladder, of course, made it very clear that it would not wait. I glanced around desperately, my eyes darting from the sleek, glass-fronted building to the carpark. There had to be somewhere, anywhere, I could go quickly before facing the pitch. And then I saw it—some bushes at the edge of the parking lot, slightly overgrown and, crucially, offering a modicum of privacy.

I took a deep breath, checked that Rhona was still engrossed in her conversation, and drove over to the bushes. I took a minute more to roll on some more deodorant, brush my hair, and wipe the worst of the sweat from my face, then headed behind a bush. When I reached the relative cover of the bush, I glanced around quickly, praying noone was watching.

With no time to lose, I crouched down, pulled my skirt up, tight across my thighs, and awkwardly held my handbag between my teeth, trying to keep my balance. The bushes rustled around me as tried to position myself in such a way that I wouldn't pee on my shoes.

I rummaged frantically in my bag for a tissue, but the only thing I found was a crumpled sweetwrapper. "Great," I muttered to myself.

Just as I was awkwardly trying to button up and regain some semblance of composure, I heard a noise. I froze, my chest drumming with adrenaline. Peering out from the bushes, I saw a man with white hair, staring at me, his eyes wide with shock. His mouth opened and closed like a fish out of water. My face burned with embarrassment.

"Um, good morning," I said weakly, trying to straighten my skirt as best I could. The man just stared, and I could see the wheels turning in his head as he tried to process what he had just witnessed.

I grabbed my handbag, finally managing to secure it over my shoulder, and walked as briskly and nonchalantly as I could towards the building entrance, mercifully locating a bottle of Purell in my bag.

As I approached the group, Rhona turned and gave me a sharp look.

"Hi, Ben.'" I smiled brightly as I held my hand out. "So sorry for being late. Several members of our team have food poisoning, so we had a bit of a logistical glitch."

He smiled warmly, giving me a firm handshake. "Yes, Rhona was just explaining. No worries. Why don't you two take a few minutes to talk while I gather the team? Oh, here's Martin. Martin, let me introduce Rhona Ballaster and Emiliah Bent, from Gant& Ballaster. Martin is a very important shareholder and I invited him to attend the pitch."

I turned to see the white-haired man who'd watched me emerge from the bushes, zipping up my skirt. *Fuck.*

He seemed to be even more shocked to have to shake my hand, but I decided not to explain that the moisture on them was Purell, not pee.

As Ben and Martin retreated, Rhona leaned towards me. "I'm very unimpressed, Bent."

"Sorry, Rhona. So sorry."

She gave me a disparaging look and walked towards a sofa, pulling out one of the presentations. "Okay, here's how we're going to do this."

16

The conference room was packed with the PeakSleek team, their expressions a mix of curiosity and expectation. The walls were adorned with large photos of rock climbers, parachutists and trail runners, and the large glass windows offered a panoramic view of the London skyline. A massive screen dominated one end of the room, ready to display our meticulously crafted presentation. As the pitch began, the room buzzed with anticipation. Rhona started with her usual commanding presence, outlining our main points and setting the stage for a brilliant presentation. I stood beside her, trying to project confidence.

Out of the corner of my eye, I noticed several members of the marketing team exchanging furtive glances and making subtle gestures. A woman wearing oversized, red glasses kept tilting her head slightly towards me. Another, who I think had introduced herself as Jessica, widened her eyes meaningfully and nodded in my direction.

Are they trying to tell me something? I turned quickly to look behind me, in case there was someone behind me, and a murmur of shock went around the room. Rhona glared at me and glanced at my skirt. *Oh my god.* I realized with horror that it was stuck in my tights, revealing a slice of backside.

My heart skipped a beat, and I felt my face turn crimson.

Desperate to fix the situation discreetly, I reached behind me and tugged at my skirt. As I adjusted it, I lost my balance, wobbling precariously on my heels. In a split second, I decided to turn my stumble into a little impromptu dance, twisting my hips and giving a small twirl as if it were all part of the plan.

The room fell silent for a heartbeat, and then there was a smattering of polite laughter. Ben, sitting at the conference table in front of us, hid his smile behind his fist, his eyes twinkling with amusement. He coughed to cover his chuckle, but I could see the corners of his mouth twitching. Martin, the investor, sitting to his right, just stared at me in shock.

"Sorry about that," I said with a bright, slightly breathless laugh. "Just getting into the spirit of things!"

Rhona gave me a sharp look, her eyes narrowing slightly, but she quickly recovered, turning back to the clients with a smooth segue. "And that brings us to our next point, where Emiliah will walk you through our key strategies."

When the pitch was in full swing, and despite my earlier mishaps, I began to enjoy myself. Rhona and I really clicked. She just needed to look at me for me to know what to say next. She took the lead, and I followed in perfect synchrony.

Rhona introduced our flashmob idea with an energy that immediately captivated the room. She clicked on the next slide, a vibrant video montage of previous successful flashmobs, and the room instantly buzzed with excitement.

"We envision a campaign that not only captures attention but engages the audience in a way they'll never forget," Rhona began, her voice steady and compelling. As the video played, showing crowds of people spontaneously breaking into dance in various cityscapes, I saw Ben, leaning forward, clearly engaged.

I picked up up where Rhona left off, detailing the strategic rollout of the campaign. I spoke about the layered advertising approach, integrating traditional media with a social media blitz. "We'll adapt the original dance to create one specifically for social media. For the first videos, we'll dress the dancers as window cleaners, construction workers, mountain rescuers, etc. Then we'll use advertising to fuel the campaign, airing the videos in strategic locations, such as Times Square," I explained, flipping to the next slide that displayed a cohesive blend of social media ads and influencer partnerships. "Everywhere you look, you'll see PeakSleek – on your morning commute, in your Instagram feed, even during your favorite TV shows."

As I spoke, I noticed nods of approval from the marketing team. They were engaged, enthralled even, by our enthusiasm and the clarity of our vision. Rhona then transitioned to the social media strategy, describing how we'd harness the power of trending challenges and hashtags to further leverage the campaign.

Rhona and I had such a great connection during the pitch that I could see the PeakSleek team was convinced. We'd nailed it. I knew it. Ben exchanged glances with his colleagues, and I could see the unspoken agreement in their eyes. This was it. This was what they had been looking for.

By the time we concluded, summarizing the campaign's potential reach and impact, the room erupted into applause. Ben stood up, clapping enthusiastically. "Ladies, thank you. Your vision for the campaign is clear, and of course I'll have to debrief with the team, but you're definitely on our shortlist."

I felt a surge of relief and triumph wash over me. We'd turned a potential disaster into an undeniable success. I still marveled at how grown, educated adults could be convinced by buzzwords, promises of extraordinary results and campaigns that twelve-year-olds could draw up, but by now, I'd come to accept that it was all just part of the game we played.

As the applause died down, Ben approached us with a broad smile. "Emiliah, Rhona, I have to say, I am genuinely impressed. The creativity, the strategy, the execution – it's all spot on."

"Thank you, Ben," Rhona replied, her voice steady but I could sense the elation underneath. "We're looking forward to bringing the vision to life."

Handshakes and congratulations followed as the

PeakSleek team filed out of the conference room, leaving us in a whirl of post-presentation adrenaline. I let out a breath I didn't realize I'd been holding, turning to Rhona with a grin.

She smiled, something I'd never seen before. It was quite scary, but at the same time, broke the tension. "How about we celebrate ?" she said.

"Won't that jinx it?" I asked.

She stared at me harshly, prompting me to grab my bag and keep my mouth shut.

We met up at the champagne bar at Harvey Nichols, and Rhona ordered a bottle of Veuve Cliquot.

"To Pigeon à la crème," she toasted, raising her glass with a grin.

I laughed, clinking my glass against hers. "To Pigeon à la crème."

The first sip of champagne was like liquid relief, washing away the remnants of the day's stress. We recounted the highlights of the presentation, each memory sparking a greater sense of camaraderie.

"I must say, that was a very well-prepared pitch, Bent. Good work."

Did she really just say that? To me?

She grabbed a handful of peanuts and scoffed them. "Now I'm counting on you to fucking deliver." Bits of peanut flew onto my suit as she crunched away. "That pretty boy, Ben Goodall, he likes you. Do what you need to do to keep him obsessed. That's how we make big bucks." She paused and looked past my shoulder as if remembering the time when she used her charms in the manner she was suggesting I use mine.

She stood up. "I'm very disappointed in Capri. I'm not sure she has the horsepower to be my number two. You, on the other hand, get it. You just lack self-confidence."

I wasn't sure what to answer. I was embarrassed, as well as a teeny bit triumphant.

I could have stayed talking to Rhona all night, but she had a flight to catch.

My phone rang just as she was leaving the bar. "Hello, this is Emiliah Bent."

"Miss Bent. I'd like to congratulate you on an excellent pitch." His voice sent shivers down my spine.

I leaned against the bar for support. "Thank you," I whispered.

He paused. "I'd like to take you out tomorrow to celebrate."

I paused for a second, then remembered Rhona's advice. "I'd love that."

"Perfect. I'll pick you up at five p.m." he said.

17

I dashed into the bathroom for a final look at my appearance. Not too bad. I'd straightened my wild curls into a sharp bob and applied a hint of bronze eye shadow and 'chocolat givré' lip-gloss. I wore a knee-length floral dress that looked surprisingly good against my pale skin. More importantly, I felt sleek, having shaved my legs and all the parts expected to be hair-free. I hoped the warm sping weather would hold for the evening.

I checked the wall clock. Ten minutes to go.

As I stood on the doorstep, the London breeze whispered secrets of the city, carrying the scent of Indian food and anticipation. A sleek black car pulled up to the curb, and the chauffeur held the door open with a polite nod.

I settled into the luxurious interior alone, and the car glided through the bustling streets of London, its sights and sounds a symphony of urban life. We passed iconic landmarks—Big Ben, the River Thames, and the charming cobblestone streets of Notting Hill, before heading north.

The car's interior cocooned me in luxury, a quiet sanctuary from the outside world. As we approached a private airstrip, the grandeur of the adventure unfurled before me. A gleaming private jet waited on the tarmac, its engines humming with anticipation.

Ben was waiting by the jet's stairway, dressed in a cream linen suit and white shirt. "Shall we?" he asked.

"Okay," I whispered.

He extended a hand to help me embark, and together, we ascended the steps.

The jet's cabin was a vision of opulence, plush leather seats, soft ambient lighting, and panoramic windows. As we settled into our seats, the jet's engines roared to life, and a waiter brought us tall, slim glasses of champagne. I sipped mine delicately.

The thrill of the unknown coursed through me as the jet soared into the boundless sky. London stretched out below us. I glanced at Ben, whose eyes held a glimmer of mischief and adventure.

As we approached the coast, Ben's phone rang. He answered, looking annoyed at the interruption. "Yes, Martin. Yes, I can send it over. Hang on." He manoeuvered himself out of the seat and held up his hand at me, indicating that the conversation would take five minutes. I nodded, mouthing "of course".

Unsurprisingly, it took longer than five minutes. He returned just as the jet began its descent towards a small airstrip surrounded by yellow and purple fields. As we disembarked, I saw a long, low building in the distance with large signage indicating that we had arrived at the *Aérodrome du Vaucluse*. We were in Provence. *Wow!*

A chauffeured car was already waiting. Ben held the car door for me as I climbed inside, suppressing a faint feeling of unease at being in the French countryside.

We embarked on a picturesque drive through the Luberon countryside, fields of lavender unfurling like a purple sea under the sun's tender caress. An ancient stone vilage, perched on a cliff overlooking the valley, came into view. Gordes. When the car parked, we were immediately immersed in the village's medieval charm. Ben took my hand in his and we strolled down a narrow cobblestone street to the village square, where an evening market offered an array of fragrant lavender, artisan cheeses, rough pottery and local wines. The air was thick with the scent of fresh bread and the buzz of tourists sampling local delights.

He led me to a discreet restaurant tucked away in a centuries-old stone building. As we entered, it was like stepping into a story book. The dining room was adorned with wrought-iron chandeliers, vintage wine barrels and linen-covered tables.

We were led to a table on a sun-dappled terrace overlooking the valley below, where and a canopy of climbing vines spilled its greenery over a massive pergola. The view stretched for miles, a tapestry of vineyards, olive groves, and fields of lavender, their hues shifting under the golden rays of the setting sun.

I gazed at Ben, as a waiter discreetly placed two glasses of champagne on the table.

His grey eyes held a spark of adventure, a subtle smile playing at his lips. "So," he began, his voice soft, "What do you think of Gordes?"

"It's breathtaking," I replied, letting the scenery soak in. "I can't believe how beautiful it is. Every corner we turned was like walking into a painting."

He nodded, pensive. "I knew you'd love it. There's something magical about this place."

He sipped his champagne. "I think you'll have guessed we'll be working with Gant & Ballaster for the PR campaign."

I glowed with pleasure, dying to share the news with Rhona and Vince, but not want to break the magic of the moment.

He leaned forward and stared straight into my eyes. "There's something very intriguing about you, Emiliah. I can't quite figure you out."

I blushed furiously and cleared my throat. "I – I suppose I just don't have a lot to say."

He shook his head. "No. No, that's not it. I've told you all about me, but I know nothing about you. I'm curious about your life. Tell me about your past."

I hesitated momentarily, a flicker of uncertainty passing

through my eyes. I took another sip of wine, gathering my thoughts. "I had a fairly typical upbringing," My words were carefully chosen. "I have fond memories of family vacations, school, and all the usual things. But, you know, it was a long time ago, and I don't have much memory. And I love the present." I smiled sweetly.

Ben smiled, his eyes inquisitive, but he didn't press further. Instead, he shifted the conversation to other topics—the Provençal countryside, the flavors of the region, and the beauty of the village surrounding us.

He raised his glass. "To unexpected adventures."

We clinked our glasses, and the breeze carried the scent of lavender.

As the courses were served—delicate salads with local herbs and artisan cheeses, followed by a succulent roasted quail—I was drawn into a captivating conversation with Ben.

He leaned in closer, his voice a velvety whisper. "I've had an idea, that I'd like to share with you. Something that's been on my mind."

I nodded, my heart quickening with anticipation. "What is it?"

He took my hand. "I'd really like you to manage my internal communications campaign. I feel like I can really trust you. I meant what I said after the concert, you know. I really like you. It feels as if I've known you for years. You really get me."

I cleared my throat, trying my best to sound professional. "Of course, we have a lot of experience with internal communications. We'd just have to understand your HR strategy, your objectives, etcetera."

He gazed at me for a few seconds. "I don't mean with Gant and Ballaster. I'd like to work directly with you on this particular subject. As an independent consultant."

His words hung in the air.

"Well, I'm not-, I don't think-"

"Just think about it, okay?" he interrupted. "I'd pay you the same hourly fee I pay G&B. I just want to be able to work with you on my own terms, and I need someone I can trust for this particular mission."

I wiped my mouth slowly, thinking. "Ben," I said after a while, "I'm very pleased you trust me, but to be honest, I don't want to do anything to jeopardize my career. And Rhona would hit the roof if she found out I'd been consulting on the side. My reputation would be destroyed."

He smiled knowingly. "I'll never put you in any kind of danger, trust me." As he said this, his shoe brushed my foot fleetingly. *Did he do that on purpose?*

Then the dessert arrived—a masterpiece of chocolate and raspberries that melted on the tongue. Ben's gaze held mine, and in that moment, the world outside faded into insignificance. It was as if the entire universe had conspired to bring us together in this enchanted corner of Provence.

I promised to think about his offer, even though I couldn't figure out what his motive could possibly be. As we ate our delicious raspberry and white chocolate domes, we talked less, enjoying the moment and the view, and smiling at each other like teenagers.

As we were leaving, I took a final look around the restaurant, savoring the vision. I gasped. A face I knew from a lifetime ago. Words, handwritten, jumped to mind. *Judge Tinner. N°128, Ludovic, one thousand pounds*. Our eyes met for a split second, and I knew he was trying to place me. I quickly turned to Ben, engaging him in conversation as I steered him away.

I was on edge all the way back to London, but I couldn't tell whether or not Ben noticed. I was quite relieved when he dropped me off in front of my building with just a peck on the cheek. There was too much to think about to abandon myself in his arms once again.

How stupid to assume I could go to that kind of establishment and not run into people from my past. Until now, I had evolved in completely different circles, but with Ben, it felt like I was dangerously close to my past life. If we were to see each other again, I was going to have to be very, very careful.

18

18

The entrance to the Louvre bathed in the glistening sunshine, presented an awe-inspiring sight. As the morning light filtered through the glass pyramid, it cast a kaleidoscope of reflections that danced across the courtyard's ancient stones. Visitors were greeted by the juxtaposition of modern and historic architectural marvels, where the sleek lines of I. M. Pei's Pyramid contrasted beautifully with the grandeur of the surrounding Haussmannian facades. The air was fresh with the promise of spring, carrying the faint scent of blossoming flowers from the nearby Tuileries Garden. The sun's rays, breaking through the crisp morning, illuminated the museum's entrance, highlighting the intricate details of the stonework and the majestic doors that had welcomed art lovers for centuries.

Beneath the Louvre, in the shadow of the inverted pyramid, lay a hall that buzzed with an almost tangible energy. This underground space, a feat of modern engineering, contrasted starkly with the classical beauty that defined the rest of the museum. The inverted pyramid, a counterpart to its above-ground sibling, hung like a jewel, its tip nearly touching the ground below.

The place was packed. Hundreds of tourists, twenty-four journalists, Rhona, and all her minions. Capri, to Rhona's right, looked sour.

Suddenly, without warning, a recorded version of Sia's powerful voice rang out, singing 'PeakSleek me' and people gradually started turning to the inverted pyramid to see what was happening.

The window cleaners were lying, immobile, on the glass panels inside the inverted pyramid. They almost looked like they were having a break, lying in the warm April sun. Quite suddenly, a gong sounded and gradually turned into a reverberating microphone-type screech. Then, a beat picked up, and the cleaners thrust their bodies erratically in rhythm. Sia's recorded voice filled the carrousel, reverberating loudly from wall to wall. The cleaners moved crazily around the glass structure, and as the words burst out, they all jumped, magically avoiding each other from one side of the pyramid to the other. They were no longer window cleaners but ballet dancers, performing the most beautiful contemporary dance I'd ever seen. They were acting the words in the most beautiful way possible. Then people around the pyramid, acting as if they were just hanging around, talking, and watching the dancers, started moving together in unison. Four people, then eight, then twenty, then forty, danced along to another of her hots, 'The Greatest'. Large, swift movements, arms lifting, hands flying, backs bending, all perfectly synchronized.

When I had envisioned it, sitting in the adjoining hall across from Ben, I'd had no idea how spectacular it could be.

People stared in disbelief at the dancing window cleaners, then sang along, mesmerized by the bodies running barefoot, dancing, then slathering the glass with soap and water, wiping it off with swift, artistic movements as they were suspended above the glass with Breathe's equipment, and prancing from corner to corner in beautiful arching movements.

Then, as another song began -*'I'm free to be the greatest here tonight, the greatest, the greatest, the greatest alive, The greatest, the greatest alive'* – four dancers, dressed in normal clothes amongst the crowd, began dancing, and all the other dancers progressively joined in. Just as suddenly as it had started, the music stopped, the window cleaners resumed normal window cleaning, and the dancers in the hall walked away. For a second, I hesitated, frantic. No one had got it. But then the crowd erupted into applause. And we all fell into each other's arms. Nora and Helen, who'd done all the leg work, hugged me tightly. The relief that it was finally over and the feeling of triumph were exhilarating. In about ten minutes, the video team produced a two-minute video showing people milling to and from the Restaurants du Monde, and then the gong sound making people turn and look around, catching sight of the dance. The video captured everything: the crowd's amazement, the mix of pleasure and pain on the dancer's faces, the slaps of feet against glass, light filtering through the glass onto the faces of the mesmerized audience, the dancers' breathing, the emotion, and the applause. It ended with the Breathe, Louvre, and Gant & Ballaster logos. Just half an hour later, it had already gone viral, with over a hundred thousand views. All the journalists present complimented us, promising excellent coverage. Arnold, the choreographer, looked pleased in his understated way. And Ben couldn't stop grinning.

He made his way through the crowd, his eyes on me, then stood in front of me. "Nice work, Miss Bent. That was amazing." He looked me up and down and leaned in close. "And I must say, you look fabulous."

I was wearning the dress I'd bought in Paris with him and the girls, back in March.

"Thank you," I said, feeling weak.

He leaned forward. "I'd like to debrief. Now."

"Oh, I've got so much to do, you know, to clear up. Could we possibly debrief in an hour or so?"

He raised his eyebrows. "Do you not trust your team to wrap up? I *am* the client, after all."

I stared at him silently. Then, locating Nora, I pushed through the crowd and told her 'the PeakSleek team' wanted to talk to me.

She hugged me. "Of course we can manage, Em. No worries! You go with them. But tell us everything afterwards, okay?"

I nodded, feeling guilty.

I made my way back to him and saw him leaning against a wall, talking to Capri. She threw back her head, laughing at something he said.

His eyes flicked over at me for a nanosecond before he turned back to her. He said something, then she smiled and walked away. She turned around, and our eyes met. She gave me a cold look.

Ben rubbed his stubble. "Have you seen the Louvre's storage space before? You've got to see it, it's incredible."

Before I could reply, he took my arm and steered me quickly through one of the restaurants, through a door marked 'Service' and into a vestibule.

"Come along, Miss Bent," he said, eyes twinkling. Without giving me a chance to protest, he took my hand and led me toward a service door on the other side of the vestibule. Pulling out a badge and pressing it against a security panel, he pressed a finger onto a fingerprint detector. The door opened with a thud onto a stone staircase leading downwards.

At the bottom, a long, dimly-lit passageway led us to a series of storage rooms full of lighting and sound equipment, each protected by a heavy metal door and security panel. We didn't say a word.

"Here we are," he whispered as he opened yet another door.

I gasped. The room was full of antique furniture and statues. Ben walked over to a statue that looked like

Napoleon. "Cool, isn't it?"

I nodded, awestruck.

"I thought you'd like it." He smiled and slowly bent down, brushing his lips against mine. He gently lifted the loose locks sticking to my face. "You've bewitched me, Miss Bent." His voice was husky as he kissed me again. "How do you do it? What's your trick?"

He pressed his tongue against my teeth, sending a thrill through my body. The kiss became more insistent as he pushed my teeth open. A moan escaped me as he stroked the nape of my neck, kissing me deeply now. I reached up and stroked the hair in the nape of his neck.

He pulled me to him urgently, and we kissed frantically, grinding our clothed bodies against each other.

"Y'a quelqu'un?" The voice was just behind the door. Ben put a finger to my lips and pushed me silently against the wall.

"Je crois qu'il y a personne," said a second voice.

I could tell they were listening at the door. Ben covered my mouth with one hand, staring into my eyes, and slid the other up my skirt. His fingers stroked my knickers. Unable to cry out, silent tears rolled down my face.

The voices became more distant as he moved my knickers to one side to gently rub my clitoris. His hand was still covering my mouth, and I cried out in pleasure. I no longer cared if anyone heard us. He slipped a strong finger inside me as I moaned into his hand. "Shush, shush," he whispered.

He pulled his hand away, gently putting my knickers back in place, and carried me towards a huge ornate bed covered in what looked like a tapestry. Pulling the tapestry off, he lay me down gently and slowly undressed me. He then pulled off his own shirt, trousers and pants, his penis springing up, hard and strong. He crawled over and lay down next to me, pulling the tapestry over us, protecting us from the cold air. He kissed me again softly, rubbing my tummy before giving each breast his full attention with soft strokes, sucks, and firm squeezes. Holding himself up on his left arm, he slid his right hand back down, slowly, over my tummy and further down. His fingers were magic.

"Inside, inside," I moaned, begging him for more. He ignored me, enjoying my frustration as his penis came tantalizingly close to the entrance before moving away again. I couldn't take it any longer. I grabbed him, pulling him inside. I cried out in pleasure and loss of control and dug my nails into his back.

When it was over, he blew air onto my moist skin. My whole body was tingling. I thought I'd die of pleasure. Then he kissed me again, and it all started over, and I felt myself melting, wanting him to become part of me, wanting him to own me.

At some point, we drifted off to sleep, exhausted.

19

As I lay in bed the following Saturday, the sun projecting slashes of bright light onto the sheets, I wondered if it had been a one-night stand. He hadn't been in touch since we'd slept together in the Louvre, and it had been a week.

I stretched my aching limbs under the sheets. It was the best sex I'd ever had. My very first orgasm. I'd completely let my guard down. I'd fallen for him. He was so intense, such a powerhouse; I doubted I'd ever meet anyone like him again.

As I lay in my tiny flat, alone, my heart echoed the silence of my phone.

I reached out and checked it again. Nada. *Well, what did you expect, for God's sake? Look at him. Look at you. Pathetic.*

I replayed the scene in my mind, over and over. Every detail was intense, heavenly. Later, when the night had worn thin and we'd had to exit without being seen, reality had seeped in and the spell had broken. He'd promised to call, his lips brushing my forehead in a vague gesture of affection.

As the days had passed, my phone had remained humiliatingly silent. I'd talked to his team of course, about next steps, news flow, press outreach, events. But nothing from Ben himself. I checked my messages every few minutes, my heart skipping a beat every time.

I replayed the scene once more, the way he leaned into me, the way he gazed into my eyes while pounding me, and wondered if it had all been an illusion. Had I misread him? Did he use those techniques with all his targets?

Rejection was a familiar lead weight in the pit of my stomach, reminding me of my worthlessness.

Stop feeling so sorry for yourself, you piece of shit.

I rolled over slowly and pulled on the sweatpants and t-shirt I'd left on the floor the night before. Pulling on my trainers, I bullied myself into preparing for the run that I knew would make me feel better. Later on, I would relax with Meloda, who I was meeting for Saturday night drinks at l'Assemblage.

I took one last look at my phone before leaving. Still nothing.

As I pulled my front door closed behind me, I stared at the stairs. On each side of each step was a huge bunch of flowers. Roses, lilies, peonies, tulips beautifully arranged into glorious bouquets. I started walking down, and it was the same on every step all the way down. I stopped on the second floor to move the bouquets preventing Mr. Hull, my elderly neighbor, from walking down, holding the railing.

By the time we reached the door to the street, Mr. Hull was muttering under his breath about 'womanizing tossers' in his thick cockney accent.

When I opened the door for Mr. Hull, my heart leapt. There he was, Ben Goodall, standing in front of the building, holding the largest bouquet yet.

20

As I hurried through the bustling city streets, the clouds above gathered ominously. Dark and brooding, they spread an eerie shadow over the city. The first few raindrops splashed onto the pavement, warning of the impending deluge. My steps quickened, matching the pace of my racing heart, as I realized I was about to be caught in a thunderstorm.

The wind picked up, carrying the scent of rain and wet litter. Umbrellas sprouted like mushrooms, and pedestrians scurried for cover, their hurried footsteps echoing in the narrow alleys. I glanced at my watch; I had promised to meet Ben at his office. Determined to keep my commitment, I continued, even as the heavens opened.

The rain fell in a relentless downpour, drenching me in seconds. My clothes clung to my skin, and my hair became a tangled mess of damp strands. Lightning streaked across the sky, followed by the deep rumble of thunder that reverberated through the streets. People sought refuge under awnings and in doorways, but I pressed on, my determination outweighing my discomfort.

Navigating the puddle-ridden pavements became a precarious endeavor. It was as if nature itself conspired against me, testing my resolve to reach the man who occupied my every thought.

As I stood there in the pouring rain, resembling more a drowned rat than a person, my luck took a turn for the worse. Just as I thought my day couldn't get wetter, a car zoomed by, drenching me in an enormous wave of muddy street water.

"Fucker!" I shouted after the departing car, then slipped and fell on my face in a huge puddle.

A nearby homeless man burst into laughter, and soon, a chorus of chuckles erupted from a group of bedraggled people holding bottles who had sought shelter under nearby awnings.

I finally arrived at Ben's office building, rain-soaked and bedraggled. I pushed through the revolving door, my clothes dripping puddles onto the marble floor. The receptionist offered a sympathetic smile as I stood there, water pooling at my feet.

Moments later, Ben was in front of me, calling for towels and blankets.

I looked into his eyes, and he stared back at me, full of amused compassion.

"Let me take you me to my place to warm up," he murmured.

What seemed like seconds later, a chauffeured car pulled

up in front of the building, and I climbed inside, wrapped in blankets.

The car navigated the dark city streets, crossed Tower Bridge, and turned left, taking a series of quick turns before stopping in front of an ultra-modern building. Ben helped me out of the car, and I took in the large piece of writing on the façade: Thames Summit.

Ben nodded at the doorman as we entered the building, and we took the lift to the penthouse level.

I gasped as Ben stepped aside to let me enter his flat. From the address and the doorman, I had guessed that his place would be expensive, but I wasn't expecting anything quite so spectacular. As soon as I stepped inside, the floor-to-ceiling views of Tower Bridge and the city, all lit up against the dusk sky, fully captured my attention.

The large, open-space room led to a terrace overlooking the Thames. His terrasse alone was bigger than my flat. The floor inside was a white, shiny stone, and the massive kitchen island was marble, but it somehow managed to be warm and welcoming thanks to ambient lighting and area rugs, soft curtains and plants. The outdoor furniture was exotic wood with plush, white cushions, and the seating area was surrounded by beautiful shrubs in low, oversized pots.

He took me by the hand, and I followed silently. We walked up a wide, glass and steel staircase. We passed a glass-walled office and I only saw a glimpse of a couple of other rooms before he opened the door to his bedroom, a dark grey and wood room with an industrial-style metal bed and more floor-to-ceiling windows overlooking Tower Bridge and the city. He led me into an adjoining bathroom with floor-to-ceiling windows overlooking Tower Bridge. He bent over and turned on the bath's hot tap. Then he stood and cupped his hand around the nape of my neck, kissing me slowly. I moaned with pleasure, feeling a dull throb between my legs. His hands moved down to my waist, and he pulled my soaking top over my head.

"No curtains," I whispered.

"No," he replied, a sly look on his face.

He slowly undid my trousers and unpeeled them from my body. He pulled down my wet, lacy thong, kissing my thighs and calves along the way. He unclipped my bra in a single movement. I stood, naked, in front of him.

I tried to cover myself, not even caring about people outside, just self-conscious under his gaze. He moved my arms to my sides. He looked at me for a few moments before turning off the water. "Get in the bath."

I did as I was told.

He washed me all over with a soft sponge, even conditioning my hair. I suppressed a hysterical laugh as Ted Bundy came to mind. *Stop it, Emiliah! You ruin everything!*

When Ben was done washing me, he pulled me out of the bath and carried me, in a towel but still wet, to his bed. He lay me down, letting his clothes fall to the ground, his large penis springing free. He lay above me, holding himself up, and proceeded to kiss me on my face, my breasts, and my stomach. He sucked hard on my left breast while gently pinching the other one.

"Ben!" I cried out. "oh God, please!"

He ignored my pleas and continued his delicious torture.

He was kissing the top of my thighs and moving closer and closer to my vulva. Then he reached over to the bedside table, pulled out several thick, leather-wrapped handcuffs, and proceeded to attach my hands and ankles to the bed rails. He then knelt and started licking my clitoris with fervor.

"Oh my god, Ben, Oh my god!" The pleasure was too intense, too strong. My face burned, and I felt myself building up to a climax. "Ahh!" I cried out.

I had never felt anything like it. I was wet and shaking. He climbed on top of me and pushed his strong penis inside. The hard thrusting brought on another climax, and I cried out in pleasure.

He slowed down and held himself above me, smiling warmly. "I love hearing you come, Emiliah. You're so perfect." He freed me from the cuffs, lay down beside me, and held me in his arms. I couldn't speak.

He kissed me hard on the cheek and pulled me closer. "I like you very much, Miss Bent."

21

We'd begun playing dangerous, sexy games. I gradually understood why he had such a sturdy, industrial bed. It was more an erotic cage than a bed, to be honest. He would slowly attach my arms and legs to each post, then take out a riding crop. I would try to wriggle free, all the while growing more and more excited. Then he would whip me, more or less lightly. Sometimes, he would blindfold me. By the time he climbed on top of me, I would be moaning with pleasure, kissing him frantically and fighting the ropes or cuffs to hold him against me. We kissed frantically, never able to get deep enough into each other's mouths. The power he had over me was incredible.

"You're mine, Emiliah. I'm never letting you go," he would whisper into my ear as I orgasmed over and over.

As the days turned into weeks and the weeks into months, I found myself reveling in the toughness and tenderness he showed me. Each moment we spent together seemed to strengthen our bond.

Our mornings began with the soft rustle of sheets and the gentle press of his lips against mine. There was a sweetness in how he would tuck a loose strand of hair behind my ear and whisper words of affection that never failed to make my heart flutter. The simple act of making breakfast together, our fingers brushing against one another as we prepared our meals, felt like a dance of intimacy.

In the evenings, we would curl up on the couch, our legs entwined, and watch the city lights twinkling through the windows. His fingers would trace lazy patterns on my skin, igniting a trail of desire that pulsed between us.

But it wasn't just the physical intimacy that bound us together. It was the way he listened to me, drinking in my words as if holding on to them for the future. I felt cherished and valued, a feeling that filled me with a warm glow.

There were moments when he would gaze into my eyes with a tenderness that left me breathless, as if he could see into the depths of my soul.

As we lay entangled in each other's arms at night, the world outside faded into insignificance. I could hear the steady rhythm of his heartbeat, a comforting lullaby that lulled me into a peaceful slumber. I found solace and security in his embrace, and everything else became insignificant.

22

The sun hung low on the horizon, illuminating the landscape with a golden hue as Ben and I made our way to a remote airfield. The vast expanse of the open sky stretched before us, an endless canvas painted with the warm tones of dusk. I had no idea where we were headed. As we approached the strip, my heartquickened, a combination of excitement and trepidation coursing through my veins.

He had a mischievous glint in his eyes as he pulled a jumpsuit, helmet and goggles out of his sports bag. "Surprise, Miss Bent," he said with a playful grin. "We're going skydiving."

The words hung in the air like a dare, and time seemed to stand still for a moment. My heart raced, and I could feel adrenaline surging through me.

He looked at me, his eyes filled with determination."I want you to have this experience, to feel the thrill of the unknown, because I want you to help me develop a PR campaign for FaraWave's new skydiving gear. I need someone who understands what it's like to take a leap of faith."

I blinked, trying to process his words. Ben had orchestrated this adventure not just for the thrill of it but as a way to immerse me in the world of skydiving, to make me a part of the story so that I could tell the world. It was an ingenious, albeit nerve-wracking, plan.

As we suited up, fear clawed at the edges of my mind, but I knew this was a moment to seize, to let go of the safety net and embrace the exhilaration of freefall.

We boarded the small plane, its engine roaring to life as we flew into the endless blue sky. The ascent was steep and swift, the ground rapidly falling away beneath us. My pulse quickened with every meter gained.

Ben's presence beside me was reassuring, a steady anchor in the midst of my rising anxiety. He leaned in close, his shout barely audible over the roar of the engine. "Remember, it's about trusting the gear, trusting yourself, and embracing the moment."

I nodded, gripping the edge of my seat as the plane leveled off. The door slid open, and a rush of cold air filled the cabin.

Ben guided me to the edge, his hands steady on my shoulders. My heart hammered in my chest as he attached our harnesses together, the closeness a small comfort in the face of the daunting leap. I felt his reassuring presence, his steady breathing against my back.

We stepped into the open doorway, the wind tugging at

our clothes and hair. For a split second, the world seemed to pause. Then, suddenly, we were falling.

We were in freefall, hurtling through the sky at breathtaking speed. The wind rushed past, whipping against my face and pulling at my limbs. The initial drop was a whirlwind of sensation—wind roaring past, the ground rushing up to meet us, and a sense of absolute terror.

The sensation of falling was unlike anything I'd ever experienced. The air rushed past at an incredible speed, the force of it pushing against my body, making it hard to breathe. But with Ben right behind me, his presence a constant reassurance, I found myself adjusting, acclimating to the sensation. It was as if I had been untethered from the earth, soaring through the sky with nothing but the wind to guide me.

Ben tapped my shoulder just before deploying the parachute. The sudden deceleration was jarring, and we were no longer in freefall. The landscape below transformed into a living map, details coming into focus as we soared through the sky, and the fear dissolved, replaced by pure exhilaration. We were gliding gently toward the earth, the ground inevitably rising to meet us.

As our descent slowed, the world below grew clearer, more tangible. Beneath us, the earth stretched out like a patchwork quilt, a mosaic of fields, rivers, and forests. I marveled at the ground's beauty from this extraordinary vantage point, the vibrant colors and the horizon seemingly endless.

In that moment, as we glided through the sky, I felt a profound sense of liberation. It was as if time had slowed, and the world had faded into the background, leaving only the exhilaration of the present moment.

We glided gracefully towards the landing zone, my heart soaring even as we descended.

When our feet finally touched the ground, I was breathless, a wide grin plastered on my face. Ben was grinning too, his eyes sparkling with shared triumph.

We made our way back to the hangar, the adrenaline still coursing through my veins.

As we shed our gear, the golden light of the setting sun bathed the airfield in a warm glow. The skydiving adventure had been a leap of faith in more ways than one, and I felt ready to take on the challenge ahead with renewed vigor and creativity.

Ben clapped a hand on my shoulder. "So, how did it feal?"

I just shook my head, tears welling in my eyes. "Terrifying. Amazing."

He smiled and took me in his arms, kissing the top of my head. "I love you, Emiliah Bent."

I pulled away and stared at him in shock. Then I kissed him hard, sinking my fingertips into the back of his neck. He pulled me closer, holding me tighter.

Suddenly, I wanted him, hard. I wanted him roughly, painfully.

23

The more I became consumed with sexual desire, the more I lost interest in my career at G&B. I was still driven, but everything I did was to please Ben. I no longer cared about my career. All that mattered was him. It was as if the world of work that had once consumed me had suddenly lost its luster.

Until Ben, I'd been determined to pay off my mortgage as early as I could possibly manage, a relentless pursuit that had driven me to be constantly on the move, pushing myself, working harder and harder. But now, the thought of my empty flat in Shoreditch felt distant and disconnected. I hadn't been home for weeks, and my once-beloved sanctuary was fast becoming a faded memory.

I didn't want to lose my job, and the thought of financial instability still gave me anxiety, but for now, I was content with the routine of receiving my paycheck and paying my bills. It was as if the materialistic goals that had once driven me had lost their grip, replaced by a newfound sense of fulfillment in the moments spent with Ben.

In Ben's arms, work worries melted away, and time stood still. And as I grappled with my changing priorities, I couldn't help but wonder if this newfound contentment was a sign that I was finally living for myself, for love, and the simple pleasures life had to offer.

My conflicting thoughts about work and Ben had become a constant undercurrent in my life, a tug-of-war between duty and desire that played out in the recesses of my mind.

During my long hours at the office, I would find myself drifting into daydreams, thoughts of Ben's smile and the way his fingers traced delicate patterns on my skin invading my consciousness. The allure of our shared moments, laughter and connection beckoned me away from my desk, tempting me to escape the confines of my life.

But then reality would set in, and the weight of responsibility would press down upon me. I couldn't simply abandon my job, not when it had been the foundation of my life for so long.

And so, I continued to immerse myself in the chaos of conference calls, emails and meetings, forcing myself to compartmentalize the burgeoning desires that had taken root within me. It was a struggle to stay focused and shut out the whispers of temptation.

During such moments, I would question the very essence of my identity. The conflict raged on, a storm of emotions that left me feeling torn and uncertain. I knew I couldn't abandon my career entirely, and there was a part of me that still craved the satisfaction that came with professional success and compliments about my work. But there was another part, a part that had awakened with a fierce intensity, that yearned for the simplicity of love and intimacy that Ben offered.

I often wondered if I could find a way to strike a balance, to merge the two worlds without sacrificing one for the other. It was a delicate dance, one that required careful navigation and introspection. Meloda was the only person to whom I confided my doubts, and she was sure it was just a phase, certain that as soon as the honeymoon phase with Ben was over, I'd regain my professional motivation. How I wish she'd been right.

24

Sunnyside Up, as its name suggested, was a place where you could get brunch, as Meloda and I often did. Usually, we came for the delicious Punjabi-English brunch, but we were meeting for coffee on that particular Sunday. Painted in yellow, the café was bright and unpretentious, and as I pushed the café door open and inhaled the familiar blend of freshly roasted beans and Punjabi folklore, I spotted Meloda at our usual corner table. She sat there, a vision of resolute beauty, nursing her espresso cup. Her deep brown eyes were pools of emotion, a hint of vulnerability lurking beneath the surface. She'd always been the strong one. Although I'd been packing for my skiing trip with Ben, I'd come immediately when she'd called, relieved that I could finally do something for her and genuinely concerned for her wellbeing. Ben was preparing a board meeting, so he was fine with me going out.

I ordered a chai tea and two almond croissants (Meloda's favorite) and wove my way through the labyrinth of tables to join her. As I slid into the seat across from her, I couldn't help but notice her forlorn look.

"Hey," I greeted, pushing a croissant towards her.

Meloda smiled weakly, picking up the pastry. "Thanks, Em."

A moment of silence hung between us, as if the café held its breath in anticipation of what was coming. Meloda sighed, her eyes distant, and then she spoke, her words a tentative thread in the tapestry of our friendship. "I need to tell you something, Em," she confessed, her voice a fragile melody. "I'm worried about you. You and Ben."

I bristled.

She reached out to take my hand. "Flit and I have the same feeling. You're moving really fast."

I frowned. "Flit?" I asked. "Really? The woman you've already moved in with."

She sighed. "I know, I know. It's just.... He's such a powerful man. In every sense of the word. You've got to admit that Flit is more like us, more grounded in the real world. And unlike you, I'm not thinking about resigning."

I remained silent.

She exhaled slowly. "Em, please. I'm just worried about you." She looked down at her hands. "I'm worried you're out of your depth."

"You mean he's out of my league?"

She leaned forward and took my hands in hers. "That's not what I meant, and you know it. It's just that you're spending all your free time with him."

"I'm here now, aren't I? And you and Flit spend most of your free time together, even though you barely know each other. What do you know about her? Maybe she's just using you."

Meloda frowned. "What would Flit be using me for?"

I decided to backtrack. "Listen, Mel. I'm fine. Really. Please just let me look after myself."

"Em," Meloda started, her voice hesitant but firm, "there's something else." She paused, pulling at a piece of skin on her index finger. "Flit's been asking questions about you. She... well, she seems to think there's something you're not saying."

Wild thoughts raced through my mind.

She looked up at me. "There's a lot I don't know about you, Em, and that's fine. You're entitled to your secrets. I'm just worried. You've made a lot of huge decisions in a short amount of time, and well, to be honest, it's not like you."

"But you don't know me, not really." I blurted out.

She looked shocked and hurt.

I felt a knot form in my stomach. "Meloda, I..." I started, my voice trailing off as I searched for the right words. "It's complicated. There are things I haven't shared, not because I don't trust you, but because I need to keep certain things private."

Meloda reached across the space between us, taking my

hand in hers. "I'm your friend. I'm supposed to be here for you through thick and thin. Whatever it is, whatever you're hiding, you can trust me. You don't have to go through it alone."

Her words, filled with sincerity and concern, broke through the walls I had built around me. The thought of confiding in her was both terrifying and relieving. But the fear of the consequences and potential fallout held me back.

"I know, and I appreciate that more than you can imagine. But it's not just about trust." I withdrew my hand, wrapping my arms around myself as if to ward off the chill of my own words. "Please, just trust me on this."

Meloda's expression was a mix of frustration and concern. "I do trust you, Em. But I'm worried. If there's something dangerous or painful, don't you think facing it with someone by your side is better?"

Her plea hung in the air between us. The weight of it all felt too heavy.

"Meloda, please," I said softly, "let's just leave this topic for now, okay? I'm fine. There's no need for you to worry about me." My voice was a whisper, barely audible over the sound of my own fears. "I'm so happy now. I never thought I'd meet someone like Ben. I'm crazy about him." Tears welled in my eyes.

We sat in silence for a moment, the unspoken words and secrets creating a distance that hadn't been there before. Meloda finally nodded, her expression resigned yet still tinged with worry.

"Okay, I'm sorry, I won't push. I am happy for you, but just remember that I'm here whenever you need to talk." She squeezed my hand gently before standing up, leaving me alone with my thoughts.

25

Once again, we were away on a weekend, reveling in the opulence of a five-star hotel in Megève, work completely forgotten.

I was captivated by the panoramic vista of the slopes from the comfort of an elegantly appointed bathroom when I felt Ben's arms surround me and that familiar throb inside. He pushed me slowly against the window and lifted my bathrobe silently.

"Ben, people will see-"

"Shhhh," he ordered as he pushed himself inside me. I cried out in pleasure and surprise as he pounded, pushing me harder and harder against the glass and sticking his fingers into my mouth.

We washed each other in the shower afterwards, lathering our bodies in soap and kissing slowly before holding each other hungrily again, kissing deeply, teeth clashing, desperate for another round of frantic sex. He lifted me effortlessly against the shower wall and stared deep into my eyes as he pushed deeper and deeper.

Lying on the bed afterwards, I stared at the morning light dusting the mountains with a golden hue, transforming the snow-covered peaks into a dazzling spectacle. The luxurious interior, with its warm wooden accents and plush furnishings, created a stark contrast with the pristine wilderness just beyond the glass. With a steaming cup of coffee in hand, I watched skiers carve graceful arcs down the mountainside, their movements almost rhythmic against the expansive backdrop of the Alps. In a rare moment of solitude, while Ben took a call, I wondered if our lust would ever abate.

Later in the day, my heart raced as I stepped into the cable car. The exhilarating prospect of ascending the mountain had initially filled me with excitement, but now, as the ground fell away, a creeping sense of fear gripped my chest.

The cable car swayed gently, and I grabbed the railing with white-knuckled intensity. The verdant valley below seemed to grow smaller with each passing second, and the ground became a distant memory.

The view, initially awe-inspiring, transformed into a source of dread. The higher we climbed, the more daunting the landscape became. Jagged rocks jutted out from the mountainside, and sheer drops into oblivion awaited any misstep.

I couldn't help but glance down at the slope we had just ascended. The sight of the steep incline and the precipice below sent shivers down my spine. A feeling of absolute doom welled within me. The realization hit me like a sledgehammer — I was trapped up here, far from the safety of flat ground.

Finally, we reached the summit, and the cable car gently came to a halt. The doors opened, revealing the breathtaking view of the world below. But instead of feeling triumphant, I was paralyzed with fear.

I knew I had to gather the courage to step out of the car, but I couldn't shake my fear. Ben took my hand, gently pulling me off the cable car with him. He helped me put my skis on, then, taking my hand, he led me to the side of the slope, letting other skiers head straight for the steep descent. Terror gripped me as the realization that there was only one way down hit.

"Do you trust me?" he whispered.

I stared back at him, tears running down my freezing cheeks.

"I love you, Emiliah. I would never hurt you. You know that, right?"

I nodded, unable to speak.

He maneuvered himself in front of me, pulling my arms close behind him. "Ready?"

"Okay", I said, trembling.

He slowly edged us forward. "Here we go then."

I tensed as I felt us sliding down, feeling every bump on the hard snow. "Push right," he said as he turned, transporting me to the right, as if by magic. "Push left", as we reached a second corner, and then we hurtled forward, picking up speed. I opened my eyes, taking in the whiteness, the speed, the cold. We continued to descend, miraculously turning and gliding on the groomed slope. My terror gradually ebbed away, replaced by a sense of euphoria, and complete, perfect connection.

"Okay, we're at the bottom now," he shouted. "I'm going to let you go."

"No!" I screamed. This wasn't the bottom, just a less steep part.

Suddenly, I was alone, gliding, rushing, free, untethered. Then I felt my skis getting caught, and the world span as I flew forward.

26

The tired-looking doctor strode in, holding my X-rays. "Rupture des ligaments croisés."

Ben shot me a questioning glance.

I inhaled deeply, already feeling a mix of frustration and pain. "My knee ligaments are ruptured."

He took my hand, his grip a little too tight. "I'm so sorry, my sweetheart. I didn't realize you couldn't ski on a flat surface. Even little kids can do that."

A flood of annoyance washed over me. His words stung, a sharp reminder of my fall. "It's okay," I murmured, though my irritation was barely concealed. Even I knew it took adults longer than a day to learn how to ski. Ben's dig was the last thing I needed right now.

The doctor proceeded to tell me about pain medication, the brace I'd have to wear for eight weeks, and the surgery. I tried to focus on his words, but Ben's earlier comment echoed in my mind, compounding my frustration.

Ben ruffled my hair, his attempt at affection feeling more

like condescension at that particular moment. "The silver lining is that you speak the language, so you'll understand everything they say," he said, a hint of a smirk playing at the corner of his mouth.

I bit back a retort, the ache in my knee flaring up as if to punctuate my frustration. Just as I was about to pull away, he seemed to sense my growing annoyance. His expression darkened.

I reached out for his hand. "Sorry, it's just really uncomfortable."

He leaned over to kiss me, smiling. "This isn't exactly what I had in mind for our holiday, but I guess I'll be able to take care of you now."

And he did. When I was finally discharged, he carried me out to the taxi, and from the taxi to our room at the hotel, being extra careful not to bang my injured leg against door openings or elevator railings. He managed to shoulder the hotel room door open and carry me over to the bed, covering me in blankets to make sure I was okay.

The next few days were bliss: he brought me food, helped me to the bathroom, washed my hair, and even carried me down to the spa so I could relax in the warm water and enjoy a heavenly massage. And every night, we made love slowly, gently, passionately.

<h1 style="text-align:center">27</h1>

The question of whether or not I should move in with Ben was never asked. We couldn't get enough of each other. I don't think I ever stayed at my place after the skiing trip in Megève. For one thing, he had a lift, which my flat didn't, so getting home on crutches was much easier at his place. And I just couldn't get enough of him. I must admit that I was also beginning to enjoy living in luxury. Fond as I was of my home, I was blown away by the floor-to-ceiling glass walls of his Thames walk flat. It was no effort to choose his Egyptian cotton sheets over my Ikea ones, his massive marble kitchen island over my homemade cement one. I'd never seen myself as superficial, but I admit I enjoyed the expensive restaurants and impromptu trips, as well as never having to worry about money. And because he was still my main client, Ben could call me over for 'client meetings' whenever he felt like it.

I received a lot of praise for my work on the PeakSleek account, bringing in hundreds of thousands of pounds for Gant & Ballaster, so it was never a problem if I spent half my time having carnal sex with Ben.

In the mornings, I would float to work in a dreamlike

state, raw and shaking, thanking the heavens that I'd been blessed with such a relationship. I did my best to concentrate on the most urgent tasks until I could finally escape back to him and lie helplessly beneath him as pinned me to the floor or tied me to his bed railings. The combination of brutality and tenderness made me his without any kind of reserve.

After one particularly exciting session involving a small amount of choking, he held me in his arms like a broken bird and told me he wanted me with him all the time. I knew I should have protested; I knew deep down that I should remain financially independent, but I couldn't bring myself to care anymore. All the work I did was to please him. I craved the praise he showered on me every time I presented him with an idea for Breathe. And I'd always been insecure and stressed at work. It had never been an enjoyable experience.

Capri was putting in more and more hours, and I knew she would succeed in exposing me for the fraud I was. I needed to escape. I knew Vince and Meloda would miss me, but they were losing more and more ground at G&B. All our days were counted, I could sense it.

Ben stared into my eyes with a hunger that made my insides tremble. "Stay home with me, Emiliah. I want to fuck you whenever I feel like it. I want you to be mine. Completely."

I remained silent, not wanting to have this conversation again.

"Will you think about it ?" He stroked my clitoris ever so

lightly.

"I can't, Ben. You know that. Please," I begged.

"Will you ?"

"Please, Ben, please." I was crying by now.

"Will you ?" He looked at me hard.

"Yes! Please, Ben, please!" Waiting just a second longer, he thrust his fingers inside me.

So, I handed in my resignation. Just like that.

Vince and Meloda were horrified.

It was in Vince's office, the familiar messy space filled with the scent of coffee and the hum of distant conversations. Vince and Meloda sat across from me at the round conference table, their faces a combination of shock and disbelief.

"Emiliah, what brought this on?" Vince asked, leaning forward, his brow furrowed with concern. "Is it something to do with Capri, Shells and Bells?"

I shook my head, trying to keep my voice steady. "No, not at all. I've just... decided it's time for a change. I need to focus on my personal life."

Meloda's eyes widened, her voice filled with worry. "But Emiliah, you're so independent. This is so sudden. Are you sure this is what you want?"

I nodded, avoiding her gaze. "Yes, I'm sure. It's been a

tough decision, but it's what I need right now."

Vince sighed, running a hand through his hair. "We'll support you, of course, but it's a huge loss for us. Is there anything we can do to make you reconsider?"

I hesitated, knowing I couldn't tell them the real reason, that Ben wanted me all to himself and that I couldn't resist him, I needed to please him. "No, Vince. My mind is made up. I appreciate everything you both have done for me, truly."

Meloda reached out, touching my hand lightly. "God, I can't believe you're leaving." She wiped a lone tear from her face.

I forced a smile, feeling a pang of guilt. "I'll really miss the team, but you are all so great, it'll be fine."

Rhona remained impassible as I announced my departure to her in her office. After a few moments of silence, she raised her eyebrows. "You'll regret leaving, believe me. And don't think we'll ever take you back. In our industry, hundreds are always waiting in line, ready to prove themselves." She nodded at the door, indicating that I should leave. Just as I reached for the handle, she said, "G&B isn't a shop you turn your back on. And if I hear that it's all a ploy to steal a client, you'll be hearing from my lawyers."

I turned back towards her. "It's not. I'm giving up work." My voice was shaking.

She shot me a look of undisguised contempt. "Well, then,

you're far more stupid than I thought. Get out."

There was no point in staying on for my notice period. Rhona clearly wanted me gone. I think she knew that I wouldn't repeat her words to Ben, that I was loyal enough not to jeopardize one of G&B's client relationships.

I returned to Vince's office to finalize my resignation. He looked up from his desk, his expression resigned but supportive. "I wish you the best, Emiliah. Just know that you're always welcome here if you change your mind."

"Thanks, Vince. That means a lot," I said, my voice a whisper. I didn't repeat what Rhona had said.

Nora and Helen hugged me fiercely and ordered me to stay in touch, which made me tear up.

Meloda walked me to the elevator, her eyes glistening with unshed tears. "We will continue to meet up for drinks on Saturdays, right? He won't forbid it, will he?"

I nodded, unable to speak past the lump in my throat and not wanting to lie about Ben's influence on my decision. As the elevator doors closed, I took a deep breath, trying to steady my nerves. This was it. I was leaving behind a career I had worked so hard to build. The thought was both terrifying and liberating.

Stepping out into the cool air, I felt a strange mix of emotions. Part of me was relieved to be free from the pressures of the job, but another part of me couldn't shake the feeling of loss. As I walked to my car, I knew this decision would change everything.

I gradually moved more and more of my stuff into Ben's flat, although I rarely used any of it, as he preferred to buy me new things. He organized outings with Amber, his personal shopper so that I had all the right clothes for each occasion. And occasions there were. We went to the opera, to dinners with friends of his and members of PeakSleek's board. We were invited to parties and gallery openings. Everything about the life I was living was a million miles away from what I had expected to live, but I loved it.

"Marry me." He was giving me one of his intense, pre-sex stares.

"Ben!" My heart pounded.

He began stroking me, but I pulled away. "Ben. Please. Listen. You can't ask me something like that. Not like that. Not now."

He sat up, an amused smile on his face. "And why not ?"

"Ben. Listen, people don't get engaged after dating for four months."

"Emiliah." He rolled on top of me, grinding my wrists into the mattress with a little too much pressure and forcing my thighs apart with his knees. "Emiliah," he repeated, thrusting himself deep inside me.

I cried out, unable to control myself.

"I'm not people," he growled into my ear. "I'm Ben Goodall. And I'll do whatever I fucking well please."

I was still crying out with pleasure when he flipped me

over, rubbed the wetness of my vagina onto my anus, and pushed himself in. I tried to move forward, to slow down the process, but he held my shoulder down, pushing my face into the pillow so that I struggled for breath and felt the searing pain at the same time. "I'm Ben fucking Goodall," he growled into my ear. "I'm Ben fucking Goodall."

"You do love me, don't you ?" he asked as I lay, crying, in his arms afterwards.

I wiped the tears from my face. "Of course I do, Ben. I love you very much."

"You do ?" he looked scared and vulnerable.

"Yes, of course I love you. I love you so much. And I'll marry you."

28

The sun was rising, a pink light illuminating the tranquil yoga retreat nestled in the rolling Hampshire hills. The scents of honeysuckle and rosemary hung in the air, mingling with the soft sounds of wind chimes. Meloda, Flit and I were having breakfast on the porch of our cozy cabin. To me, this was the perfect hen do.

"Emiliah, can we talk?" Meloda began, her voice gentle but firm. I could see the worry etched on her face as she took a sip of chamomile tea.

I sighed, sensing where this conversation was heading. "I know what you're going to say," I replied, trying to keep my tone light. "And I appreciate your concern, but I'm fine. Really."

Flit reached out, placing a hand on Meloda's knee before speaking. "Emiliah, we just want to make sure you're making this decision for the right reasons. Marrying Ben so soon... it feels rushed. Are you absolutely sure this is what you want?"

I looked out at the horizon, the sky a canvas of pink and

orange hues. The truth was, I had been asking myself the same question. But every time doubt crept in, I pushed it aside, convincing myself that this was the path I needed to take. "I love Ben," I said, turning back to face them. "He wants us to be together, fully committed. And I want that too."

Meloda leaned forward, her eyes searching mine. "But Emiliah, what about your career? You worked so hard to get where you got. Are you really giving it all up?"

A lump formed in my throat, and I took a deep breath, trying to steady my emotions. "It's not about giving up. It's about choosing a different path. One that includes Ben."

Flit's eyes softened with understanding. "I get that, Emiliah. But you don't have to sacrifice everything for him. A relationship should be a partnership, not an ultimatum."

I looked down at my hands, the engagement ring sparkling in the fading light. "I know," I whispered, my voice barely audible. "But Ben... needs me. He wants me to be there for him whenever he needs me."

Meloda reached out and took my hand, her grip warm and reassuring. "And what about what you need? Have you thought about that?"

Tears welled in my eyes, and I blinked them away, not wanting to break down.

Flit moved closer, her presence a steady anchor. "Emiliah,

you deserve to be happy too. Don't lose yourself in someone else's life. Your happiness matters just as much as his."

We sat in silence for a few moments, the weight of their words sinking in. Part of me knew they were right, but I'd had enough of being reasonable. I'd been making calculated decisions for most of my life. I wanted to let go for once.

"I know what I'm doing," I said defiantly.

Meloda shifted uneasily in her seat, her eyes flicking to Flit before she spoke again. "Emiliah," she said, her tone soft but laced with concern. "We noticed the marks... on your wrists and shoulder."

My heart skipped a beat, and I instinctively pulled my sleeves down and adjusted my top. "It's nothing," I said quickly, trying to brush it off.

Flit leaned forward, her expression earnest. "Emiliah, those marks look serious. Is everything okay with Ben?"

I sighed, a little annoyed, and forced a smile. "It's fine," I insisted. "We... we like rough sex." I felt myself blushing. "He ties my hands, sometimes bites me a little. It's exciting," I said. "Fun."

Meloda's eyes widened with alarm. "Rough? Emiliah, no-one should be leaving marks on you, especially not someone who's supposed to love and protect you."

I looked away, frustration bubbling beneath the surface. "You don't understand," I whispered. "It's passionate. I love it."

They looked at each other fleetingly, obviously concerned, but not pushing me any further.

Meloda nodded. "We just care about you, Em. You know how much I care. I want you to be safe and happy. You deserve the best."

Flit glanced at her watch and then at me, her worry still evident but tempered by a small smile. "It's time for our morning yoga session," she said softly, her tone inviting rather than insistent.

Meloda and I nodded in agreement. I sighed, feeling the weight of their concern mixed with my own swirling thoughts.

We gathered our mats and water bottles, the air filled with the soft rustling of leaves and the distant chirping of birds. The path to the yoga pavilion was lined with blooming flowers, their vibrant colors a stark contrast to the heaviness in my heart.

As we walked, Meloda and Flit remained silent. The yoga space was open to the elements, with a panoramic view of the surrounding hills. We laid out our mats, the cool morning air brushing against our skin.

Our instructor, a serene Indian woman with flowing hair and a calming aura, began the session with a gentle meditation. "Focus on your breath," she intoned softly. "Let go of any worries or fears. This time is for you."

29

I took a deep breath and surveyed myself in the mirror, the soft morning light emitting a warm glow, making my makeup look flawless. The anticipation of the day filled the air with a palpable energy, and I could feel my heart beating with excitement and nervousness. I had never seen myself as particularly attractive, but in that moment, I felt truly beautiful.

The minimalist dress I had chosen was a masterpiece of design, made of rich, thick matte satin that clung to my curves. Its simplicity was its elegance—a timeless silhouette accentuating my figure without overwhelming it.

Looking at myself in the mirror, I couldn't help but smile. The neckline was modest yet flattering, framing my collarbone with rich fabric. The back of the dress dipped into a gentle V, revealing most of my back.

My wild curls had been subtly tamed, and tiny flowers added, giving me an elegant, celtic allure, rather than my naturally messy look. I had chosen a simple pearl necklace and matching earrings despite Meloda's suggestion that I go for something bolder.

I took one last look in the mirror, my heart swelling with anticipation.

I stood at the chapel entrance, clutching a bouquet of white roses, my heart pounding in my chest. Then, the moment arrived. The chapel doors swung open, and the strains of the bridal march filled the air. I took a deep breath and began to walk, Vince's arm linked with mine and Fiona, Ben's sister, in a beautifu white bridemaid's dress, behind us. I would have loved to have Katie as a second bridesmaid, but Davina's tolerance didn't stretch quite that far. The soft glow of candlelight bathed the wooden pews inside, creating an intimate and romantic ambiance. The scent of fresh flowers, carefully arranged by the florist, filled the air with their delicate fragrance. A string quartet played an instrumental version of Metallica's 'Nothing Else Matters', setting the tone for the momentous occasion.

As I made the final steps towards the altar, my eyes were drawn to Ben, waiting patiently at the end of the aisle, his expression a blend of anticipation and sheer adoration.

The ceremony was a blur, the priest's voice fading as all I could take in, was the tall, muscular, grey-eyed man standing in front of me. He squeezed my hand when it was time to say my vows, which I did without hesitation, in a strong, clear voice.

Then it was his time to speak. "Emiliah, my darling Emiliah, from the moment I set eyes on you when you were teaching French, German, Italian and Swedish colleagues to write limericks, I was hooked." Laughter rippled through the crowd. I glanced anxiously at the Minister, as these weren't the vows we'd practiced. "You were so sweet, so naïve and yet so determined to make it work, that I knew then and there that you were the woman I would marry. I so look forward to spending the rest of my life with you. I just know that you are the perfect person for me and that you will bring me so much satisfaction. You are my muse, my confidante, my true love. Today, I choose you, Emiliah, and I promise to choose you every day for the rest of our lives. With all that I am and all that I have, I pledge to be your partner, your true love, and your best friend."

Tears welled in my eyes as I took in every word he said, still unable to believe he'd picked me.

As we exchanged rings, our eyes locked in a silent exchange. The chapel seemed to radiate with the warmth of our union.

Finally, the priest pronounced us husband and wife, and we sealed our vows with a tender kiss. The chapel erupted in applause, and my heart swelled with an overwhelming sense of joy and gratitude.

The reception was set against the picturesque backdrop of Winchester College, a place that held a special significance in Ben's life. It was here that he had spent his formative years after suffering through boarding school in Hong Kong, forging lasting friendships and creating cherished memories. Whenever his group of friends gathered, they were loud and boisterous, with Gavin, Ben's closest friend, occasionally hinting at illegal activities they had gotten away with in their youth. Ben insisted that Gavin fabricated the stories, but I wasn't completely convinced. In this particular day though, they were all well-behaved.

The historic grounds of the medieval school provided an enchanting backdrop for the photographs captured by Togar, London's most renowned photographer, known for his artistic documentary-style shots. After the ceremony, we were treated to a sumptuous wedding breakfast featuring traditional English cuisine, artfully crafted by the Michelin-starred chef Geoffrey Dax, including a gastronomical revisit of the classic Ploughman's Lunch, with artisanal cheeses, pickled vegetables, devilled quail eggs, and delicate pâté en croute with a citrusy emulsioned mayonnaise. Every detail, from the smooth linen tablecloths to the delicate crystal glasses, exuded an unmistakable air of opulence and sophistication.

As we mingled among the two hundred elegantly attired guests, I couldn't help but feel a vague sadness that there were only four people from my side, all of them former colleagues. They were the best guests I could have wished for though, and they all hugged me fiercely, congratulating me without reserve.

Amidst the celebration, Augusta, Ben's statuesque mother, gracefully excused herself from a group of well-wishers and made her way over to where I stood with Meloda, Nora, Helen, and Vince. Ben was momentarily absent, lost in the joyful chaos of the festivities.

I steeled myself, knowing that Ben's decision not to sign a prenup was a sore spot for my mother-in-law. I hoped she realized that I wasn't with Ben for his money but because I was deeply, desperately in love with him. She greeted me with a warm smile, raising her champagne glass. "Darling, congratulations. You will make him happy, won't you?"

"Of course," I replied, returning her smile, genuinely appreciative of her warmth and kindness on our special day. I sighed. My life felt complete, and I couldn't fathom how, after such a great start to our marriage, anything could possibly go wrong.

30

"This way. Turn here."

"Okay. Here we go." Ben grinned at me as he pulled the Jeep off the bumpy track into the monkey sanctuary's car park. He was so sexy in his thin white tee-shit, cotton shorts, flip-flops and shades. We were on day three of our honeymoon, and apart from a bout of diarrhea for Ben, which, I was confident, was mostly over, based on the heated sex we'd had just before leaving for the sanctuary, everything had been heavenly so far. Every so often, I would pinch myself. *What have I done to deserve such an amazing life? How isit that I, Emeliah Bent, get to be married to Ben Goodwall?*

He unbuckled his seatbelt. "Okay, let's go."

Walking towards the entrance, he lazily took my little finger in his. In this heat, anything more than that would have been uncomfortable.

A man with several teeth missing appeared from inside the dark building. "Mister Goodall? Missus Goodall?"

Ben grinned at me. "Yes, that's us."

"Liv bags here. Pliz. No worries. No worries."

Ben shifted. "No, thanks. I'll keep my stuff on me."

I squeezed his hand. "Sweetie, um, I read that monkeys steal pretty much everything you carry. I'm sure it's safe to leave your rucksack and glasses here."

"It's fine, Babe. I'll hold on to them tightly."

He waited patiently while I handed the man whose name I had not properly understood (it sounded something like 'Shash') my own bag, and we followed him through the building. As soon as we emerged into the lush vegetation on the other side, a large Tucan flew past us and headed for a sycamore ahead of us.

"Oh my God, did you see that?" I could feel tears about to well up.

Ben turned towards me and planted an affectionate kiss on my head.

We continued to follow Shash, who pointed at various monkeys and explained things in what sounded like tongues. "Sheisholashash. Shaloushamifash." After which, he'd look at us, nodding. I nodded back enthusiastically.

We walked on and on through the vegetation, breathing in the sweet smell of copals and guarumos, listening to the Chickadee whistle and the Nightingale sing.

Shash beckoned for us to follow him along a small path, through thick vegetation before stopping in front of a tree covered in what looked like ants. He grabbed my hand and put it on the truck, letting the ants walk all over it, then pulled it away and rubbed his rough hands around mine, squashing the ants.

"Shgood. For moshquitoesh."

He tried to grab Ben's hand, but Ben pulled away just in time. He placed his right hand tentatively against the tree and waited for the ants to roam over him. Rubbing his hands together, he gave me one of his intense stares and rubbed his forearms and face with the ant 'juice'.

We were both in awe as we followed Shash further into the forest. The birdsong was louder here, and we could hear other animal sounds, although the branches and lianas around us prevented us from seeing any of them.

Shash suddenly stopped and pointed through a large opening in the trees above us to what looked like some kind of temple. "Sheagles. Up. Up."

It was incredible. An entire family of eagles was up on one of the temple's ledges, only fifty or so feet from the ground. The mother was bending over a nest, while what must have been the male eagle stood next to her, looking around keenly.

"Wow." We stared up in awe.

Then something landed on my back, and I screamed. 'Monksheesh,' shouted Shash as the creature climbed to the top of my head. Ben belly-laughed as I stood there, cringing, the monkey perched on my head and playing with my hair. Then one landed on him, and he shouted out, too, making me laugh. He tried to shake it off, but it clang onto his shoulder as if its life depended on it. Then it looked really pissed off and opened Ben's rucksack with its deft little fingers, pushed its arm deep inside, and leaped off, running away.

"What did it take? What did it take?" Ben shouted.

I gently prised my monkey off my head and put it on the ground. It gave me an aggressive smile before prancing off into the trees. "Let's take it off and have a look."

He pushed me away impatiently. "Wallet, shades, passport. I can't see what's miss- Fuck! My anti-diarrhea pills. Fuck!"

I searched the trees around us, and sure enough, there was a very annoyed-looking monkey on a branch just a few meters away, popping pill after pill from Ben's packet.

I looked at him in shock, then turned to Shash, who was looking on, smiling widely. "IT TOOK PILLS," I enunciated very slowly. "WILL IT BE OK?"

Ben turned towards me angrily. "Are you fucking kidding me, Emiliah? Who gives a shit about the fucking monkey? What about me? Where am I supposed to get new medication for my diarrhea? I have to finish the treatment. Mérida is four hours away. We're in the middle of fucking nowhere!"

Suddenly, the monkey stopped munching on pills and threw the packet at Ben, hitting him on the head. I bent down and picked up the aluminium packet, which still contained six pills. I looked up, and the monkey stuck a finger up at Ben and turned its back to us.

"It's eaten most of the packet! It could be seriously ill!" I looked at Shash, who shrugged, having no idea what I was trying to say. So I held up the packed and pointed at the monkey, saying "DIARRHOEA MEDICINE. DIARRHOEA MEDICINE." Shash looked at me for a second before bursting into laughter. "Shokay. Itsh jush shitting bricksh. No worries. No worries." He shook his head, laughing, as he took in Ben's rage at having lost his medication.

Ben closed his rucksack and pulled it round to the front, protecting the rest of its contents with his arms. "Come on. We're leaving."

"But Ben, we're supposed to do a whole circuit. And he's taking us to another temple. You've still got six pills. That'll get you to tommorow night. Surely we can-"

He stared at me, livid. "I'm leaving. You can stay if you like."

I didn't insist. We quickly collected our belongings, and I thanked Shash, shaking his hand profusely. Ben just turned and headed out to the Jeep.

Once inside, I turned to him. "Sweetie. We'll buy some more pills. Don't worry; we'll be okay."

He grunted.

I giggled. "did you hear what he said about the monkey shitting bricks? I don't know if I misheard, but if that's what he said, you've got to admit it's quite funny." I gave him a playful nudge.

"Yeah, so fucking funny," he said coldly.

I searched his face, looking for signs it was a joke. It wasn't.

"Little miss humor," he spat. "So damn fucking hilarious. Ha. Ha. Ha."

I stared at the road, a familiar pit of hurt in my stomach. *Don't cry. Whatever you do, don't you dare cry.*

31

He didn't speak for the rest of the drive back to the hotel, despite my attempts to start a conversation. When we arrived, he parked the rental car and got out, taking his ruck sack from the back seat.

I followed him inside, desperate to talk, but he ignored me and headed straight for the stairs.

I decided to let him cool off, and walked out to the terrace. It was so beautiful : the massive infinity pool looked out over a lush jungle, dense with mahogany trees, and animated by the loud cries of grackles.

I undressed until I was wearing only the undersized bikini that Ben had given me on our first night here, one of the swimsuits I wore under my clothes, in lieu of underwear. The top consisted of tiny triangular cups, barely enough to contain my curves, held together by thin straps tied around my neck and back. The rich, earthy brown fabric contrasted against my lightly sun-kissed skin, accentuating the natural glow I'd developed since our arrival. The bottoms sat low on my hips, with narrow strips of fabric that left little to the imagination. Each movement seemed to stretch the material to its limit, emphasizing the apparel's tenuous grasp on functionality. I washed the day's anxiety off under the large outdoor shower and slipped into the pool. I swam a few laps before pulling myself out and heading over to the nearest sunbed.

A waiter arrived on cue, handing me a soft white towel. "Madam, would you like your usual cocktail?"

I smiled up at him, covering my eyes against the low sun. "Yes, please. Thank you."

As he disappeared inside, I rubbed myself off with the soft, fluffy towel, looking around at the few other couples, holding hands, speaking softly or dozing after a long day of excursions. Why wasn't he here with me? Why weren't we talking? This was our honeymoon. I stayed, watching the sunset and sipping my margarita, until the sky turned dark and the other guests moved inside for dinner. I realized I was ravenous.

I pulled my grubby clothes back on and headed inside, towards the lifts.

When I opened the bedroom door, he was lying on the bed, facing the wall. I undressed and lay down, naked, against him. I sensed he was awake but he didn't react. I kissed him softly on the neck and edged closer still. He grunted and shook me off, still facing the wall.

I turned around to face the door and wept silently, knowing instinctively that I shouldn't make a sound.

Eventually, I dried my tears, headed to the shower to wash,

dressed in a simple linen slip dress and flip-flops, and headed downstairs for something to eat.

32

By the time we returned to London, we were back to normal. Ben had spent the rest of the honeymoon on his laptop, by the pool. I had also read, and practiced yoga, and got to know Jojo, the cook, who showed me how to make real tacos, chilaquiles and Pozole. I'd had margaritas with the restaurant staff in the evenings, and they'd even taken me to see Chichen Itza, one of the most incredible experiences I'd ever had, and we'd had drinks in a shack on the beach, a place so beautifully simple, I could have moved there. So, all in all, it was a wonderful honeymoon, although not quite what I'd expected.

On the flight back to London, Ben stopped sulking and became sweet and loving once again, focused on our relationship and eager to make plans for our future together.

Outside the cab, on the way from Heathrow to central London, it was pouring rain.

"I'll have quite a lot of work this week, Babe, so feel free to go shopping, to the hairdresser's, the beautician's, whatever you like." He didn't look up from his smartphone as he spoke.

I patted his thigh. "Of course."

We remained silent for the rest of the journey while he read his emails.

Before leaving Mexico, I'd messaged Meloda to see if we could meet up when we returned. I hadn't gone into any detail in my message, but I wanted her opinion on how the honeymoon had played out. After dropping Ben off at the flat, our driver took me to one of Meloda and my favourite places, the Star of Bethnal Green.

I was nervous on entering the pub, as I no longer knew what to tell Meloda. She hadn't really expressed a clear opinion on Ben, and she'd tried to talk me out of marrying so soon and giving up my job. I didn't want to tarnish Ben's image, but at the same time, I was interested in her opinion.

I settled down and ordered an Indian tonic. After all the margaritas in Mexico, I was determined to lay off the alcohol for a while.

A few minutes later, Meloda entered the colorful, art nouveau restaurant. As usual, several heads turned her way. She was particularly striking today in a white pencil dress that hugged her tall, slim figure. She beamed her gorgeous smile when she spotted me. We hugged as if we'd been apart for months, although it had only been three weeks.

She looked me up and down. "You look amazing." She

lowered her voice. "Must be all the sex you've been having."

I gave her a scolding look. "You think I look amazing? Look at you! You look as if you've just walked off the front page of Grazia."

She beamed again. "Flit picked it out for me. I never would have dared."

I nodded, thinking how interesting a couple they made. Flit herself was not the stylish type. She was attractive, but nothing like as attractive as Mel, and very simply dressed. Yet she encouraged Mel to nurture her fashionista side. There was no judgement, no trying to make Mel more like herself. Flit was definitely growing on me, although I was glad she wasn't with us tonight.

"Go on, tell me what it was like," Meloda said, gliding graciously into the velvet-covered armchair opposite me.

"It was great. Amazing," I replied. "Mexico is such a beautiful country, with such a rich culture. I loved it. And the food! Oh my god, I had no idea how good it was. Nothing like the Mexican food you get here."

Meloda looked at me suspiciously. "I wasn't talking about Mexico. How was it with Ben?"

I played with my napkin. "Oh it was great. Really relaxing and romantic."

Meloda stared at me, not speaking. Her eyes seemed to probe deeper, looking for the truth behind my words.

Nervous, I carried on. "It was really, really good. On our first night there, we were all over each other, ripping each other's clothes off." That much was true, I thought, remembering Ben ripping my shirt open, lifting my skirt up and pinning me against the hotel room door.

She tilted her head slightly, her gaze never wavering. "And after the first night? How was the rest of the trip?"

I forced a smile. "It was lovely. Sightseeing, relaxing on the beach, dinners, cocktails... It was amazing."

Meloda raised an eyebrow, her skepticism clear. "Why are you so tense?"

I sighed, feeling the weight of her concern and the truth I had been avoiding. "It's just... you know. Ben was a bit... moody at times."

"Moody?" Meloda echoed, her tone gentle but firm. "That's putting it lightly, isn't it?"

I bit my lip, the memories of his stony silence flooding back. "I was unthoughtful - it's been stressful for him lately."

"Em," Meloda said softly, leaning forward. "I'm your friend. I can see you're anxious. You don't have to pretend with me."

I looked down, feeling tears prick at the corners of my eyes. I wanted to say more, but I felt as if I was betraying Ben, which I couldn't stand. "It's just... sometimes..."

"Sometimes it's too much?" Meloda finished for me, her

voice filled with understanding.

I nodded, unable to speak past the lump in my throat. Meloda reached across the table, taking my hand in hers. "You know what? You deserve to be happy. Just as much as he does."

I squeezed her hand, grateful for her tenacious support. "Thanks, Mel. I just... I need to give the relationship time. We need to get to know each other better."

She smiled, her eyes warm and encouraging. "Take your time. I'm here for you, no matter what."

We sat in silence for a few moments, the bustling sounds of the pub around us.

As the evening wore on, she filled me in on the latest gossip from work. Capri was back in Rhona's good books after the betrayal of my departure.

The evening ended with Meloda giving me a tight hug before we parted ways. As I walked home, I felt a strange mix of emotions—sadness, relief, and a spark of determination.

When I opened the door to the flat, exhausted and ready for bed, Ben, who was standing at one of the windows, walked over to me purposefully. He bent down towards my lips and kissed me. He played with the hair on the nape of my neck, sending shivers down my spine and awakening a deep longing. He kissed me again with the tiniest of licks on my lips. I opened my mouth a fraction and responded with my tongue, and then we were kissing frantically, pulling at each other's clothes with fervor. He grabbed my breasts, squeezing hard, and then pushed me against the door we'd just closed and slid one of his hands up my thigh to my knickers.

He slipped a finger inside me and until moaned for more. Then he freed his penis and pushed me down to my knees. Grabbing my hair, he pushed his penis so deep into my throat that I gagged as he groaned with pleasure. I pushed him away, unable to breathe. He stared down at me, snarling. "What's wrong?"

"No, I'm sorry, it was just hurting my throat."

He looked at me in disgust. "God, you always have to ruin everything, don't you? They told me this would happen as soon as I got married. Great." He turned around and walked away. A few seconds later, I heard a door slam.

33

"That smells delicious." He held my waist with his left arm as he leaned over my right shoulder. I turned towards him and held out a spoon.

He tasted the stew. "Hmmmm. Quite the cook, aren't you?"

"Thank you." I was touched. He'd never complimented my cooking before.

"Hey, listen." He looked at his watch. "I promised Gavin we'd meet Sally and him for drinks at 5.30. Just a quick one down at Chapter's. Then we'll easily be back in time for dinner at seven."

"But Sweetie, I want to lay the table nicely for Meloda and Flit and have time to get ready."

He looked at me with his begging puppy eyes.

I sighed. "Okay. But we leave at 6.15 on the dot, okay?"

"I love you, Babe." And he lifted me off the ground into a bear hug, which turned into frantic sex on the counter.

Three hours later, we were sitting at a table at the Panorama Tower bar, Ben entertaining Gavin and Sally with the monkey story over gin and tonics. I checked my watch. 6.30 pm. I looked at him intensely, urging him to understand that we had to leave.

Ben frowned. "What is it, Babe?"

"Nothing. It's just that, you know, Meloda and Flit are coming over at seven."

"Just call them and say we'll start a bit later. We're all having such a good time, aren't we, Gav? Sally?"

Gavin and Sally looked at me, beaming.

I smiled back. "Of course. I'll just give her a call."

When I returned, I felt a bit better. Meloda was fine with eight. She wasn't actually ready yet. I settled down and listened to the men discuss bonds while Sally raised her eyebrows at me. "So, what have you been up to recently, Emiliah?"

We made small talk until a quarter to eight when I spoke directly to Gavin and Sally. "Guys, thank you so much for this. It was so nice. We'll definitely have to do something soon. Sally, why don't you message me some dates and we'll set something up ASAP?" I was getting desperate. "Come on, Ben. Meloda'll be wondering what happened."

"Thanks, Mate." Ben squeezed Gavin's shoulder and leaned down to kiss Sally on the cheek.

As soon as we were in the car, I texted Meloda, saying we'd

be home at 8.30. Ben took a long time to put on his seatbelt and adjust his seat and the rearview mirror of the Ferrari.

"Ben, can we please hurry up? I've already changed the time twice."

He reversed out of the space at top speed, without looking behind him, and sped towards the car park exit at top speed.

"Oh my God, Ben. Slow down."

He braked violently. "Do you want to drive?"

"Please, Ben. I just want to be back in time to spend the evening with Meloda and Flit, as planned."

As he accelerated again up the ramp and into the street, something in me snapped. "I feel as though every time I want to see one of *my* friends, you make a scene, so that doesn't go well."

He pulled the car to a stop and stared at the dashboard. Then he started thumping it. Bits of plastic and metal came flying out toward me as he screamed, smashing the dashboard with all his strength. "YOU ALWAYS HAVE TO DO THIS, DON'T YOU? THINGS CAN NEVER BE SIMPLE, CAN THEY?"

I stared at the smashed dashboard in shock.

He closed his eyes and took a deep breath. "Get out."

"What?" I didn't understand.

"Get out. GET THE FUCK OUT OF MY CAR!" he

roared.

I undid my seatbelt, and he revved up the car again. I barely had time to get out before he drove off at top speed.

I pulled out my phone and dialed Meloda's number. "I'm so sorry, Mel. I think I have food poisoning from lunch. Yes, yes, I'm fine. I just need to rest. No, I wasn't going to poison you, of course not," I giggled weakly. "Yes, yes, I'll call you. I'm so sorry, Mel. I have to go now." And I pressed the red button before she could hear me cry.

I pulled my anorak hood up and kept my head down. I searched my pockets for tissues but couldn't find any. I'd left my bag in the car. All I had was my mobile phone and my coat. I looked around. Lamb Walk. I needed somewhere hidden to blow my nose into my sleeve. I could feel it all running down my face, the salty taste on my tongue. Surely, Leathermarket Gardens were somewhere around here. I kept my head down, walking forward. Morrocco Street. Black railings. Buses rushing past. Shouts. Finally, I saw the trees ahead of me. I maintained my pace, not wanting to be conspicuous until I reached the safety of the oaks and birch trees. I wasn't sure what time it was, but it was dark, and the park seemed empty. Leaning against a sturdy tree, I pulled off my coat and crumpled to the ground. As I sobbed into the lining of my Burberry Trench, I felt sure my behavior hadn't been that bad. We'd planned to have Meloda over, I'd agreed to go out with Gavin and Sally, and I'd wanted to be back on time. Yes, I'd accused him of sabotaging evenings with my friends, but I'd expressed it as a feeling. What was wrong with me that made me ruin every relationship I had? I thought back to the Limerelease training, the Louvre, everything. Our relationship was so perfect, so loving. And yet, I felt such despair. I breathed heavily, wiping my face clean. *You're going to make this work, Emiliah Bent. You just need to try harder.*

34

The moment the Bugatti pulled up in front of the luxury spa, ironically called 'The Factory', I felt a swell of anticipation.

As we exited the car, the crisp London air brushed against my skin. The spa's staff greeted us with a warmth that felt both professional and genuinely caring. Ben, ever the perfectionist, had orchestrated this day with meticulous attention to detail, ensuring every moment would be tailored to my liking.

The grand entrance of the building, a renovated industrial structure, welcomed us into a world of indulgence. Ben squeezed my hand, his eyes meeting mine with an unspoken promise of relaxation and rejuvenation.

The interior was a sanctuary of calm. Soft, ambient music floated through the air, mingling with the subtle scent of ylang ylang and jasmine. The decor struck a perfect balance between comfort and style, with plush furnishings, exotic plants and serene water features creating an oasis of tranquility against a backdrop of distressed brick walls and steel beams. Ben led me by hand, as we were shown to the changing area.

I slipped into a plush robe and slippers, the fabric soft against my skin.

Ben had chosen a couple's massage. As we down lay side by side, the therapists held out bowls of scented oil for us to smell. Then, once we had made our choice, they set to work, easing away the tension of the preceding days.

I felt my therapist's warm, oil-slicked hands glide over my back, pressing firmly but gently into the knots that had been bothering me for days. Each stroke was deliberate, expertly targeting areas of stress and tightness. The rhythmic kneading of my muscles sent waves of relaxation through my body, starting from my shoulders and spreading down my spine. I closed my eyes, surrendering to the blissful sensation.

I could hear Ben's relaxed breathing, deep and even, and occasionally, I would feel the subtle movements of his body as his therapist worked on him.

The final part of the massage was focused on my neck and scalp. The therapist's fingers worked through my hair, massaging my scalp in slow, circular motions.

Ben's hand found mine, our fingers intertwining. I turned my head slightly to look at him, and he gave me a small, contented smile. In that moment, it felt like everything was right again. We were connected, both physically and emotionally, sharing this intimate experience of relaxation and healing.

As the massage came to an end, the therapists slowly brought us back to the present, their touch becoming lighter and more delicate. They gently patted our shoulders, signaling the end of the session.

We lay there for a few more moments, basking in the afterglow of the massage. Ben squeezed my hand, and I squeezed back.

After our massage, we explored the spa's many amenities, from the sauna's steamy embrace to the ice fountain's refreshing chill. Each experience was a delight to the senses.

Ben had even arranged for a private lunch in the spa's garden, a spot where we could enjoy the beauty of of our surroundings while savoring delicious, healthy dishes. The space was elegantly set, with crisp white tablecloths, shiny silver cutlery and tall, slim champagne glasses.

Yet I sensed a subtle shift in Ben's demeanor. It was a slight furrowing of his brow, a tightening of his jaw, signaling his discontent before he uttered a single word to our waiter.

"This isn't what I was promised," Ben's voice cut through the calm, his tone sharp. "We were supposed to have a private area, away from other guests. This," he gestured at the table, "is hardly secluded."

I glanced around, noting the few other patrons in the area, each absorbed in their own quiet conversations.

I put my hand on his arm. "Ben, it's fine. The other guests are really not that close."

He stared at me angrily, and I stopped, understanding that

I'd gone too far again.

The manager, a stocky, energetic man, sensing the tension, approached with practiced ease, ready to diffuse the situation. But Ben was already past the point of easy assurances. "I specifically requested a secluded dining experience for my wife and me. This is unacceptable," he said, his voice rising enough to draw a few discreet glances our way. The warmth I had felt cocooning us dissipated. "Ben, it's okay," I found myself insisting. "Really, it doesn't matter. The day has been perfect as is. Let's not let this spoil it."

"Let's not let this spoil it," he sang. "It's already fucking spoiled."

I felt the heat of shame creep over my face.

The manager led us to another spot, and Ben followed in frustrated silence. When we arrived in a completely secluded corner of the garden, Ben looked at him. "Now, that wasn't so hard, was it?"

"No sir," replied the manager quietly. "Please let us offer you a complimentary glass of champagne."

Ben gave a curt nod and waved him away. He breathed deeply as we sat and took my hand in his. "Emiliah," he said, not unkindly but with an intensity that left no room for argument. "It matters because today was supposed to be about us, about creating a perfect moment. When something falls short, it feels like a breach of that promise, not just by the spa but by me, for being unable to give you the day you deserve."

I nodded and patted his arm. He was so dedicated. And yet, there was a gnawing discomfort telling me that this wouldn't be as easy and natural as I'd imagined.

35

It was a chilly Sunday when Meloda, Flit, and I managed to meet up again, this time for dinner at Dhal Palace in Shoreditch, my favorite Indian restaurant. The air was scented with oils, spices, and garlicky naan, and a gentle hum of conversation filled the space. We found a quiet corner, a small haven where we could talk. Despite the warm, welcoming setting, I the remnants of our conversation at my hen do lingered like a shadow, making me instinctively guard my words and emotions.

Flit seemed to sense the delicate balance of the day, opting to steer clear of topics that had anything to do with Ben or romantic relationships. "Have you guys seen the documentary 'The Keepers' on Netflix?" she asked, her tone deliberately casual. "It's sad and intense, but really good."

Meloda's eyes lit up. "Yes! I watched it a while ago. It's incredibly gripping."

I nodded, feeling a mix of curiosity and unease. "I haven't seen it yet. What's it about?"

Flit leaned forward, her expression serious. "It's about the unsolved murder of a nun in Baltimore and the secrets that were uncovered during the investigation. It touches on themes of abuse and corruption. It's a difficult watch but very powerful."

"The really shocking part," Meloda added, her voice lowering slightly, "is how the investigators didn't seem interested in finding out the truth. It was a group of middle-aged women who led their own investigation, piecing together clues that the authorities ignored."

A shiver ran down my spine, the mention of negligent investigators stirring up a whirlpool of buried memories and emotions. I took a deep breath, trying to steady myself, but a knot of unease settled in my stomach. I forced a smile and nodded.

"It's amazing how the story unfolds," Meloda said, breaking a piece of naan and dipping it into the rich, flavorful dhal. "The bravery of the survivors who came forward is incredible."

Flit nodded in agreement. "And the way those women connected all the pieces of the puzzle... it's heartbreaking but also inspiring to see people fight for justice on their own terms."

I listened intently, intrigued by Flit's perspective, even though I was uncomfortable with the topic. "I'll have to watch it," I said, even though I knew I wouldn't. "It sounds really good."

Flit seemed to sense my unease, opting for a lighter

approach. "Have you ever played outdoor laser tag?" she asked, her tone deliberately casual.

I shook my head. "No, but I'm up for it, if you guys want to give it a try," I said.

"Maybe we could all next weekend," she suggested with a warm smile. "It could be a nice day out."

"That sounds great," I agreed, feeling a bit of the tension ease away.

The conversation flowed more smoothly from there, touching on everything from our favorite books and movies to plans for the upcoming holidays. As we dipped naan into the best dhal in London, Flit contributed with anecdotes from her work, careful to steer clear of anything too personal or probing. She was clearly trying to respect my boundaries, for which I was silently thankful.

When it was time to leave, we all shared promises get together again soon. I felt such a surge of affection for them both when I hugged them goodbye that it brought tears to my eyes.

"Take care, Em," Meloda whispered, her hug lingering a moment longer than usual."

"Thank you," I whispered back.

36

"Good morning, Mrs. Goodwall," he said, as I rolled over and opened my eyes. His tall, muscular body towered over me, a dark outline against the bright bay window overlooking the Thames.

"Continental or English?" He placed a tray on the bed beside me, with two large plates covered in shiny metal domes, as well as a cup of steaming black coffee and a tall glass of orange juice.

He lifted one, revealing a plate of croissants, baguette, butter and dark red jam. Then, replacing the first dome, lifted the other, revealing bacon, sausages, mushrooms, tomatoes and spicy baked beans.

"Mmm," I sighed blissfully. "Definitely the English breakfast. It's been ages."

I pulled myself up and he placed the tray on my lap, removing the continental plate. I tucked in, savoring the meaty taste and realizing as I ate the bacon that he'd bought the plant-based version, as I'd confided I wanted to transition to veganism, even though it was a struggle. I felt a surge of affection for him for supporting me in my goal.

Mopping up the last of the plate with a piece of baguette, I smiled at my gorgeous husband, sitting, topless, at the end of the bed, drinking coffee. "Are you busy today?" I asked.

"No. Well, nothing I can't postpone." He stroked my bare lags lazily. "I was thinking we could maybe drive down to Brighton for the day, and if we feel like it, maybe stay the night there?"

I pulled his hand further up my leg. "I would love that. Just maybe in an hour or two?"

Three hours later, we were strolling, hand in hand, through the colorful Brighton lanes. The late summer sunshine bathed everything in a warm, golden glow, creating a perfect backdrop for our spontaneous getaway.

Ben seemed relaxed in the bright, bustling atmosphere. We stopped to admire the display of a vintage record store, some old vinyls catching his eye. He squeezed my hand and smiled, making my heart flutter.

We wandered further, drawn by the scent of fresh pastries to a nearby bakery. The aroma of warm bread and sweet treats wafted through the air, making our mouths water, even after the huge breakfast. Ben suggested we grab a snack, and we entered the charming little bakery, its shelves filled with an array of delectable pastries. We shared a flaky pain suisse, its buttery layers melting in our mouths, and laughed as we smiled at each other with dark chocolate on our teeth.

Continuing our walk, we passed a series of art galleries, each showcasing eclectic collections that ranged from contemporary pieces to more traditional works. Ben paused in front of one, captivated by a striking abstract painting, then, on a whim, went inside and bought it, and the gallery manager took down his contact details for the delivery.

We'd already booked a room at the Grand Hotel, its elegant façade promising a night of luxury and comfort. We'd also secured a table at The Ivy, a place I'd long wanted to try out for its creative food and colorful, art deco ambiance.

After visiting bookstores, vintage clothes shops and vinyl stores, we stopped in front of Erotica, a bright red erotic shop. We walked around, looking at various BDSM devices. I smiled at the idea of coming here with Meloda, how we'd giggle, showing each other ever larger dildos in horror. Yet, here I was with Ben, browsing quite seriously. Everything he showed me sent a shiver of excitement down my spine, and I was suddenly impatient to check out the Grand Hotel's luxurious presidential suite.

We made our way towards the seafront, the sound of waves crashing against the shore growing louder with each step. The beach was dotted with families and couples, all enjoying the sun-soaked afternoon.

In front of the hotel, Ben wrapped his arms around me and I leaned into him. *This can't be real. It's too perfect.*

37

The following Monday, I was making a dinner of tian with vegan cheese when he slammed the door, the suddenness of the sound causing my heart to race. Panic welled inside me as I watched him storm away from the dining room, his footsteps echoing in the hallway.

"What's wrong? Did something happen at work?" I called out, abandoning my uncooked dish.

He stopped abruptly in the hallway, his back still turned to me. His shoulders rose and fell with each labored breath, and his hands clenched into fists.

He turned to face me, his expression twisted in disgust. "You know very well what's wrong," he spat out, his words dripping with resentment.

I took a hesitant step closer, my heart pounding and the lump in my throat growing. "No, no, I don't," I stammered. "Ben, what's going on? Have I done something wrong?"

His eyes bore into mine, filled with rage. He seemed on the verge of saying something, but then, with a shake of the head, he shot me another look of disgust and walked out of the room, leaving me alone and bewildered.

Almost absentmindedly, I opened the freezer and took out a single caramel cheesecake to defrost in the microwave. I waited impatiently for the ping before diving my spoon into the creamy dessert. When I finished, I realized it wasn't enough and looked around quickly before taking out two more. So much for veganism.

38

On one unassuming Tuesday afternoon, I decided to embark on a journey to the public library. I needed answers, but after a brief online search, I had the feeling that maybe it wasn't a great idea to conduct internet searches at home. I left behind the opulent confines of Thames Summit, where I'd already prepared the evening meal, and headed south to the John Harvard Library.

As I stepped outside, the crisp autumn air greeted me, a welcome change from the stifling warmth inside. The Thames shimmered in the midday sun, its waters reflecting the life and energy of the city around it. The walk was invigorating, the hustle and bustle of the city providing a comforting backdrop. I made my way down Tower Bridge Road, the iconic bridge itself a silent guardian of my thoughts.

On the way, I stopped for a cappuccino and a cinnamon roll at Starbucks, the familiar aroma of coffee and baked goods enveloping me like a warm hug. The barista smiled as she handed me my order, and I found a moment of solace in the simple act of taking a sip of my cappuccino, the frothy milk and rich espresso a small delight. Still hungry, I bought a slice of carrot cake to eat on the way, its sweet, creamy frosting a decadent treat.

I passed the bustling entrance of London Bridge station, the crowds ebbing and flowing.

The John Harvard Library was not far. The streets were quieter here, the noise of the city giving way to a more subdued, almost contemplative atmosphere.

The anticipation of what lay inside the library quickened my steps, and I hurriedly finished the carrot cake, shoving the last bite into my mouth as I drew closer to the entrance.

Pushing open the heavy wooden doors, a gentle hush enveloped me. The musty scent of old books embraced my senses, and I felt an inexplicable thrill coursing through my veins. I pulled out my phone and put it on airplane mode.

The soft glow of the library's lamps diffused a warm light, creating an atmosphere of quiet introspection. I passed through the novel section, my fingers brushing against the books. I was looking for something far more specific.

Navigating the aisles, I finally found the section I was looking for: self-help and personal growth. The titles ranged from familiar bestsellers to obscure works, each promising insight and guidance. I pulled down a worn copy of a book I'd read about online. The cover was faded, the pages slightly yellowed. Hopefully, it would give me the advice I desperately needed.

I found a quiet corner by a window, the late afternoon sun casting a golden hue across the wooden table. Sitting down, as I began to read, the noise and chaos of my life felt distant, replaced by the tranquility of the library and the promise of understanding.

The advice within the book started to unfold, each sentence offering a glimmer of hope, a potential path forward. The words introduced me to other couples who had had challenges, transported me to far-off possibilities, igniting a spark of hope.

The hours slipped by unnoticed as I delved deeper into different books.

As I emerged from the depths of the building, it was already dark. I took out my phone and saw that Ben had left seventeen texts and twenty-one voice messages. *Shit*.

39

I hesitated before unlocking my phone, knowing the barrage I was about to face. The notifications blinked urgently on the screen, a digital manifestation of Ben's mounting anxiety and anger. With a deep breath, I opened them.

The first few texts seemed relatively benign:

"Where are you?"

"Hey, just checking in. Call me when you can."

But as I scrolled further, the tone quickly changed:

"Why aren't you answering?"

"This isn't funny, Emiliah. Where the hell are you?"

"I'm starting to get really worried. CALL ME NOW."

My heart pounded as I skimmed through the increasingly frantic and angry messages. Bracing myself, I moved on to the voice messages.

The first message was calm, almost gentle. "Hey, it's me.

Just wondering where you are. Give me a call when you get this."

By the fifth message, his voice had a noticeable edge. "Emiliah, I've called and texted you a bunch of times. What's going on? Are you okay?"

The tenth message was sharper, anger seeping through. "This is ridiculous. I don't understand why you're ignoring me. Answer your damn phone."

By the fifteenth message, he sounded furious and desperate. "You can't just disappear like this! I'm worried sick! What if something happened to you? This is so irresponsible."

The final message sent a shiver down my spine. His voice was low and controlled, the anger barely restrained. "You'd better have a good explanation for this, Emiliah. We're going to have a serious talk when you get home."

I felt a knot tighten in my stomach. The library's peace and solitude felt worlds away now. I hastened my pace, my mind racing.

I quickly typed out a text message. "On my way. Nearly home. Sorry xx".

As I walked briskly back to the apartment, the city's vibrant nightlife blurred around me. My thoughts were consumed by the impending confrontation. What was I going to say? How would I explain myself without making things worse?

By the time I reached the familiar entrance, I was mentally

and physically exhausted. I paused outside the door, taking a deep breath to steady myself before stepping inside.

The apartment was dimly lit, and the atmosphere was tense. Ben was pacing around the living room, his face a mask of worry and anger. He looked up as I entered, his eyes narrowing.

"Where have you been?" he demanded, his voice tight with barely controlled emotion.

"I went to the library," I said, trying to keep my voice steady. "I wanted to find a new novel."

"For five hours?" he shot back, his tone incredulous. "Do you have any idea how worried I was? I thought you'd had an accident!"

"I'm sorry, Ben," I replied softly. "I didn't mean to worry you. I just needed a break."

"A break?" he asked with a snort. "From what? Lounging around all day?"

"I'm sorry," I repeated, feeling both guilty and frustrated. "I'll try to be better about letting you know where I am." I stepped closer and reached out to take his hand. "I didn't mean to upset you.

He squeezed my hand, his grip firm. "Next time, just call me, okay? I worry because I care about you."

"I will," I promised.

I set about laying the coffee table in front of the TV and

heating the shepherd's pie I'd made in the morning.

When we finished eating, he dabbed at his mouth. "We should probably eat lighter meals."

I flushed.

"You know what I mean, don't you, Emiliah?"

I nodded, keeping my head down. I'd put on weight. I'd been trying to lose some of it, especially given that we had a big event coming up at the Dorchester for his fortieth.

He stared at me. "You've been buying a lot of cakes and cappuccinos at Starbucks, haven't you?"

Tears welled in my eyes.

"Emiliah, I'm just looking out for you." He reached out and took my hand. "I want to help you, babe. I don't want you to be tempted like this all the time. No more snacks at home or cakes when you're out, okay?"

"Okay," I whispered.

He cracked his knuckles. "I think it best if you don't have a card anymore. Tell me when you need to buy something, and I'll give you the cash you need. That'll really help you control yourself."

I looked up sharply.

He stood up and came towards me, lifting me up and folding me into his arms. "I want to help you, Emiliah. I know you don't want be fat. Look at you. You were so beautiful. I hardly recognize you anymore. Let me help you."

He lifted my chin and kissed me, pushing his tongue into my mouth.

40

The grand ballroom at the Dorchester was ablaze with dazzling lights, and the air was filled with the lively chatter of guests. The opulence of the occasion was staggering, a reflection of the life we led.

As I navigated the sea of well-dressed guests, I couldn't help but feel like a stranger in my own life. Everyone around me was caught up in the festivities, sipping champagne, laughing, and mingling, but I felt detached, a silent observer of the play that had become my existence.

My husband, the center of attention, was the life of the party. He charmed the guests with his charisma, his laughter ringing throughout the room. He was the epitome of success, and everyone wanted to be near him, as if beauty and success were contagious.

As I watched him from across the room, my heart pounded.

I smiled, laughed, engaged in polite conversation.

Gavin gave a toast, of which I heard parts ("best mate", "incredible", "genuine", "generous", "best right hook", then laughs, and more jokes that I didn't get). I plastered another smile on my face and raised my glass, wondering what I was doing there. *What is wrong with me that I can't even enjoy a celebration? Maybe he's right. Maybe there's something very off with me.*

Amid the extravagant birthday celebration, I stood with a group of his colleagues from Breathe—charming, successful individuals who were delightful to the CEO's wife, oblivious to what was going on in my mind. Their laughter and banter filled the air. I kept the smile plastered on.

One of Ben's Wintonian friends, Mark, raised his glass, his face slushed with alcohol. "To the birthday boy! You've got it all, my friend."

The group joked, regaling stories of my husband's achievements and adventures, his personality and his accomplishments in both his career and personal life. But when they started talking about an accident in Bangkok involving a prostitute, he glared at them, prompting them to switch topics.

Lisa, Breathe's independent board member, in a long green silk gown hugging her slim frame, sidled up to me. "You two are such a great couple."

I nodded, playing my part. "Thank you, Lisa."

She leaned in, conspiringly, allowing me to smell her heady musk. "I must ask, Dahling, are you expecting?"

My mind flashed to cream cheese and Biscoff spread

bought in secret with change taken from Ben's leather jacket, that I'd scoffed greedily behind the local Tesco's. "Erm, no, I've just... well." I couldn't finish. It was too humiliating.

Lisa turned to Ben and congratulated him on the recent sale of all the retail stores and focus on the growing e-commerce activity. My husband beamed with pride, soaking in the accolades. "Well, none of it would be possible without my incredible wife," he said, enlacing me.

I smiled back at him, my gaze never faltering. "And I'm blessed to have him."

His friends continued to compliment us, extolling our perfect life. Lisa smiled condescendingly, making me briefly wonder whether she and Ben were having an affair.

She thinks he's too good for you.

Shut up, I told my inner voice.

The conversation moved on, and I kept up the game, sharing stories and anecdotes that painted a picture of a happy, loving couple. In the midst of the laughter and admiration, I couldn't help but feel a profound sense of isolation.

As the night wore on, I felt a weight pressing down on me. And it wasn't just the extra weight bulging against the seams of the dress I'd purchased two months earlier. Part of me longed to escape, to break free from the suffocating confines of the party, but I couldn't. To leave would be to risk exposing Ben, letting people see that he'd made the mistake of his life by marrying such a misfit.

I moved through the crowd like a ghost, a phantom in my own life. I watched people dancing, realizing they weren't aware of the pain in the music. I mean, when you actually listen to the lyrics of 'Mr. Brightside', how can you possibly dance to it?

The disconnect was terrifying.

Just make an effort to fit in, for fuck's sake. Why all the drama? You're so melodramatic, such a martyr. Just get a grip and grow up.

41

I sat in the dimly lit living room, my heart pounding like a caged bird. The weight of dread settled upon me like a suffocating blanket, and I waited anxiously for Ben to return home.

When he walked through the door, I forced a smile, my fingers trembling beneath the facade of composure.

"Hey, welcome home," I greeted him, my voice carefully measured to hide the quiver of anxiety beneath.

He stared at me, unsmiling. My heart skipped a beat, but I couldn't let it show. "What is it?" he snapped, his impatience palpable.

I took a deep breath, summoning every ounce of strength to speak without revealing the terror that gripped me. "I think we should talk," I said, my voice as steady as possible.

He scoffed, his irritation deepening. "Talk? About what?"

My mind raced, searching for the right words. "We've been through a lot lately, and it's taking a toll on us," I began, my words carefully chosen. "I think we should consider getting some help, you know, for our relationship."

He stared at me, face twisted in anger, and my heart raced faster. I had hit a nerve, but I couldn't back down now. He took a step towards me. "Help? You think I need help?"

I shook my head, desperate for him to understand. "*We* need help. It's not easy for either of us, and I just want us to be happy."

He paced the room, his frustration evident in every step. "I don't know what more I'm supposed to do. It's you who keeps creating problems."

I fought to keep my emotions in check, to hide my feelings. "I just want us to be okay, that's all."

He looked out at the city skyline for a few seconds. "Fine, we'll get help," he said.

Relief washed over me, even though discomfort still lurked beneath the surface. The conversation had been a small step towards addressing the problem, but I couldn't be sure it would work.

42

I sat in an uncomfortable chair, staring at the sterile white walls of the doctor's waiting room. Ben was beside me, his leg jittering with nervous energy.

The room was cold, and the air carried the unmistakable scent of medical hostility. The receptionist's desk was adorned with a potted plant, struggling to survive in the clinical environment. The floor was covered in a wood-imitation PVC, worn down by countless feet that had shuffled through here over the years.

My gaze wandered to the posters on the walls, all about mental health. They were meant to offer comfort and reassurance, but to me, they were just reminders of my inadequacy. One poster featured a serene beach scene, promising relief from anxiety and stress. Another showcased a field of wildflowers, symbolizing hope and renewal.

Ben flipped through a magazine, his eyes darting across the pages without absorbing a word. He was often restless these days, unable to sit still for long. I almost reached out to place my hand on his, but thought better of it.

We waited in silence, the minutes ticking by slowly.

When we'd arrived in front of the building, I had asked Ben why we were there.

He had looked down at me questioningly. "You said you wanted help."

I'd wanted to explain that I had meant a therapist, not a doctor, but I hadn't wanted to start an argument.

The receptionist called our names, and we followed her into the doctor's consultation room. The room was barely more welcoming than the waiting area, with harsh lighting and framed medical certificates on the wall.

Dr. Mitchell, a middle-aged man with a friendly demeanor, greeted us as we entered. "Ben. Mrs. Goodall. Good afternoon," he said, motioning for us to sit across from his desk.

We settled into the chairs, and he leaned forward, his expression attentive. "So, what brings you both in today? How can I help?"

Ben hesitated for a moment, glancing at me as if seeking confirmation. I nodded encouragingly, and he began to explain.

His voice filled with concern, he described my struggles with anxiety, paranoia and signs of hysteria. He talked about the sleepless nights, the constant worrying,and the moments when my fear seemed to take over, making it difficult for me to function in our daily lives.

Dr. Mitchell listened attentively, nodding in understanding as he tried to piece together the puzzle of my mental health. He asked for specific examples of my behavior and any triggers that might have contributed to my heightened anxiety.

I sat quietly, feeling mixed emotions as Ben talked. It was difficult to hear my struggles laid out so openly, and I felt he was leaving out key parts.

I opened my mouth to explain, but Dr. Mitchell lifted his right hand, gesturing for me to let Ben finish.

I put my head down.

When Ben had finished telling the doctor about my issues, I took a deep breath, feeling a knot of anxiety in my chest as I tried to find the right words. "Dr. Mitchell," I began, "it's not just my issues. Ben's behavior has been... different lately." I shot a quick look at Ben, who was glaring at me. But I was determined to continue. "He's become more angry, easily irritable, and I don't know how to please him anymore."

Ben turned to Dr. Mitchell. "Do you see? This is what I mean. I don't have an aggressive bone in my body."

Dr. Mitchell nodded. "Quite," he said.

I felt a pang of frustration as Ben's words casted doubt on my concerns. I tried to explain that my observations were not mere paranoia but genuine worries about our relationship and his anger.

Dr. Mitchell's gaze shifted from me to Ben, and I sensed

a subtle change. He turned to my husband and explained the issues I faced, carefully avoiding any overt judgment. He spoke about anxiety disorders and how medication could help.

As he delved into the details, I couldn't help but feel a growing sense of isolation. It was as if Dr. Mitchell had already made up his mind, siding with Ben's perspective and implying that my concerns were solely a product of my mental health issues.

Ben nodded gravely in agreement with the doctor's assessment.

Dr. Mitchell leaned forward, his expression compassionate but firm. "Emiliah," he said, "based on what we've discussed today and your symptoms, I believe it would be beneficial for you to start a course of medication to help calm your anxiety. These pills can be very effective in providing relief from the type of distress you've been experiencing."

As he explained the potential benefits of the medication, the idea of finding relief from the overwhelming anxiety became increasingly appealing, but the thought of relying on medication scared me.

Dr. Mitchell continued to explain the treatment plan, emphasizing that the medication was just one part of the process and that the support of my husband would also play a crucial role in my recovery. I nodded absently.

As we were leaving, Dr. Mitchell put his arm on Ben's shoulder. "Do give Augusta my regards."

43

"They're breathing down my fucking neck." Ben was pacing back and forth. He'd been stressing about the board meeting for weeks. Martin, the lead investor, the white-haired man who'd witnessed me coming out of the bushes with my skirt stuck in my knickers at PeakSleek's headquarters eighteen months earlier, had apparently been challenging Ben's leadership over the past few weeks.

I had originally understood that Ben had crafted the PeakSleek Me campaign, as that was how it had been presented to the press, but apparently it had been crafted by a marketing manager, who had since left the company to become a full-time mother. Ben had been 'brought in' by Martin Vanken soon after the campaign's creation. Martin was an old friend of Augusta's, and he'd been at our wedding. He'd been charming and had never referred to the 'bush episode', and the few times I'd seen him since, he'd been completely absorbed by his phone. I often wondered what made work so important for these people. I'd worked long hours at G&B, but it had been more about survival than anything else, as well as, I suppose, the delicious taste of positive feedback. But in these power-hungry types, I just didn't get it. They were already loaded, but they continued to work every waking hour. Martin was apparently dissatisfied with PeakSleek's quarterly results, and with the fact that the two acquisitions Ben had initiated hadn't generated the expected results.

Ben punched the wall, leaving a small dent and making me jump. "They're so fucking small-minded. They just don't get the long-term vision."

I walked over to him, encircling him in my arms and kissing his muscular arm. But he shook me off and climbed the stairs two at a time to his glass study.

It definitely wasn't the right time to tell him I was pregnant. I wasn't even sure how I felt about it myself. When the pregnancy test had shown a plus sign, I'd gasped. Most women I knew had struggled to get pregnant. We'd only been married for six months. I wasn't sure how I felt about it.

I decided to focus on dinner. I had started taking a keener interest in Mexican food since our honeymoon. I began chopping red onions, cucumber and cilantro, juicing limes, and cutting oyster mushrooms to replace the shrimp. I lost myself in the process so when I placed the potatoes in the oven and checked the clock, it was already 6 pm. I prepared a margarita for Ben and a virgin margarita for myself, poured some tortilla chips into a bowl, and sat on the sofa, relaxing with Ken Follett's *Column of Fire* until Ben finished his work.

"Something smells good." I jumped up to see Ben reaching

out for a margarita. I realized I must have drifted off to sleep; the book was on the floor. "Oh God, the potatoes." I rushed over and pulled them out of the oven, receiving a blast of hot air in the face as I opened it. "Damn. They're slightly burnt. Not all of them though, thankfully."

"I think I'll pass on the burnt spuds, thanks." He sipped his margarita.

"I'm sorry, Ben. I just dropped off."

"It's okay. I didn't marry you for your cooking skills."

I sipped my drink, feeling deflated. Realizing it was the alcoholic version, I swapped our glasses.

Ben stared at my glass. "What did you do that for?"

I just stared back.

He took my glass from my hand, took a gulp, and then sipped his own. "Why is there no alcohol in yours?" He was holding my wrist, and his grip tightened.

"I, I'm pregnant," I whispered.

He stared at me, his face getting redder and redder. "And you were *keeping* it from me?"

"I just wanted to find the right moment, I-"

"I wanted to find the right moment," he repeated in a sing-song voice, a look of disgust on his face. "Do I not have a say in this?" he roared. "And you lie to me about it?" he poked me in the shoulder as the words came out of his mouth. I took a step backwards. The veins on his forehead were bulging, and his skin had taken on a reddish hue. I needed to calm him down.

"Ben, Ben, my darling. Please. I just wanted to-"

The force of the slap sent me staggering sideways, my left shoulder hitting the fridge handle. He stared at me, heaving with rage, as I held my cheek with both hands. I didn't move. I knew I had to stay silent and immobile. No noise came out as tears streamed silently down my face.

His face came close to mine, pulsing with rage. "Don't act as if I punched you, for God's sake. You really know how to play the victim card, don't you?"

With that, he sat down and waited for me to serve dinner.

44

As I was clearing the table later in the evening, the doorbell rang. It was Augusta and Timothy, on their way back from a concert at the Albert Hall, Burberry jackets folded over their arms. Their grandeur seemed to amplify the tension, and I couldn't shake the feeling that I was in greater danger with them present.

Ben greeted them with warm hugs and smiles, his charm on full display. To his parents, he was the embodiment of success and marital devotion, a man they adored without reservation.

As we all sat down to talk, the men drinking cognac and the women chamomile tea, I kept my eyes lowered, my hands shaking slightly as I tried to maintain the role of dutiful daughter-in-law. The conversation flowed around me, filled with polite inquiries. Augusta and Timothy praised Ben once again for his achievements and the life he had built, comparing to Fiona, who, at boarding school in Switzerland, was proving to be less academically inclined than her older brother.

I forced a smile and nodded at the appropriate moments

while feeling the weight of their scrutiny. They had known me for almost a year now, had seen me evolve from the woman their son had fallen in love with, into the wife I had become.

Timothy, a stern figure, fixed his gaze on me, his eyes piercing through my carefully constructed veneer. "And how have you been, Emiliah?" he asked, his tone deceptively polite.

I struggled to keep my composure, to maintain the illusion of normalcy. "I've been well, thank you," I replied, my voice trembling slightly.

Augusta chimed in, her voice sweet but laced with an underlying curiosity. "You seem a bit... tense, dear. Is something bothering you?"

I swallowed hard. "Oh, it's just been a busy week, that's all. You know how it can be sometimes."

Augusta scoffed. "But you're a housewife, dear, married to a very wealthy man. What on earth could you possibly be busy with?"

All their eyes fixed on me, and I couldn't help but feel as though they were peeling away the layers of my persona, layer by layer.

I shrugged, forcing a small smile. "Shopping, lunches and teas, you know."

Ben stared hard at me, fully aware I did none of those things. "Emiliah is pregnant," he said.

Augusta and Timothy stared at me, then smiled widely. "How wonderful!" Augusta gushed at Ben. "Bravo, that was quick," added Timothy in surprised admiration. He was talking to Ben.

STOP IT! I screamed silently.

Ben smiled smugly. "We were planning to go skydiving again next week, but this changes things, obviously," he said.

Skydiving? He may have been planning to kill you. And make it look like an accident.

"But," began Augusta before stopping herself.

"What?" demanded Ben.

"Well, you know," she continued hesitantly, turning to me. "The medication – for your depression, dear. I hope it hasn't harmed the baby."

I blushed fiercely, engulfed in humiliation. He'd told his parents about my medication. They saw me as the poor, fragile, crazy wife. I couldn't, of course, point out that I hadn't been taking the pills, because Ben would have blown his top.

"Good Lord, yes," added Timothy. "You'll have to run all the tests. You wouldn't want some deformity ruining your marriage."

"What do you mean?" I asked.

Augusta leaned forward, placing a comforting hand on

my knee. "A... damaged child would ruin your marriage, dear. You must be aware of that. And marriage always comes first." She stole a look at Timothy, who nodded in agreement. Ben stood up to serve himself another cognac. Augusta lowered her voice. "Emiliah dear, Timothy and I agreed that if we ever had a handicapped child, we would suffocate it with a pillow."

"What?" I asked, confused, as an image of Mildred, a girl with Down's syndrome I'd babysat as a student, came to mind. Mildred was the sweetest, most cheerful child I'd ever met.

"Don't be naïve, Emiliah," said Ben sharply. "No one wants a handicapped child."

Once again, I felt trapped in a world I didn't understand. I didn't even realize people thought like this. It was alien. It felt wrong, but I was the misfit. *Am I wrong to be shocked?*

I suddenly felt a desperate need to talk to Meloda, as I was sure she would agree with me, and I trusted her opinion more than anyone's. But I'd distanced myself over the past couple of months, claiming headaches or conflicting schedules, when in fact I'd just wanted to avoid her questions.

I watched my husband's parents as the conversation switched to PeakSleek's board and Ben voiced his frustration with Martin. Their voices faded into a distant hum as my mind ventured into another realm. I couldn't help but wonder if, in the event my husband's anger spiraled out of control, his parents would become his allies, and help him conceal my body.

The idea seemed preposterous, even to me. His parents were respected members of the community, pillars of society. But the shadows of doubt and mistrust had begun to creep into my mind, eroding my ability to trust.

I tried to shake off the unsettling fantasy to focus on the conversation at hand, but the fear had taken hold, and it was impossible to ignore. My parents in law's words became a blur as I grappled with the terrifying possibility that they might be complicit in my demise.

As I forced a smile and nodded along to the conversation, I couldn't help but wonder how much of the danger I felt was in my head, a product of my own spiraling mental illness. But the fear remained, an ever-present shadow that held a pall over the dinner table, a reminder that trust had become a rare and precious commodity in my world, and that even those closest to me were not exempt from the web of suspicion that had ensnared my mind.

The murmur of conversation filled the air, but I felt detached, as though I were a spectator in my own home.

45

Three weeks later, I sat in Ben's home office chair, fingers trembling as I turned on his computer. Each keystroke felt like a thunderclap in the silent room, echoing my mounting anxiety.

I had to complete the task before he returned home. The weight of his suspicions pressed down on me like a suffocating blanket, choking every rational thought. My breaths came in shallow gasps, my pulse thundering in my ears.

What I was doing was my only lifeline, my escape route, a fragile thread holding back the flood of panic threatening to consume me. Sweat beaded on my forehead as I prayed fervently for each digit to be correct, for the screen to unlock before it was too late.

Suddenly, I heard a key in the lock. Ben's voice cut through the silence like a knife, freezing me in place.

"Emiliah?" he shouted.

I closed the PC without turning it off and slipped out of his office into the large adjacent bathroom.

He appeared at the door. "What are you doing here?" he demanded, his tone laced with suspicion.

My heart stopped as I looked at him. "Just doing my makeup," I replied, putting down the mascara I'd grabbed seconds ago.

He stepped towards me. "You know I don't like mascara. It makes you look cheap."

I put my head down. "Sorry," I said.

"Where's the paracetamol?" he asked. "I've got a splitting headache. That wine you opened yesterday was trash."

I opened one of the drawers and pulled out a jar of tablets. "Here. Sorry."

He grabbed the jar. "I'm going to work from home today. I'm too fucking tired to go to the office."

He started walking towards his office. *If he sees the computer, he'll kill you.*

I touched his arm, and he whipped around angrily.

I tried to look at him coquettishly but felt grotesque. "D'you remember when I used to work from home?" I moved closer, putting my arms around him.

He stared at me. "Turn around."

I obeyed.

He bent me over and pulled my tracksuit bottoms down roughly. "You want to remember, do you? I'll give you something to remember."

It seemed never-ending, as if he couldn't finish. Halfway through, he dragged me into the closest guest bedroom and threw me, roughly, onto the bed. I didn't even need to pretend to enjoy it. He very obviously wanted to hurt me. But when he was done, he fell into a deep sleep, and I rushed off to finish what I'd started.

46

I was chopping tomatoes. Bruschetta. I longed for a sip of Chapoutier Côtes du Rhône to give me strength, but I had to make do with sparkling water. It was the day of the board meeting, and he wasn't due home for another hour. I rubbed garlic cloves on toasted ciabatta.

The door slammed. The ensuing silence was deafening. He stood in front of me. Enraged.

I froze.

"What's for dinner?" He was drunk.

"Bruschetta," I whispered.

"It's pronounced '"bru-SKET-ta', not 'bru-shetta,'" he repeated, his words laced with contempt. His eyes were wild, unfocused, yet full of a simmering rage that made my blood run cold.

I slowly reached out to turn off the gas, not moving any other part of my body. The sizzling stopped, leaving a tense silence hanging in the air.

"It's pronounced 'bru-SKET-ta,' not 'bru-shetta,'" he snapped again.

My breath hitched as I carefully placed the knife on the edge of the counter, every movement slow and deliberate, as if any sudden action might provoke him further. The tension in the room was palpable, a coiled spring ready to snap.

His eyes bore into me, dark and unforgiving. "You can't even get something as simple as pronunciation right, can you?" he spat, his voice dripping with disdain. "So pedestrian, so suburban..."

His words trailed off into a growl, the alcohol making his anger unpredictable. "Give me some wine." He slumped onto one of the Knoll bar stools, his movements heavy and uncoordinated.

I fought to keep my composure, my hands trembling as I reached for the bottle of wine. The bottle was heavy, my fingers slick with sweat.

You can do this. Stay calm.

I walked over to him, heart pounding, holding the bottle. Hands trembling, I poured the dark red liquid into the glass I'd got out earlier. The bottle hit the side of the glass, knocking it over and spilling wine all over trousers and his stark white shirt.

"You CUNT! You stupid fucking CUNT!" His scream was a jagged knife in the silence. He lunged at me, face red, veins bulging, eyes wide with fury.

I backed away as fast as I could, but his punch caught my cheek before I could react. The pain was indescribable. Bile rose up my throat and into my mouth. I swallowed it down. It tasted of blood. I fell to one knee when he kicked me in the thigh, sending me crashing into the cabinet doors.

Get out! Get the fuck out! It's not worth it.

I lifted myself up, my body screaming with pain, but my mouth shut. My hand reached the counter and grabbed a handle, but he pulled me back down towards him, holding his fist back. The world narrowed to the space between us, filled with his rage and my terror. He punched me again, the blow hitting me square on the nose this time.

He'll kill you.

In a desperate move, I grappled blindly, trying to manoeuver the handle I was still holding, but unable to open my eyes. My fingers closed around it as I felt a new wave of pain in my mouth, as if my jaw was being torn apart. I pulled my right hand in front of me, holding the handle with all my strength, and pushed the blade inside him. I forced my eyes open, despite the pain. Placing a hand on his chest, I pulled the knife out and thrust it higher up in his chest, moving the knife upwards. His eyes widened and a gurgling sound escaped his lips. We stayed like that for a few moments, me staring into his eyes, him in shock, uncomprehending. Blood filled his mouth, bubbling over his lips as he looked at me, the confusion slowly giving way to fear.

He staggered backwards, his hands clutching the knife

protruding from his chest. He took a step towards me, then another, before collapsing to the floor, face down. The sound of his body hitting the tiles was a dull thud with a sharp knock, as the knife handle struck the floor, the final note in a symphony of violence. I turned him over and pulled the knife out again, using all my strength, my eyesight blurry and stabbed him a third time, this time in the throat.

Then I stood there, trembling, the kitchen around me suddenly unreal, like a stage set. The smell of garlic mingled with the coppery scent of blood. My hands were stained, my body ached, but my mind was strangely clear.

47

The figure sitting across from me puts down his pen and leans back. "You're pregnant?"

"No, I miscarried that day. The day I killed him. There was quite a lot of blood by the time the ambulance arrived." I paused. "It should all be in the hospital records."

He nods slowly, seemingly unbothered by my lack of emotion. I'd always been very emotional, the first to cry when watching a sad film, or even a not-so-sad film, the first to blush when complimented, and the first to feel angry when accused unfairly. But when the ambulance had arrived and the police had questioned me in hospital, I'd felt no emotion. I'd heard them talking to the doctors, who'd explained that I was in a state of deep shock. And now, a week later, as I finish telling David Shaw, my lawyer, the full story, I still feel no emotion, no regret. Mr. Shaw shows little emotion himself; he's all business. So far, he's made a good enough impression. After all, he did manage to convince the judge to place me in a psychiatric institution whilst awaiting trial, invoking the fact that I'd already been under psychiatric treatment.

He rubs his eyes. "Okay, I think we can wrap up for today. I'll be back on Tuesday."

"Okay." I rise slowly, holding my hand out for him to shake.

He shakes it firmly. Mine remains limp.

He gives me what is, I suppose, an appropriately subdued smile and turns around to leave.

I'm not sure he believes me.

48

Now that the meeting with David Shaw is over, I head to the TV room.

"Welcome to Purgatory", Rav, one of the nurses, said three days ago when I arrived, handing me a bundle of blankets and toiletries.

When the Magistrate's court agreed, under Section 37 of the Mental Health Act, to send me to a psych ward instead of prison until my trial was heard, I had expected a prison-like institution. I was, after all, a murderer. But here I was, in a sprawling, albeit decrepit, country estate. And judging by the yellowed posters peeling off the walls, talking about 'Skills, Not Pills' and 'Mindfulness', the approach to psychiatric treatment seems decidedly relaxed.

'Purgatory' or Saint George's Resting Clinic, its official name, is located on the South Downs, in an ancient, badly insulated manor, surrounded by woods, fields, and hiking trails. The interior of the clinic exudes a sense of faded grandeur, a ghost of its former opulence lingering in the air, now crumbling like the minds of its inhabitants.

The wooden floors creak underfoot, their dark polish worn away by years of foot traffic. Rich tapestries hang on the walls, their intricate patterns muted by dust and age, depicting scenes of pastoral tranquility.

The entrance hall is dominated by a sweeping staircase with an intricately carved banister. A musty smell permeates the air, mingling with the faint scent of antiseptic, reminding us all of the building's current use.

To the right of the foyer is a spacious lounge, furnished with a mismatched assortment of armchairs and sofas, their upholstery faded and threadbare. A large, stone fireplace dominates one wall, though it remains cold and unused, its mantelpiece adorned with a clutter of homemade knickknacks. The walls are lined with bookshelves, filled with a haphazard collection of worn books, their spines cracked and pages yellowed. The room, once a place of lively gatherings, now echoes with the quiet murmurs of patients lost in their own fractured realities.

To one side of the lounge, an ancient conservatory overlooks the Downs, its glass panes cloudy with age, allowing only a hazy view of the rolling landscape beyond. The air inside is humid and thick with the smell of mold. It has been haphazardly furnished with donated furniture, including a large Formica table and mismatched chairs, threadbare armchairs, and a few plastic garden stools, creating a disjointed and forlorn atmosphere.

The dining hall, accessible through a set of heavy oak doors, features a long, dark wooden table that stretches almost the entire length of the room. High-backed chairs, their seats sunken and fabric frayed, line both sides. Large windows, covered with thick, dusty curtains, let in minimal light, keeping the room in a perpetual twilight.

Down the dimly lit corridors, the clinic's age becomes more apparent. Peeling wallpaper reveals patches of plaster, and the occasional flicker of the old, brass sconces adds an eerie, haunted feel. The patient rooms are sparsely furnished, each with a single bed, a small wooden dresser and a nightstand.

After the sleek perfection of Thames Summit, the faded tapestries and creaking floors of the clinic seem somehow more rooted in real life, as if everything I experienced with Ben was a strange dream.

I'm not sure how I feel about being here. I stayed afloat for years, but now that everything has crashed to pieces, I don't feel the terrifying doom I'd expected. I feel nothing. Emptiness.

Entering the lounge, I keep my head down as I head for a battered old armchair facing the French windows that look out onto the rolling Downs. I watch a group of people enter a tiny chapel on the edge of the woods that surround the clinic and make a mental note to take a look inside sometime. A man with neatly combed, graying hair approaches me, his steps measured and purposeful. He pulls up a folding plastic chair and sits beside me silently for a few minutes. Then, leaning closely, he says, "This place, it's not really a psychiatric ward."

I shift in my seat. "Oh?"

He's wearing a crisply ironed shirt with glasses perched on the bridge of his nose, framing his deep-set eyes. There's a subtle confidence in his posture, a sense that he's used to being taken seriously.

Psychiatrist? Careful what you say, Emiliah.

He continues to stare out of the window. "They're testing on us."

"Testing," I echo, my mind blank.

He nods. "Yes, vaccines."

I turn my head slowly towards him. "I thought we only had to take anti-depressants or anxiety medication here, if required by a doctor?"

He pulls off his glasses and cleans them with a handkerchief while casually glancing left and right. "It's a smokescreen. Do you see those lines in the sky?"

I look out, seeing the crisscrossing of vapor trails left by planes flying in and out of Gatwick.

He leans closer. "Chemtrails," he whispers.

I feel strangely detached. "Chemtrails?"

He nods gravely, removing his glasses to clean them with a handkerchief. His gaze darts left and right as if ensuring no one else is eavesdropping on our conversation. "Chemtrails," he repeats, his voice filled with urgency. "It's a government experiment. They dump a mind-controlling substance on us. Then they test the latest Flu vaccine on us." He makes an inverted comma gesture when saying 'Flu' and 'vaccine'.

I feel tired. "But they don't give injections here, do they? They told me they didn't."

He looks around again, obviously on edge. "Those who've been drugged by chemtrails don't remember the injections. That's why you must stay inside. Spending as much time as possible in the basement is even better, as the chemicals sometimes permeate the walls, but they can't reach the basement."

A muscular middle-aged lady with cropped hair, wearing a *McShit* t-shirt, appears beside the man. "Cut ze crap, Gerald. Keep your zeories to yourself and leave ze rest of us alone."

The man, 'Gerald', looks up at the lady and scuttles away.

The woman eases herself onto the empty chair beside me and looks outside. "Some of the people in here are bat-shit crazy. Don't hesitate to tell zem to piss off."

I smile at her weakly. Strangely, I feel more at ease here than in the outside world.

She gives me a quick squeeze on the shoulder and lifts herself up. I turn and watch her walk towards the kitchen.

49

I've been told I'm to see a therapist. His name is James, and he's late. As I sit, waiting in his office, I study his desk, which is messy. Books, piles of paper, mugs, paperclips, post-it notes, and scrunched-up pieces of cello tape. Ben would have lost his mind. Even I'm a bit annoyed by all the clutter.

In contrast, the 'therapy area' is very tidy. Here he is. Short, plump, bearded, wearing glasses. Unremarkable. *Safe*, I think immediately. He sits on an armchair covered with a purple blanket, holding a large pad. Just above his seat, to the right, is an impressionist-style painting of a mountain.

He asks me how I am.

"Okay, I think."

"Would you like to talk about what happened?"

"Erm, no. Not really."

"Okay."

He sits and waits, looking at me.

I wait, too.

He clicks his pen closed and attaches it to the pad. 'Would you be willing to share a childhood memory?'

"Erm, okay."

He waits for me to begin.

So I tell him about the Channel crossing. It usually amuses people.

50

When my parents had announced we were moving to France, the four of us, Davina, Ralph, Fergus, and I, were horrified. When they explained we'd be sailing across the Channel, we'd thought it was a joke.

We set off from a jetty at Southampton Marina. Mummy had put deck chairs and a champagne bucket on the deck, but the wind had already blown over one of the chairs, and the champagne bucket looked as if it might topple over. You could tell how happy Mummy was; she was all dressed up, sporting a white floaty Chloé number, with loose wavy hair and leather sandals.

She talked animatedly about the French way of life, the warmth and simplicity, the long summer evenings, the rosé. I hoped she wouldn't be disappointed.

Davina inspected the boat carefully, while Fergus and Ralph had scuttled off below deck, probably to avoid being asked to help out. "Where are the lifeboats, Mummy?"

"Don't be silly, Davina. There *are* no lifeboats. How often do I have to explain that this is a *canal boat*? Come on, girls, hurry up. We have to embark before nightfall."

Even I was a bit worried, looking at the sea. Dark waves were slapping the jetty. I wondered if drowning hurt.

Davina looked horrified. "Mummy, we'll all die of we try crossing the Channel on this."

Daddy's head appeared through the hold. "Don't be silly. We've done lots of research. Perfectly feasible."

Mummy was staring at the horizon. "Isn't this exciting?" She said this to no one in particular. "We'll be sipping champagne and sailing into the sunset in half an hour."

"But Mummy," I ventured, "there aren't any sails on the boat."

"Oh, don't be so literal, Emiliah. Come and help me prepare the drinks."

My parents seemed completely oblivious to the fact that this long, flat boat was rocking violently from side to side. Daddy untied the ropes, singing 'L'amour est enfant de bohème.' Mummy grabbed the magnum Veuve Cliquot before it fell off the rickety table. Davina was hanging onto a rail, looking ill.

"Humpf. Humpf. HUMPF." Daddy tried desperately to get the motor started, but it kept stalling. We were slowly drifting towards the beach. People on the pier stopped walking to stare at us.

"HUMPF! HUMPF!" Daddy struggled on.

'POP' Mummy half poured, half spilled champagne into six plastic flutes. The whole situation was so surreal that I didn't properly register that I was being offered champagne at the age of ten.

A crowd gathered on the pier and slowly made their way down to the beach. Were they following us? Was that couple filming us?

BANG! The engine came to life with a burst. CHUG! Then it stalled, sending all six glasses of champagne flying and the bottle toppling off the table, spilling its contents onto the deck.

The crowd on the beach grew, lights flashing. People were waving, shouting out their encouragement.

"Hang on!" Mummy was trying to catch the bottle of Veuve Cliquot as it rolled all over the place, banging the edges of the boat, froth escaping uncontrollably. When she finally retrieved the bottle, the motor came to life with a second 'BANG!' sending Mummy to her knees and the last of the champagne onto the deck.

"Yeah!" cried Daddy in a very American, un-Daddy-like way. "France, here we come!"

A loud cheer sounded on the beach. I leaned over the hull and saw the crowd clapping and cheering wildly. Davina was livid. Mummy just stared at the empty bottle of Veuve Clicquot, and Daddy waved back enthusiastically.

The clapping faded as Daddy turned the steering wheel away from the beach and towards the horizon. My shoulders relaxed as I took in the vibrant reds, pinks and oranges that were by now lighting up the sky. I had never seen anything quite so beautiful. On the other hand, Mummy was clinging to the guardrail, looking decidedly green.

I slid over to her, careful not to let go of the rail. "Are you okay, Mummy?"

She looked at me as if I'd asked the most stupid question possible. "Just go and get Da-UGGGHHHLARRR!" The largest volume of vomit I have ever seen gushed out of her. She just stared as it poured from one side of the boat to the other in rhythm with the sea. Horrified, I wondered what I could do. She vomited again, "UGGGHHHLARRR!" repeatedly, until there was nothing left, and she crumpled to the floor. She looked up at me helplessly, like a rag doll that'd been dragged through a puddle by an overenthusiastic dog. "Davina. Where's Davina?"

Building a pile of blankets around her in the manner of a makeshift flood barrier, I did my best to protect her from the river of vomit sliding from one side of the deck to the other, and then covered her upper body with the softest one I could find (still extremely scratchy). I grabbed a rope attached to the side of the boat with a snap hook, less than a foot from where she was crumpled, and pulled the rest of it onto the blankets surrounding her, in an attempt to weigh them down. "Hold on to this rope, Mummy."

She looked up again, pleadingly. "Davina."

I nodded. "Yes, I'll get her."

I sidled further down the boat until I reached Davina, who ignored me. I tapped her shoulder. "She wants you."

She turned around, fury burning her eyes, pushed past me and made her way over to Mummy, who was now bent over, making snoring noises, but still clinging to the rope.

The sky had gone from heavenly pink to dark blue in a matter of minutes, and now we were all alone, a cork on a sea of peril.

"Daddy, um, how long do you think it'll take to get to France?" I had to shout to make myself heard over the roaring waves.

"Well, dear" (he actually looked up at the sky as if the moon was going to tell him), "I'd say it's about thirteen hours to Dieppe."

"Thirteen *hours*?" I looked over at Davina, hanging onto the rail and bending over Mummy, whose body was still lumped against the edge of the boat. . I couldn't see which way we were going. Could Daddy see? Suddenly, I was drenched to the bone by a violent spray of freezing water. Teeth chattering and hands shaking, I held on for dear life. I needed to get inside. Shivering violently, I launched myself at the hold, which was now only a few feet away, and wrenched open the lock. Slamming the door behind me, I descended carefully into the dimly-lit cabin. I thought it would be better down here, but nausea hit me like a sledgehammer as soon as my feet touched the floor. Ralph and Fergus, white with shock, were holding onto each other and clinging to a couple of handles behind the fitted sofa. Our two cats, Talleyrand and Pichegru, were in their crate, crouching low and meowing loudly. Here, too, a pile of vomit was swirling around on the floor, but unlike outside, the smell was overwhelming. I was pretty sure some of it was cat vomit; I decided I'd rather freeze to death.

I climbed back out and felt the slap of bitterly cold wind. *There must be clothes that are designed for this kind of weather. Why aren't we wearing them?* As we moved further into the Channel, the waves became deeper and deeper, rocking the houseboat until it was practically on its side after each wave.

Daddy looked doubtful all of a sudden. "Good Lord. I must say, it *is* getting rather choppy."

Rather choppy? We were going to die. And I'd never even kissed anyone.

My dear father now seemed to have cottoned on to the fact that we were all about to die. He started wildly turning the steering wheel away as if he was in control. Up and down we went, up, down, further up and further down. Every freezing wave that crashed onto the boat drenched us until we were numb with cold. He was shouting at the sea now, in a fit of rage: "Will you just stop for a minute, so I can get my bearings, you stupid berk of a sea!"

BOOOOOOOOOOOOOOOOM!

Davina screamed. I looked around frantically, searching for the origin of the deafening sound.

"Look!" shouted Daddy.

And quite suddenly, right next to us was a *massive* ship. The loud horn sounded again.

"Help! Help!" I screamed. "Help!"

Daddy was shouting at me, but I couldn't hear what he was saying.

"Help!" I waved frantically at the ship while holding onto the hull for dear life, begging them to see us and come to our rescue. But it was moving on, abandoning us. As soon as the ship moved past, we were again hit by angry slaps of water. From the corner of my eye, I saw Davina gesturing wildly at the ship with one arm. I stood next to her and screamed at the bulk with her.

"What do you think you're doing?" Daddy grabbed my arm.

"They can save us, Daddy." I was shouting and crying at the same time.

"No," he shouted back. "I said we'd sail across; we're sailing across."

But something deep inside, a primal urge to stay alive, gave me the strength to stand up to him. "Help!" I screamed once again at the steel monster moving away. Davina was screaming, too. For once, we were acting together, united against our parents' craziness.

Suddenly, we were alight, blinded by spotlights. I couldn't see a thing.

"Please! Help us!" screamed Davina, her voice hoarse.

Suddenly, the narrow boat stopped being hurled around by the waves. After a few seconds, we realized what had happened. The sea behind the ship was flat, due to the size and the power of its motors, and we were now in its wake.

Daddy carried on steering, looking pleased with himself, as if he had been in control all along. Davina was trying to pull Mummy to her feet and into the warmth of the cabin. I was too tired and too cold to even try to help them.

I pried the hold door open with my frozen fingers and made my way down the steep steps. Ralph and Fergus were fast asleep, having strapped themselves together on one of the bunks. The smell of vomit was overwhelming, but I didn't care anymore. I peeled off my clothes and climbed into the bunk above the sofa, wrapping myself in the coarse blanket. Thankfully, there were three straps to prevent me from rolling out onto the hard floor. I curled into a ball and drifted into oblivion.

51

Apparently, I am one of four criminals here. Only one other, Vero, the woman who warned me about the crazies, is on trial for murder. The other two have committed slightly less serious crimes but are still considered 'potentially dangerous.'

Paris, the arsonist, approaches my armchair, playing nervously with his hair. I'm actually surprised he uses the pronoun 'he,' but I heard him explaining to a group of baffled patients a few days ago that he's 'simply androgynous'. "Wanna come for a smoke?"

I stand up, stretching. "Yeah, okay, why not?"

Paris's extravagant demeanor does not go unnoticed in a place where everyone else wears tracksuits. He leads the way outside, sporting shiny black platform shoes, a gauzy leopard-skin top and tight leather trousers. Compared with yesterday's, his makeup is quite light: gold lipstick and black mascara; no eye shadow; no blusher. He's pulled his long, blonde hair into a bun high on the top of his head. He flashes a large, white smile at me. His transparent silicon implant, which he usually carries around and strokes like a cat, is in a small fake Gucci clutch. I've heard that Paris used to sell breast implants until he discovered that his company had replaced the high quality silicon with a cheaper, toxic gel, making a lot of patients seriously ill. The discovery triggered him to burn down the company's factory.

We walk across the old stone terrace, Paris's heels clicking on the paving stones. "Had therapy yet?"

"Yeah." I don't elaborate.

He pulls out a lighter and lights two slim cigarettes before passing one to me. I inhale deeply. Funny, I never thought I'd smoke. After just six days, I'm hooked, despite the foul taste.

Paris inhales sharply, then blows out a thin line of smoke and bites his nails.

I look out at the overgrown garden. The patients are supposed to look after the grounds, but Vero is the only one who gardens. She told me she ran an 'underground' operation in Bulgaria, offering everything from fake passports to escort services, male and female ("But always over eighteen," she insisted). She also ran an online sex service where married men, mainly in the US and the UK, exchanged messages with what they believed to be young, beautiful women. Vero had chuckled when she'd explained that almost everyone in her family, including her great-aunt, exchanged raunchy messages with such men. Then she'd become serious when she explained that one client had decided to come and 'save' one of the 'young women', who turned out to be Vero's middle-aged brother. The client had strangled Vero's brother when he'd discovered the woman he'd intended to save was, in face, a man. Vero had tracked the client all the way to Surrey, where he lived a normal, married life. She'd waited until he was alone and stabbed him seventeen times. Vero is the only other murderer here.

As usual, she is digging disturbingly deep holes in the garden, pausing occasionally to wipe sweat from her brow with her muscular forearm. If I cared, I'd probably find her terrifying.

Paris grinds out his cigarette with a fake Louboutin. "D'you think she's planning to escape?"

Given that the grounds are surrounded with rickety wooden fences, I very much doubt it. "Mmm, probably not," I reply.

52

James is waiting, a concerned look on his face. "How are you today, Emiliah?"

"OK," I mumble.

He places his notepad on his knees. "I want to make sure you understand something important. What's said and shared here in this psychiatric ward is confidential. It can't be used against you in any legal proceedings."

His words hang in the air, and I'm not sure what to answer, so I remain silent.

He clears his throat. "Would you like to tell me what happened when you arrived in France?"

"We traveled down to the Lot et Garonne region and lived there for a few years, before moving back to London."

"What was that like, living in France?"

I think for a moment, my mind wandering to places I'd tried to forget about for years. I think about that first day in Biffière.

After a lengthy ordeal at the canal locks, where my parents had painfully maneuvered Whimsy, the boat we'd crossed the Channel on, through the Agen lock, we made our entrance into Biffière sur Garonne. The canal, an engineering marvel to my parents, was to me a tedious barrier that tested my patience. Progress had been painfully slow, and I was sick to the core of living inside the damp, cramped space with five other people, a place filled with books, knickknacks, lists scribbled on the backs of envelopes, crumbs, cat hair, and condensation. When Mummy and Daddy announced that we'd finally arrived, I ignored the canal and focused on the terrain, which seemed unwelcoming, yet intriguing.

The land bordering the canal was sodden, with the kind of mud that threatened to swallow anything too curious to tread upon it, but further in, it was firm and dry, and the allure of adventure drew us forward. A group of ancient farm buildings bore marks of neglect, standing as relics of a bygone era. Among them, the barn was particularly striking, its structure compromised by age, leaning heavily as though burdened by untold stories. Encased in moss and ivy, its walls spoke of years spent battling the elements.

Davina was the first of us to speak. "Mummy, where's the house?"

Mummy smiled sheepishly. "We're going to stay onboard Whimsy until the first building is renovated."

Davina just stared at her, once again in disbelief.

While my parents viewed the property through the lens of restoration and dreams of what could be and Davina saw only a wreck, I saw a playground of possibilities, a place where my imagination could run wild, unencumbered by the realities of adult responsibilities.

As soon as we moored the boat and my parents busied themselves with plans and discussions, Fergus, Ralph and I disappeared before Davina could bully us into helping clean Whimsy. We embarked on an expedition across our new domain, a trio of explorers eager to claim the land's hidden treasures for ourselves.

The outbuildings, with their old stone facades, were our first stops. Each building was a new world, albeit a dusty and spider-webbed one. But it was the barn, with its massive hay loft and piles and piles of hay, that captured our attention.

Inside, the air was thick with the scent of old hay. The barn's ground floor was a maze of forgotten tools and rusty machinery on one side and stacks of hay on the other; but our sights were set higher. The hay loft, accessible by a rickety ladder, was our destination. Climbing it was a challenge we accepted without hesitation, each rung bringing us closer to our lofty castle in the sky.

Once aloft, the hay became our domain. We built forts and moats, the hay bales serving as bricks and battlements. Laughter echoed throughout the barn. For a moment, the world outside—the uncertainties and the changes—faded away, leaving only the joy of the present.

Davina, our older sister, stayed behind with our parents, lending her hands and her maturity to the tasks that demanded immediate attention. Her absence in our games was a silent reminder of our uselessness, but escaping our obligations and having fun was our usual modus operandi.

A few days after our arrival, my brothers and I ventured into another realm entirely—the local school.

The French spoken around me was completely foreign and incredibly fast. It was as if children here had a thousand things to say in a very limited amount of time, barely stopping for breath before continuing their passionate, incomprehensible tirades.

Time seemed to have paused inside the classroom, holding its breath in a bygone era. The desks were arranged in meticulous rows, each an island of polished wood aged by countless years of schooling. Upon the desks lay slates and pieces of chalk. The slates were wiped clean for the day's lessons, waiting to be marked by the careful scrawl of calculations and script.

The atmosphere was one of reverence, underscored by an absolute silence that enveloped the room. This silence was not empty but filled with the weight of concentration, each student engrossed in their work. The only sounds were the scratch of chalk on slate and the occasional shuffle of feet.

The headmaster and teacher of my class, which included children ages of seven to ten, paced around the room. The man, referred to as 'Maître', regularly smoked Gitanes as he strolled around the classroom, smoke curling into the air. The strong smell, mingled with old wood and chalk dust, created a unique fragrance that would remain etched in my mind for many years. Each of his steps was measured, and his control over the class total.

In the midst of a deep, concentrated silence on the second day of school, a sudden shift occurred. Maître paused beside a boy sitting just in front of me. There was a moment, brief and charged, where the atmosphere seemed to condense, drawing the entire class's attention to the silent exchange. The master leaned down slightly, his hand reaching out in a gesture that, at first, appeared almost tender. He stroked the boy's cheek slowly, his fingers tracing the line of the boy's jaw. Then, without warning, the sharp crack of a slap shattered the quiet. Maître's hand moved from gentleness to severity in an instant, the sound echoing off the classroom walls, a stark reminder of the discipline that underpinned our learning environment. The boy's head jerked to the side under the force of the blow, a red mark blooming on his cheek, his eyes wide with shock and pain.

The master spoke then, his voice low but carrying, uttering words in French I didn't understand. The tone was admonishing, the words flowing with an ease that contrasted sharply with the physical reprimand. It was an alien and unsettling discipline method to me, steeped in a tradition where such actions might still find a place.

Around me, the classroom remained silent, the other children avoiding eye contact.

53

Life in Purgatory continues to unfold in its peculiar, suspended rhythm, with each day promising a fresh dose of eccentricity. As I settle into my armchair, which people now recognize as mine, my gaze wanders to the sprawling South Downs, offering a brief respite from the occasional shouts and screams within the building.

Beatrice, an anorexic-looking, ancient lady who claims to be an animal whisperer, acknowledges me with a nod, before opening the French windows and letting in a breath of crisp air.

Gerald, the man who explained the dangers of chemtrails to me, runs over to close it again. "Beatrice, you mustn't open the windows. You'll let the chemicals in!"

Beatrice struggles to open the windows, fighting Gerald's clasp. "It's stuffy. The fish need to breathe."

I watch the scuffle with detached curiosity.

Gerald's anxiety is palpable. "But the chemicals! They'll poison us!"

Beatrice adopts a soothing tone, "Don't worry, Gerald. Trust the process. Let it go. The fish need fresh air."

Gerald seems briefly torn before hastily retreating.

Then Rav, the nurse who greeted me on my arrival, approaches us and explains that the mindfulness session is about to start, and that it would probably do us good to join. Beatrice smiles absently. "I do love filling my mind," before walking away towards the bedroom wing.

I decide to give mindfulness a go.

Somehow Paris, fidgety and intense, seems an unlikely volunteer for mindfulness. But here he is, this time with his hair in a bun, wearing a sarong and crop top, his feet bare.

To my right is Gerald, looking around uneasily.

Next to Gerald is Vero, flexing her muscles

My musings are interrupted as Lola, all loose grey hair, earthy clothes and wooden beads, pads in, sits silently and nods at each of us in turn.

"Hello Vero, hi Emiliah. Hi Paris. Gerald," she says finally, eyes half closed. Then she smiles brightly and plucks a packet of something from the pocket of her long corduroy skirt. "Here you go." She has a dreamy look as she hands out what look like raisins. Absent-mindedly, I pop mine into my mouth and eat it.

"Now, everyone. I want you to look at your raisin."

Oh dear. I shift from one buttock to the other. "Erm, could I possibly have another one, please? I... um... seem to have eaten mine."

Paris giggles.

Blushing, I take the raisin Lola holds out.

She smiles her vague smile again. "So, I was saying. Look at your raisin. Look at the details, the little wrinkles on it."

As Lola describes every little detail of the raisin, I can feel Paris's tiny shoulders shaking beside me. I steal a look at Vero, who's twisting her finger into the side of her forehead, indicating which category of people here in Purgatory she believes Lola belongs to.

Lola hasn't noticed, or else she's pretending she hasn't. "Smell the raisin. Inhale its wonderful fragrance."

Don't laugh. I pull the raisin up to my nose, which just makes Paris shake harder.

Think of something sad. Something terrible. War. Famine. The tiniest gurgle erupts from deep inside me.

Lola rubs her raisin against her cheek, and everyone follows suit. "Now *feeeeel* the raisin. Feel its softness."

Tears are streaming down my cheeks, and I'm shuddering uncontrollably.

Lola looks as if she's having an orgasm when she shouts, "Now *taste* the raisin. *Taste* its delicious sweetness, its warmth. *Taste* the wonder and ask yourself how you feel when the—"

She stares at Paris and me, aghast, as we collapse, rolling around on the floor and laughing uncontrollably. From the corner of my eye, I see Vero breaking into a smile and Gerald covering his ears. Despite the disruption, he remains focused on his raisin, mesmerized.

Lola stares at us coldly. "You two can leave. You're free to try again next time. Please go and calm down elsewhere." And even as I continue to giggle, I feel that familiar sense of shame wash over me.

Why the hell can't I control myself? I can tell I've hurt Lola's feelings, but I just can't stop laughing. *Why am I even giggling? Do I not care? Am I a monster?*

54

James waits, a kind look on his face. "How are you today, Emiliah?"

"OK," I mumble.

"I was hoping you could tell me more about France, your school, and your life there."

I don't want to, but I suppose I should.

My mind wanders back to Biffière sur Garonne nineteen years ago.

Life in Biffière unfolded at a different pace from that of West London. In Richmond, where I'd grown up, people were always in a rush, rushing to work, to and from school, shopping in a hurry. In Biffière, it was as if time was suspended.

The village church's bell rang every morning at eight, and from that first ring, the villagers would slowly emerge, and many of the local men would make their way to the bar, drinking wine, even in the morning.

On Saturday mornings, as the sun lit up the yellow stone of the buildings huddled around the *mairie*, the village square came to life with bustling activity. Stalls lined the cobblestone streets, creating a kaleidoscope of sights and sounds. The air was filled with the melodic chatter of vendors and the fragrant aromas of freshly baked bread, aromatic cheese and ripe fruit.

Women in floral overcoats strolled energetically through the market, *bising* each other twice on each cheek, knowing instinctively which cheek to kiss first. Their laughter mingled with the noise from the bar, which grew gradually more raucous, and the bells of the church again at eleven, when a trickle of ancient, pious villagers made their way out.

My parents loved rambling around the market, trying out their broken French on the tanned, frowning locals.

And then there was Maître, ever-present, omnipotent. Teacher, headmaster and village mayor, shaking hands, tasting cheese, laughing with the villagers.

It didn't take long for Ralph, Fergus, Davina, and me to pick up French. It was that or forego any kind of social life with our peers.

Davina went to the local lycée, so she didn't experience the local school classroom, which seemed to hum with malevolent energy as if the very walls themselves were conspiring to perpetuate the reign of terror that Maître wielded like a twisted scepter.

On school days, when Maître entered the classroom, his

presence sent a collective shiver down our spines. We all stood in silence, heads down until he signalled for us to sit. His eyes, cold and calculating, scanned the room with an unsettling hunger, searching for the day's victim. Invariably, it was Ludovic, one of the school's ten or so foster children, who found himself in the crosshairs of the headmaster's sadistic pleasure.

On one occasion, Maître's voice, soft but dripping with malice, addressed the young boy. "Have you written your two thousand lines?"

Ludovic shook his head.

Maître's cruel smile widened, relishing the power he held over the boy. "Which punishment do you choose? Twenty sandwiches or twenty open sandwiches?"

Ludovic stared, uncomprehending.

Maître signaled for Ludovic to stand, which he did slowly, head bowed. Maître led him to the front of the classroom. Then, without further warning, he clapped both hands hard and simultaneously against Ludovic's cheeks, leaving red, angry marks. "That is a sandwich".

Tears welled in Ludovic's eyes, but he fought not to cry.

Maître then gave him a hard slap on the left cheek, followed a split-second later by a hard slap on the right. "That is an open sandwich. So, which do you choose?"

Ludovic, cheeks burning red, tears in his eyes, looked up at the sadistic man, holding his gaze. "twenty sandwiches".

We all watched silently as Maître put all his strength into the slaps that pounded against Ludovic's cheeks. After the third sandwich, the ten year-old burst into tears, still standing, still rooted in obedience.

As I watched the torment unfold before my young eyes, a torrent of emotions welled within me. Anger surged through my veins. It was a feeling I had long suppressed - the awakening of a primal rage that stirred within the depths of my being.

The headmaster's cruelty, which had until then been an abstract horror, now took on a tangible form. Ludovic's tears, his trembling voice, his humiliation—all of it fueled the fire of my hatred. I couldn't bear to be a passive witness to the sadistic spectacle that played out before me.

In that moment, I felt the stirrings of rebellion, a defiance against the injustice that permeated the classroom. But I wasn't brave enough to voice my anger yet. As the true coward that I was, I just watched the show, along with the rest of the class.

When Maître finished, and Ludovic returned to his seat, sobbing and red, the classroom fell into an eerie silence, and Maître smiled to himself.

As I sat there, I knew the sadistic bastard's reign of terror would go unopposed.

As the final bell rang, signaling the end of another grueling day at school, a knot of terror tightened in the pit of my stomach. I resolved to put an end to the old man's reign of terror. How, I didn't know, but my determination was strong.

55

It's two-thirty am, and I'm staring at the ceiling when the walls of my tiny room reverberate with an unexpected burst of sound—a solitary voice singing. At first, it's just a faint murmur, a distant melody that catches my attention. But then, as if on cue, the familiar words and melody of 'I Want It That Way' by the Backstreet Boys fill the air.

The singer is belting out the lyrics with surprising enthusiasm. His voice wavers slightly, but it's clear he's giving it his all. It's a moment of pure spontaneity in a place known for its routines and rules.

As the first few lines of the chorus roll around, something magical happens. Others start to join in, their voices timid but growing stronger with each lyric.

A few other patients begin to harmonize, their voices a surprising blend of timbres and tones. The ward comes alive with the sound of the impromptu choir, and the weight of individual struggles is forgotten for a few precious minutes.

As the song reaches its crescendo, and I join in for one

final, exuberant chorus, our voices rising in unison. Then, suddenly, I feel it, a giant wave of loss.

Grief crashes over me, raw and unrelenting. My baby, the tiny, innocent being I was carrying, the child I was supposed to protect. I can't bear the loss.

As the song fades into silence, I'm left with guilt, a heavy, suffocating blanket, wrapped around me. Tears stream down my face. I curl up, clutching my pillow as if it could somehow absorb the pain. But guilt seeps into every thought, every memory.

56

I'm back with James, back with the memories that I've pushed down for so many years.

During the spring and summer months, many people from England visited us in Biffière sur Garonne. Most were Mummy and Daddy's former colleagues or university friends, barristers, judges, politicians, CPS prosecutors, a couple of junior ministers. Some would camp on the land, but mostly, they stayed in the second narrow boat my parents had acquired shortly after moving there. By September of the first year, we had three additional caravans for guests.

Sometimes, the visitors would bring their children, and we would all run around the fields and outbuildings like maniacs, but most of the time, it was just men traveling alone or in groups. There would be late-night talks around the firepit near the buildings, lots of local cheese and wine, Armagnac and cigars, talk of politics, budget votes, disappointment in the latest Tory leader.

Sometimes, we were allowed to stay up late and play while the adults talked around the fire, but most of the time, we'd be ordered to bed early. There was no explanation for the fluctuation of rules, but the days when we were ordered to bed were the days when Maître came over. He would always bring a child, sometimes Ludovic, sometimes another child. Always a foster child.

At first, I was envious of these French children being allowed to stay up late when we were being ordered to bed, but they never seemed to enjoy being there. I just couldn't figure out why they were there. As I understood it, most adults viewed children as nuisances.

One day, a small girl called Federica was accompanied by her foster father, a local farmer my parents called 'Monsieur'. Federica was one of Maître's favorite targets at school, even though she wasn't in his class, being just six. One time, he'd pulled her across the playground by the hair while she ran, screaming, trying to keep up with his pace. When he'd finished, he'd shaken off the hair in his hand and she'd scuffled off, crying.

Monsieur, Federica's foster father, wasn't as intimidating as Maître, but he had empty blue eyes which scared me.

Most of the time, the children were brought to our place in the evening, but one time, it was broad daylight when Monsieur left Federica in the care of my parents and Gerry, a solicitor from Weybridge.

Once he'd dropped off Federica, Monsieur came over to me as I was swinging on the heavy barn door, pushing it back and forth with my feet. "Would you like me to show you a really good hiding place in the woods?" he asked.

I looked around uncertainly. "I'd better stay here in case my parents need me."

He smiled. "They told me you could come with me. Come on."

He led me to his truck. I climbed in. It took almost an hour of driving through woodland to reach the spot. I had no idea where we were or how to get back home.

"Come on," he said, climbing out.

I followed him. He took me by the hand and we walked. He showed me what looked like a grave with a makeshift wooden cross. "A girl died here," he said.

In that moment, I understood what was about to happen.

"Come on, this way," he said, and we walked hand in hand down a rocky track.

I could feel sweat running down my back and my heart pounding.

"I think we should turn back," I managed.

"Okay," he said, and we turned around. As we turned, he placed his arm around my shoulder, and we walked back up the track with his arm tightly around me.

When we arrived at his truck, he kissed my cheek. Then he kissed it again, a fraction closer to my mouth. Then again, next to my mouth. When he bent down to kiss my lips, I turned my face away. "My parents will be wondering where I am. We need to go back."

He smiled and said, "No, they won't. They don't care." And kissed me on the mouth, forcing my teeth open with his tongue.

After that day, I hardly left my bunk, except to go to school. I couldn't bear the thought of ever seeing Monsieur again, even if it meant spending the rest of my life inside the boat. I heard my parents joking with their friends about my 'adolescent phase' being a 'bloody relief'.

Then, one day, everything changed. Our barn burned down, and Maître and Monsieur's corpses were found dead inside the burnt-out building. No one understood what they had been doing in our barn or how it had caught fire with them trapped inside.

The arrival of the Gendarmes in our small village sent ripples of unease through the community. I watched from a distance, hidden among the trees, as they descended upon the scene of the gruesome discovery.

I observed the stern expressions on the Gendarmes' faces and the air of authority that clung to them like an invisible cloak. They were emissaries of the law, their presence an undeniable sign that the events of that night were far from forgotten.

More police were hailed from the nearby town of Agen, bringing a sense of detachment that set them apart from the close-knit village.

As they examined the barn, I couldn't help but feel fear and curiosity. What would they uncover? They spent days scrutinizing every detail of the crime scene and talking to my parents and the villagers. I listened to snippets of conversation that carried on the breeze, their words like fragments of a puzzle.

As the investigation continued, I remained hidden, an unseen observer of the unfolding drama. As the investigation into the deaths of Maître and Monsieur continued, the focus of the police began to shift. Their inquiries led them to the local foster children, secondary citizens in our village's society.

I heard my parents whispering that the police had begun questioning the children. It was as though the police had stumbled upon a trail of secrets that led directly to our hidden world.

The police seemed particularly interested in the children's visits to the second narrowboat, Lovely. Our boats had long been a source of curiosity and intrigue for the villagers, and it appeared that the police were determined to uncover their mysteries.

As the questioning continued, I couldn't help but feel a growing sense of unease. The police were peeling back the layers of our carefully constructed façade, and the truth we had hidden was becoming increasingly fragile.

Then, something even more ominous occurred. Police officers from Toulouse, dressed in normal clothes but exuding an air of authority, arrived in the village. These were not the local Gendarmes who patrolled the streets on occasion, nor the police from Agen; these were true outsiders, strangers who had descended upon the village like a dark cloud. They delved deeper into the lives of the foster children. I watched from the shadows as the police from Toulouse combed through the caravans, their faces inscrutable as they collected evidence and pieced together a puzzle that had remained concealed for what seemed like years but had only been eighteen months.

The investigation took a serious turn one afternoon, when Mummy and Daddy were kept overnight at the Toulouse *commissariat* for questioning.

The boat was engulfed in chaos and confusion. Davina, Ralph, Fergus, and I watched in wide-eyed apprehension as our parents were escorted away by the stern police officers from Toulouse, leaving us in the care of a social worker and a gendarme.

Late in the evening, after playing in the woods for hours, we huddled in the dimly lit cabin of our narrow boat, our young hearts heavy with worry. With kind but tired eyes, the social worker tried to reassure us that everything would be fine. We said nothing. We knew better than to talk about anything in the presence of outside adults.

Whispers of speculation floated through the community, and the next day, some of the children at school refused to talk to Fergus, Ralph or me.

Mummy and Daddy's return in the late afternoon the next day brought relief and trepidation. I could see weariness etched into their faces, reflecting the long night they had endured. The questions and uncertainty that loomed over the family had not been resolved.

Then we, the children, were taken in for questioning,

one after the other. The questioning occurred in a small, nondescript room at the Toulouse commissariat. The room was small and plain, with walls painted a dull shade of beige that seemed to absorb all the color from the world.

I sat in one of the wooden chairs, my feet barely touching the floor. The table in front of me looked old and scratched, like a well-used school table. Two more chairs were set on the other side of the table, and I knew that that was where the police officers would sit.

I fidgeted nervously in my chair, my fingers picking at the edge of the table. The overhead light was too bright, casting harsh shadows that danced on the walls.

Then they came in—two police officers, one a woman and one a man. The woman, Detective Sophie Laurent, had a stern face and sharp eyes that seemed to see right through me. Her dark hair was pulled back into a tight bun, and her suit looked stiff and official.

Detective Antoine Vivier had a beard that was neatly trimmed, and his gaze was serious but not unkind.

"Good morning, Emiliah," Detective Laurent said, her voice firm but not unfriendly. "We appreciate your cooperation in helping us with our investigation."

I nodded, my heart thudding in my chest like a drum. I tried to sit up straight and act brave, but couldn't help feeling small and vulnerable.

They began with simple questions, like my name and where I lived. Detective Laurent asked about my family, my school, and my life in the village. Her calm and patient tone made me feel a little more at ease, and I started to talk, answering her questions as best as I could.

However, as the interview went on, Detective Laurent's questions became more serious. She wanted to know about that night—the night when Maître and Monsieur trapped in the barn, and about Lovely, the second narrow boat, what it was used for, who stayed there. Her questions felt like they were closing in on me, leaving no room to hide.

I hesitated, glancing between the two detectives. I knew I had a choice to make.

In that small, stark room, surrounded by plain walls and unforgiving light, and without my sister's disapproving presence, I found myself opening up. I told them about Maître, Monsieur and the foster children. I told them about the people who came to visit from England.

The detectives listened, their expressions grave but not unkind. They wrote things down in their notebooks, and several times asked me to clarify or explain further. It was like a floodgate had been opened, and many things I'd kept hidden were pouring out. I couldn't tell them about Monsieur and me though. I was too ashamed. And scared. Certain details remained closed off.

As the interview came to an end, I felt a combination of relief and uncertainty. I had revealed so much, and the weight of those secrets had been lifted, at least for now. But I also knew that the world outside that room was waiting for me, and it was a world that would change because of what I had revealed.

The detectives exchanged a look, a silent understanding that what I had shared was important. They assured me that they would keep investigating, and then they left the room, leaving me alone with my thoughts.

In that moment, I felt like a child who had just stepped into a grown-up world—one filled with questions and uncertainty. The room felt even emptier now, and the shadows on the walls seemed to stretch out as if trying to recover the secrets I had revealed.

As the days passed, a massive veil of guilt descended upon me. I hadn't meant to say all that I had. I hadn't meant to talk, but their questioning had unsettled me. I wished I had been able to keep my stupid mouth shut. The investigation had taken a serious turn, and I knew the secrets my family had guarded for so long were now out in the open. I feared the consequences that might follow, how our lives might change.

Mummy and Daddy were taken in for questioning again. The evening after their second round of questioning, there was a big fight, urgent whispering, and silence.

Then, a few days later, something unexpected happened—the investigation came to an abrupt halt. The questions stopped, the interviews ceased, and it was as if the affair had never occurred to begin with. I didn't understand why, and couldn't help but feel bewildered.

I watched as the police officers left our village, their cars disappearing down the dusty road. There were no arrests, no charges filed, and in the end, the deaths of Monsieur and Maître were ruled an accident.

Relief washed over me as I realized my parents were safe and wouldn't have to face the consequences of my inability to keep my mouth shut. But at the same time, a heavy cloud of tension settled over our family. It was as if the secrets we'd kept hidden for so long had been exposed to the harsh light of day, and the consequences of my revelations were swift and unforgiving.

In the days that followed the revelation of our family secrets and the ensuing rift within our household, I made several attempts to bridge the gap that had formed between my parents and Davina, and me. Each effort was met with a stony silence that seemed impenetrable. Davina was the most vocal and virulent in her criticism of me. She said I had betrayed our family by revealing our secrets to the police. Her words were like daggers, each one laced with raw hatred. She accused me of tearing our family apart, of endangering our parents. The atmosphere at home became unbearable, with Davina's harsh words echoing in my ears. While not as openly critical as Davina, my parents were distant and reserved. I would sit at the dinner table, my heart heavy, longing for some sort of connection. I'd attempt to start a conversation, to ask about their day, or share a piece of news I had heard, but my words hung in the air, unanswered and ignored. Davina would eventually resort to throwing me icy glances and refusing to engage in any conversation.

I was an outcast in my own home, a pariah whose actions had brought shame and disgrace upon our family. As the days turned into weeks, I tried to make amends, apologize, and mend the rift between us.

I cried many nights silently into my pillow, not wanting anyone to hear my pain. I hated myself. I wished with all my might that I could travel back in time and prevent myself from saying anything. If the investigation had continued, I would have backtracked and told the police I'd lied. I would have done anything to restore the fragile thread of connection that I'd lost. The pain of rejection engulfed me completely, and I had no reason to continue living.

57

Today is 'walk in the woods day'. Re-connect day. Every Thursday, we have to try and reconnect with nature. We're supposed to do this as often as possible, but on Thursdays, the staff makes sure there's no one inside unless there's a hurricane, in which case re-connecting is postponed until the next day. It's another of Lola's initiatives.

If I could, I'd go straight back to bed and listen to Sia. I've been revisiting her music, and really paying attention to the lyrics helps me process my grief. But I know they won't let me. Thankfully, today the weather is okay. Maybe a walk will do me some good.

I know a few people are smoking joints in the woods. Vero runs a small operation, having marijuana delivered here. She's offered me weed several times, as well as escape assistance, a fake passport, whatever I may need to start over. I'm pretty sure the staff knows about the weed but turns a blind eye. Part of the program here involves making healthy choices (a healthy body makes a healthy mind and so on), and alcohol is strictly forbidden, but there's a certain level of tolerance when it comes to fags and joints. I've also seen patients smuggle in crates and crates of Coke and guzzling the stuff as if it were bourbon during the Prohibition.

Before the first reconnexion session, Lola encouraged us to find a tree to hug: 'Not a bent tree, mind. A proper, strong, upright tree.' She actually demonstrated tree-hugging for us by earnestly embracing the large Chestnut standing in front of the manor. Closing her eyes, she said, "*Feel* the energy it emits. Feel it!" I avoided looking at Paris and kept a straight face.

There's no way I'm hugging a tree, but I've decided to give the re-connecting thing a shot. I've always loved the English countryside. Walking, listening to birdsong, all that. So here I am, trudging through mud on the outskirts of the grounds, about to join the hiking trail ahead. I hear a short cry coming from the trail in front of me and pick up my pace, soon catching up with Paris, who's negotiating the rocky terrain in fuchsia high heels and a shiny silver raincoat.

"What the hell, Emiliah? Why would anyone want to walk here? Can you tell me? I. CAN. NOT. DO. THIS. It's hell."

I look at his ridiculous attire and smile. "You're not exactly dressed for a walk, Paris."

"What do you mean? I walk miles, *miles* I tell you, in these." He lifts up a twelve-inch heel.

I offer my arm for support. "Here. Let me help." And so we walk along, me guiding him and him picking out the less treacherous areas with his dainty feet.

As the trail winds upwards, Paris stumbles more and more often. "This is exhausting, Emiliah. Leave me here. I simply CANNOT go on."

"Oh, come on, Paris. Look, there's a clearing." We climb up the last hundred yards of the track and arrive at the edge of a field overlooking a picturesque valley. I PeakSleek in and feel myself relaxing. "Shall we have a rest?"

Paris looks at me with tears in his eyes. "Oh Emiliah, I so need a rest. I think we'll have to call a helicopter to come and rescue us."

I can't help but smile. "Paris. It's a fifteen-minute walk back to Purgatory. There's no need-". But he's not listening. He seems to be completely absorbed by something to my left. I swivel just as a couple of wild horses run up the field towards us. When they're about twenty feet away, they turn and canter away.

Paris looks as if he's seen a ghost. "WHAT. WAS. THAT?"

"What?"

"That thing? Hanging down from the horse?"

"You mean its penis?"

"That was a *penis*?! Are you kidding me? Did you see the size of it? Oh my God, oh my God. That must *hurt*. Imagine the poor lady-horse."

"The mare?"

"What*ever*. It's *huge*!"

"Have you never seen a horse with an erection before?"

"I've never seen a real horse before."

I widen my eyes, and he becomes defensive. "Well, there aren't many horses trotting around Croydon."

I stare at the horses cantering across the field below us, as if I'd never seen horses before. Their muscular legs are rhythmically pounding forward, hooves hitting the turf, manes and tails flying. The one with the erection, which is slowly receding, slows to a walk, snorting, breathing in the clean air. The other one turns and joins its companion.

They graze side by side, their companionship seeming so effortless. My mind wanders to Ben and me, sitting on a bench by the Thames, watching the boats drift by, our hands entwined.

Tears well in my eyes. The horses' heads stoop gracefully to the ground, pulling grass with their teeth. Suddenly, once again, I'm overwhelmed with grief. I watch them, their simple movements and contentment, and I can't help but wonder why I couldn't have a relationship as straightforward and uncomplicated as theirs.

I wipe away my tears, feeling the ache in my chest deepen. The horses lift their heads, looking our way. There is a calmness in their gaze, a quiet understanding. I envy their simplicity, their ability to just be, without the burdens of guilt and grief that weigh me down.

Paris, still in shock, takes my arm. "Are you okay? You look like you're in a trance or something."

I can't stand it, the scene, the situation, Paris standing next to me, staring at the landscape, wondering what I've seen, what's triggered this reaction. "I need to go."

"Wait, wait, Emiliah. You can't leave me here. I can't make it back alone."

"Oh, for goodness sake, Paris, just take your bloody heels off and walk the half-mile back. Here, take mine." I throw my trainers at him and walk back towards the trail, my socks soaked after about two steps. I jog and stumble, stones digging into the soles of my feet, away from it all, until I'm hidden in the woods, finally alone, sobbing, and hitting the ground hard with my fists. *Why did it have to come to this? Why?*

I thump the ground with my fist, and it hurts so much that I burst into tears. I cry and cry and finally lie down on the damp leaves, breathing in the moisture.

58

In my twelfth year, as the days of silence and isolation stretched on within the family, my parents grew increasingly convinced that one of the villagers had stolen their money, which had been hidden somewhere on our land. Their suspicions fell on the baker's wife, a woman known for her cunning ways and knack for eavesdropping the village's secrets.

I listened carefully as my parents whispered about their suspicions, their hushed conversations taking place behind closed doors. They believed that the money had been taken by someone we knew, someone close enough to the family to learn of our hidden treasure.

Progressively, all the doors in the village closed on my parents, just as Ralph, Fergus, and I were shunned at school. Davina, who went to the lycée in Agen, didn't face the same rejection, but she hated it there anyway. And so, inevitably, the decision was made to return to England. Our life in Biffière sur Garonne had been a failure. My parents were enraged about the lost money but had no other choice than to leave.

Whimsy, the narrow boat that had changed all of our lives, was simply left there, along with Lovely and the caravans, and one sunny Tuesday morning in October, we boarded a flight in Toulouse airport that would bring us back to the land where I'd grown up. But I knew I'd be back in Biffière sur Garonne one day.

59

The sun beats down mercilessly on the courtyard of Saint George's Resting Clinic, throwing long shadows on the cracked flagstones. It's a sweltering day, and I find myself seeking refuge in the chapel. As I step into the cool interior, a group, huddled together in a conspiratorial circle, looks up.

Paris grins mischievously, his eyes sparkling. "Emiliah darling!" he exclaims, taking a long drag from a joint.

Vero nods at me, acknowledging me gruffly while holding her hand out for the spliff.

I'm surprised to see Gerald, as he spends most of his time in the basement. He definitely doesn't look the type to smoke weed. He looks at his feet, obviously embarrassed. "Too hot in the basement. No toxic chemicals in the chapel."

Beatrice simply smiles a vague, gappy grin.

It's an unlikely group, brought together by the quirks and eccentricities that landed us in this place. But in this moment, as we gather in this place of worship, our shared boredom and search for escape binds us together.

I take the offering with a grateful nod and join them. As we pass around a joint and lighter, the tension of our shared predicament dissipates in a cloud of smoke and laughter.

Paris, always the entertainer, regales us with her tales of silicon breast sales, industry conferences, and doctors who hit on him endlessly.

The weed makes me lightheaded, removing inhibitions, and I decide to tell them about the Limerelease debacle.

They all roar with laughter as I explain the Limerelease training sessions given to the Italian, French, German, and Swedish teams.

"And they call us crazy. Your Rhona sounds mental!" exclaims Paris, fanning himself to stop himself from crying.

Vero pulls a line of tobacco from her teeth and gives limerick creation a go, winking at Paris.

"Zere was once an andro named Paris,

Whose style was a little bit precious,

He burned down a factory,

But claims it's a mystery,

He's now known as ze arsonist duchess!"

Paris looks shocked for a second before giggling and fanning himself furiously, which makes us all laugh in turn.

He calms himself, patting his chest daintily, then looks around at us all and says:

"There was once a psycho named Vero,

Who had a few businesses, ya know?

Shovel in hand,

She dug holes in the ground,

But her gardening skills were fucking zero!"

Vero laughs hard, making a deep, scary noise, then becomes serious about three seconds later, calming us all down. She frowns at us and we all look at our feet.

"Good stuff, isn't it?" she says, smiling, and we all laugh again.

As the sun sinks lower in the sky and the air begins to cool, I can't help but feel a strange sense of belonging among this group of weirdos, but maybe that's just the weed.

60

You can only escape with drugs for so long. As the poster in the dining hall, citing Carl Jung, says, 'what you resist, persists'.

James looks at me with concern. "Take your time, Emiliah."

"OK." *Breathe.*

"My parents started suspecting that Ralph stole the money."

James writes something on his pad. "How did they express their suspicions?"

I look past his shoulder, remembering the scene.

"WHAT did you do with it, you little PRICK?" Daddy snarled. His face was red.

Ralph held up his chin. "I didn't take your money."

Daddy put his hands around Ralph's neck and started squeezing. I felt sick. "You fucking piece of shit! I KNOW you stole our money."

"Stop!" I screamed. The old man turned on me. "You! Don't you *EVER* tell lies about us again." With the 'EVER' came a sharp pain in my stomach. I fell to my knees.

He stood above me, heaving with rage. "You *FUCKING* lying, little *BITCH*." There was spittle at the corners of his mouth. "You told those fucking policemen *LIES* about us. How dare you, you sick little piece of *SHIT*? Don't you EVER do that again! DO you understand, you little FUCK?" I was being dragged to my feet, his fingers digging deep into my shoulders.

"Yes," I cried.

"Yes, who? You *CUNT*."

"Yes, Daddy."

A final push and I was lying on the floor, my face stuck to the carpet in a pool of drool and snot, shaking quietly as I watched him walk away towards the kitchen of the small rental flat in Reading. He was walking along the wall. Or was I on the ceiling?

I heaved myself to my hands and feet, shaking, and crawled towards the stairs, sobbing quietly as I climbed to the room I shared with Davina, closed the door, and pulled myself into bed. I cried into my pillow so they wouldn't hear me. *What's wrong with me? Why can't I be like Davina? She never does anything wrong.* But deep down, somewhere inside, I knew that wasn't true. Davina and Fergus were the favorites, so they embraced the family system. *I hate you all!* I screamed silently, pounding my pillow. *I hate you!*

I was awakened by Mummy shouting up the stairs. 'Emiliah! Down. Now. It's supper time.'

Don't look at anyone. They'll call you a crybaby. A martyr.

Davina was poking her plate anxiously. 'I'm so stressed out at the idea of starting at a new school...again."

Mummy patted her hand. "You'll be fine, Divvy, don't be silly."

"But Mummy, I really can't-" she began.

Mummy glared at her, and Davina stopped talking and looked down at her plate. Then she looked up at me. 'What are you looking at?'

I lowered my eyes, face burning. I hadn't realized I'd been staring. I stole a look at Ralph, who was eating silently, too. He didn't look at me.

I waited until everyone had left the table before plucking up enough courage to talk to Mummy. She was scraping ketchup from a plate into the bin.

I kept my eyes on the fork. "Mummy, why does Daddy hit Ralph and me and not Davina and Fergus?"

She carried on scraping. "I can't hear you, Emiliah. Speak up. You've really got to stop mumbling."

I looked at her for just a second. "Why does Daddy hit Ralph and me and not Davina and Fergus?"

She stared at me in disbelief. "What are you talking about? He doesn't hit you. Do you have any idea what hitting is?"

"But..."

"No. I don't want to hear another word. You have no idea what you're talking about."

Don't push it.

"But Mummy—"

She turned away and ignored me. Tears welled in my eyes.

The next morning, there was a folder on my desk. Inside was a stack of photos. The boy in the pictures was younger than Fergus, really young, maybe five or six. One side of his face was red and puffy, his eye closed. Parts of his cheek were purple and yellow. On one picture, he had small black circles on his arm, with red haloes around each mark, and I don't know how I knew this, but I knew they were cigarette burns.

"I'm sorry," I whispered. *I didn't mean to be ungrateful. I'm sorry. Thank you, God, for not putting me in that kind of family. I promise I'll be good now.*

61

James's face is full of concern. "You poor child. You've been through hell, haven't you?"

I break down, sobbing as I take in the words. Words I've always needed to hear without realizing it.

"You cry, Emiliah, you just keep on crying." And I do. I cry and I cry and I cry.

James is waiting patiently, compassionately, in his worn purple armchair, as I cry. Late summer sunshine is streaming through the window, flecks of dust flying over the desk, lighting up his collection of books. His face is not dissimilar to that of a wise owl with warm, intelligent eyes.

This is our twelfth session since my arrival. I'm folded into myself on the battered old sofa, listening to his soothing words and crying softly.

"Grieving your childhood is a long process," he says. "When you were young, you needed to believe you were loved, even if you were aware it was dysfunctional. Every child needs love and affection, Emiliah, as much as food and water. We can't survive otherwise. When there *is* no love, children will bend reality to equate what they receive with love." He looks at me intently. "It's not just courage that's needed to realize that abuse is abuse; it's distance. So don't be harsh on yourself."

More than the memories, the beatings, the neglect, what makes me cry is his compassion. I can take a lot of shit from people without having any kind of emotional reaction, but sympathy really gets me. I hate it.

He closes his owl eyes, thinking before he speaks. He's careful with his words. I can see that, as he looks into the middle distance, his gaze intense, his mind is working to find the right words. "Denial was a great help to you in childhood. It's what got you through it all. After denial, there can be one or more of the other stages of grief. You've experienced anger, bargaining, and sadness. The final stage is acceptance. Eventually, you'll be able to accept what happened."

My sobs are subsiding and turn into a kind of ugly snort-hiccup combo. Everything he says is perfect, *perfect*. Why did I have to wait this long to meet him? Why didn't I meet him before Ben? How different my life would have turned out.

I wish our sessions lasted longer. I could listen to him for *hours*. As soon as one meeting is over, I count the hours until the next one. Nothing matters more these days than my time with James. I talk to him all week in my mind, and when we actually meet, I wallow in the warm fuzziness of his compassion and acceptance.

He half-smiles. "Right now, you just need to accept your

feelings. Let them in and process them."

Sometimes, when he tells me what love should be like, what sex should be like, I see us together, me lying in his arms in front of a wood-burning stove, talking.

As he sits down across from me, the late summer light playing on his soft brown hair, a worn scarf over his blazer, I realize I've fallen in love. Just like that. He started out as someone to dump my feelings on, someone who would collect, store and analyze, holding my hand and guiding me through the haze, and now he's the love of my life. Which is really, really weird because I definitely didn't find him attractive when we started these sessions, and I was in no state to even think about romance. But now, nothing feels more natural, and I want more. A lot more. But at the same time, I know it's wrong. He's explained, several times, why I've developed inadequate feelings over the years. "Neglected children, deprived of parental affection, will go to all kinds of extremes to connect with people, and often, the wrong kind of people. They're not taught about boundaries. They're not taught to protect themselves. You're not the only one. And it's not your fault."

62

I've got three entire days until my next session with James. Three days of emptiness. I want to spend every waking hour with him, watching his face, listening to his strong, firm voice, smelling his earthy smell.

The feelings battling inside me are unbearable, and I feel the need to be alone. Back in my room, I lie on the bed, imagining us. Walking through a market in Guatemala. In front of our hut on a deserted beach, wrapped in each other's arms, talking, laughing, watching the waves hit the shore.

I realize I've been living in black and white for years. Now, I'm in a world of vivid reds, blues and yellows. Full Technicolor. Sharp contrast. Rich hues. Bloody hell, I could be writing a press release about the latest in HDTV technology.

I can't focus on anything else. It crept up on me without warning, and the intensity of the feeling has blown me off kilter. His image torments me constantly. It's unbearable because I know, I *know* it's wrong. But it feels so right. No one is more alluring to me than he is. He's the only one I want to talk to, the only person I can really trust.

Everything he says is perfect. He doesn't see the patients here as mentally ill. He just sees their pain. He also pointed out that being well-adapted to a dysfunctional world isn't necessarily a good thing, and that it may even be preferable to be unaligned with modern society. It has removed all judgement of the other patients, despite their quirks. Of course, he doesn't know everything about us, but his point of view is comforting nonetheless.

I flick through an old copy of House & Garden and imagine us choosing our dream house. I want to see all his childhood photos. I want to meet his friends, but I'm afraid they won't like me. I'm afraid of being too weak for him to love me.

The next three days are excruciating. I lie on my bed, my MP3 player pumping Metallica's 'Nothing else matters' into my ears. Bittersweet tears roll down my cheeks as, even though I know it's all wrong, I can't help wondering whether he feels the same. His concern, his insistence that I break certain habits and take care of myself, is that not love?

I don't know anything about him. I don't want to be a stalker, but I want to find out everything I can about him. I borrow one of Vero's phones and do a little digging. There's nothing. Nada. The only thing I *do* know, because one of the other patients mentioned it, is that he consults for a refugee center. I mean, how perfect can you be?

The love inside me swells to the point that it's intolerable. How will he react if I tell him? What if he no longer wants to see me? The idea of being left by James, the only person to whom I have ever truly opened up, fills me with despair.

63

I end up telling him.

He leans forward, placing his pen and pad on the table in front of him. "It's called transference. It's quite common." Another warm smile. "It's also misguided. You're transferring onto me the love you felt for your parents because you've finally found someone you trust."

I nod, silent tears streaming down my face. As I wipe my face with my sleeve, I let his words sink in.

"Believe it or not, Emiliah, this is good."

Seeing the look of horror on my face, he nods, pushing his point. "Therapy works a lot better with transference. A certain level of transference is actually *necessary* in therapy. I know it's hard, Emiliah, but you'll get through this. You're projecting loving feelings onto me, but you'll soon realize it's not really *me* you love."

"It is, though," I whisper.

He smiles. "I'm the first person you've really talked to about your pain, and the first to show you compassion.

Whether or not you were aware of it, you've been craving this kind of connection all your life. The mere fact that you're directing your affection towards someone compassionate, who wants you to be happy, means you're changing your old habits. It means you're less likely to invite abusers in. We can use your feelings to explore your psyche; understand what you've been missing in your past relationships."

I shudder, unable to really believe that this heartbreak can be good for me. "But you're perfect. I couldn't feel this for anyone else."

He raises his eyebrows. "Nobody's perfect, Emiliah. Believe me. I have many imperfections. You don't see them because I'm in a professional setting, doing my job, but I have just as many flaws as the next person. In fact, therapists are a bit like prostitutes: we can't allow ourselves to love because we're paid to do what we do."

"Maybe you can see me for free?"

He laughs.

I smile.

He becomes serious again. "What you need to learn is critical thinking. Nobody's perfect. No-one. The human brain is wired to think less critically when it's in love. That's merely to ensure reproduction and survival of the species.

James pulls himself up and walks over to the kettle. "What we're going to do, you, me, and the rest of the team here, is help you re-direct all those loving feelings towards yourself. You have to learn to love *yourself*. You have to learn to stop blaming yourself. You're a victim of the abuse you've suffered. But you're also a survivor."

When the session ends, I feel somewhat better, less emotional. I decide to go outside, walk around the garden, feel the sunshine. I head downstairs. As I reach the bottom of the staircase, I come to a halt. "Meloda," I whisper.

64

As soon as I set eyes on her, I start blubbing. Tears stream down my face uncontrollably, a mix of relief and overwhelming emotion. She takes a step forward, and we're in each other's arms, hugging fiercely. Her embrace is warm and familiar, instantly soothing the raw edges of my heart.

"I've missed you so much," I manage to choke out between sobs, clinging to her as if she might disappear.

Meloda pulls back slightly, just enough to look into my eyes, her own glistening. "I've missed you too, Em. Every single day."

I give Flit a quick hug as well, her presence offering an additional layer of comfort. She pats my back gently, a silent reassurance that she too is here for me.

Stepping back, I rub my eyes, trying to compose myself. "What are you doing here? How come you're allowed to visit me?"

Meloda beams. "David Shaw. We've seen quite a lot of him recently. He arranged it. He's great, Em. You're in good hands."

The mention of David Shaw brings a flicker of anxiety. "I can't believe you're here," I whisper, still in awe of their presence.

I lead them to the moldy conservatory, which is always empty. The air is thick with humidity, and the smell of damp and decay clings to the walls. It's the only place where we can have complete privacy. We all sit at the Formica table, the mismatched chairs creaking under our weight.

Meloda takes my hand across the table, her grip firm and reassuring. "We're going to get through this, Em. You're not alone."

We sit in silence for a while. Then Meloda and Flit exchange glances and Flit clears her throat. "Emiliah," she begins, her voice carrying a gentle firmness and her eyes scanning my face. "I've been doing some digging," she says, her tone still gentle but now edged with a seriousness that makes my heart race. "There's something about your past... inconsistencies that have come to light."

My defenses go up immediately, a wall erected by years of hiding and running from the truth. "What do you mean?"

Flit pauses, perhaps considering her next words carefully. "I went to Biffière-sur-Garonne, asked around. I heard about the operation your family ran."

Flit's expression softens slightly, but the determination in her eyes doesn't waver. "Emiliah, I believe your childhood story could help you. It could shed light on why you did what you did, help the public, maybe even the jury, understand the trauma you've been through. It's not just about the trial; it's about your life, your experiences."

A cold shiver runs down my spine. My past is a shadow I had hoped to bury forever, now threatening to engulf me once more. "Flit, please," I plead, the fear evident in my voice. "You don't understand. The legal system can't be trusted." I pause for a second. "When I was a child, there was an investigation."

They both stare at me in shock.

I nod. "The investigation was squashed. It didn't just... go away on its own. It was squashed by people with a lot of power who are still out there and won't let the story come out.

Flit slowly closes her notebook. "How will they manage to kill the story once it's published?" Her question is more than professional curiosity; it is an acknowledgment of the risk we are both taking.

I lean forward, fueled by urgency. "Flit, the people involved own the newspapers. They have all the power." I sigh. "They run the country."

Flit stays silent for a few moments, her hands in a praying position. "Emiliah, I get it. I really do, but times have changed. We have social media now. It's much, much harder to kill a story."

I give her a cold stare. "If you destroy all the evidence and the witnesses, there is no story."

She shifts in her seat. "That's why we need to be smart about how and when we release this. Listen-"

I interrupt her, raising a hand, and turn to Meloda. "Mel, would you mind giving Flit and me a moment?"

Nodding slowly, Meloda rises and leaves the conservatory.

As the tension between Flit and me thickens, a desperate thought forms. "Flit, if you publish this story now without my consent, I don't know if Meloda will forgive you. For not respecting my wishes, my safety."

Flit's response is immediate, her demeanor shifting. "Emiliah," she says, her voice steady but icy, "I thought better of you than to use our friendship—Meloda's friendship—as a bargaining chip. This isn't about Meloda. This is about you and me, deciding what's right."

She's right; I crossed a line, letting my fear cloud my judgment, but I need to prevent her from pushing forward. I use another approach, voice trembling. "Sorry, Flit. I'm scared, and I'm not thinking straight. I shouldn't have said that. It's just... this story, my past, it's all so much to bear. I wish I'd just left the country months ago. I wish I could just disappear," I whisper, realizing I'm voicing a wish that's been under the surface for a while.

Flit's expression softens slightly, the edge in her voice receding as she acknowledges my apology. "I understand you're scared. But I want to help you."

We sit in silence for a moment, the gravity of our

conversation hanging heavily in the air. Finally, she nods, a compromise forming behind her thoughtful gaze. "Okay, how about this," she says. "After your acquittal, you leave for a while, and I'll publish the story. We show the world the real Emiliah and the circumstances that led you here. Not as a sensational piece. We'll use it to shed light on the systemic failures that led to this point—your past, the circumstances of your self-defense, everything. It's a chance to change the narrative, to possibly influence a more compassionate understanding of your actions. Maybe it won't change the outcome, but at least people will understand your truth."

"And if I'm convicted?" I ask.

She stares at me levelly, understanding that I won't be convinced by empty reassurance. "Then I'll bin the story. Or we can wait for an appeal. But it'll be your choice. You have my word."

It's a compromise fraught with risk, yet it offers a chance for my story to be told on my terms, a way to control the narrative that could spiral so wildly out of my grasp. "Okay," I agree. "If I'm acquitted, you publish when I'm safely outside the country. If not, we forget all about it."

Flit reaches across the table, her hand briefly covering mine in a gesture of solidarity. "Emiliah, whatever happens, I want you to know that your story matters. And I'll do it justice."

As she stands to leave, I realize that, in the most unexpected way, Flit has become an ally, offering me a sliver of control.

We join Meloda, who's being talked at by Paris, dramatically explaining a disagreement with Vero in great detail. I gently maneuver Meloda away, explaining to Paris that my friends have to leave now.

As they depart, I'm left with mixed emotions—fear of what lies ahead and a strange sense of relief. The trial is looming, and I need to focus on preparing myself. David has given me notes to go over, and I have work to do.

65

No one looks more out-of-place in Purgatory than my lawyer, David Shaw. A man of precision and determination, dressed in impeccably tailored suits, he stands out against the backdrop of faded wallpaper, worn floors, track suits and empty stares.

With his Hugo Boss suit and shiny briefcase, David is an outsider in this world of crumbling elegance.

His polished exterior is not just a façade. David is a truly committed lawyer.

As I sit across from him in the conservatory, looking out onto the rainy downs, my heart pounds with anxiety as our talk of the trial brings me back to reality, like a slap in the face.

He clears his throat, his brow furrowed with concern. "I'm afraid I going to have to be blunt, Emiliah," he begins, his voice measured and somber. "Things are not looking great."

I swallow hard, my throat dry. "Why? What's happening?"

He leans forward, his expression grave. "Firstly, a significant portion of your husband's money is untraceable. The police are looking into it. They think your stabbing Ben was maybe not just self-defense."

I feel a knot tighten in my stomach.

David continues, "But that's not the only problem. Your ex-boyfriend, Peter, has come forward, and he's claiming you stalked him."

"Stalked him?" I hear myself asking.

David nods, visibly concerned. "Yes. He's given video footage of you breaking and entering his art studio to the police. What were you doing there, Emiliah?"

I take a deep breath, trying to calm the emotions swirling within me. "I didn't break and enter. I kept a key. I went there sometimes to remember what it was like when we first met."

David sighs, the weariness in his expression betraying the weight of our predicament. "Okay. We'll start by gathering character witnesses—people who can vouch for your behavior and establish a pattern of normalcy in your life. We'll also need to investigate Peter's motivations more deeply. It could discredit his claims if we can find evidence of ulterior motives."

The weight of the situation presses down on me, and I realize the uphill battle ahead. The murder trial is turning from a self-defense, domestic abuse case into a complex web of financial mysteries and ulterior motives.

The task ahead seems daunting, but I know I have no choice but to fight. "What about Ben's money?," I ask. "How can we prove that I don't know anything about it? Can't they trace it?"

David leans back in his chair, fingers steepled in thought. "That's a trickier issue. We need to find out where the funds went. If we can show that they weren't connected to you in any way, it might help. But it won't be easy."

I nod, my heart thumping.

"Emiliah," he says carefully, "I appreciate you sharing your story about Ben, but I can't shake the feeling that there might be more you're not telling me. Are there any other details, no matter how small, that you haven't disclosed?"

I feel a pang of guilt as his words hang in the air. I understand his concern, but instinct tells me I can't reveal everything. He's a lawyer, and I know those creatures all too well.

I lean towards him. "David, I promise you, I've told you everything I know."

His gaze doesn't shift. "Alright. I'll take you at your word. But if you remember anything else, no matter how insignificant, please tell me."

I offer a reassuring smile, attempting to dispel his concerns. "Thank you, David, for everything."

He regards me with a blend of sympathy and determination. "We'll do everything we can, Emiliah. But I won't sugarcoat it—this is going to be a tough fight. You need to prepare yourself for a long and grueling process."

As our conversation continues, we delve into the details of our strategy. David explains that we'll need to hire a private investigator to dig into Peter's past and uncover any possible motives he might have for making stalking allegations. We also start compiling a short list of character witnesses who can testify to my behavior and credibility. I mention Vince and Meloda. *Oh God. Will the police talk to Rhona? To Capri?* I feel sick.

Eventually, our conversation shifts to the trial itself. David outlines the challenges we'll face in the courtroom—cross-examinations, hostile witnesses, and the relentless pursuit of the truth.

"Remember," David says, his voice firm, "the truth is on our side. We'll present a compelling case and fight to expose the flaws in their allegations."

I take a deep breath, the knot in my stomach tightening.

66

As I lie in bed, I think about the baby I lost that night. I let myself grieve. I grapple with the feeling that it was probably for the best.

I know deep down that it was, but I'd begun feeling excited about the idea of holding a baby, despite the circumstances. Had I not lost it, there would have been a custody battle with Augusta before it was even born. And if I hadn't killed Ben, who knows how he would have treated a child. One thing is for certain: he would never have let me leave with his baby.

Had that night gone differently, he would have continued to hit me. If I hadn't miscarried, my baby would have had to endure great stress in utero and maybe be born in a psychiatric hospital or in prison. Still, for the first time in the nine months since I arrived here, I have room to properly grieve, and I weep silently.

Just as I'm drifting off to sleep, having wept every tear in my body, I hear a soft knock.

I drag myself out of bed and walk over to open the door,

which is surrounded by ripped wallpaper.

Paris is smiling sheepishly on the other side.

I sigh. "What's up, Paris?"

He lowers his head and looks up at me coquettishly. "We've decided to escape."

"Escape?" I repeat, incredulous.

"Yes," he says. "You're leaving for your trial on Monday, and we reckoned it was time to escape."

"Who's 'we'?" I ask, fearing the worst.

He starts dramatically counting on his fingers. "Well, there's you and me."

"Yeees?"

"And Vero, Beatrice, and Gerald."

There you go. The worst escape crew ever.

I know we won't get far, but the idea of a night-time escapade suddenly feels amazing. And why shouldn't we have some fun? Maybe it's exactly what we need.

A few minutes later, we're all huddled in my tiny room, under a sliver of moonlight, preparing to climb out of the window, down the gutters, and run across the grounds to... well, I suppose we'll find out when we get there.

I'm the first to swing my legs out, the cool night air kissing my skin, a stark contrast to the warmth of the building I'm leaving behind. As soon as I'm clinging on to the gutter, I realize what a terrible idea this is, but it's too late. Paris is already climbing out. In high heels. Fake Louboutins have no business being part of an escape outfit. Yet, there they are, defying logic and gravity with equal disdain. I start to descend despite the terror that engulfs me.

Vero follows, muscles bulging. The gutter groans under her weight, a precarious symphony of metal and determination. She's a force of nature, but even forces of nature have to respect the laws of physics. There's no way the gutter will hold all of our weight.

"Tell them to wait!" I whisper loudly to Paris, who is clinging on for dear life above me. "Well them to bait!" Paris hisses at Vero.

Vero looks down, puzzled, then turns to Beatrice, who has one leg over the sill. "Close the gate," she says.

Beatrice nods enthusiastically and climbs out onto the gutter, barefoot and dressed in a white, flowy sleeping gown. The gutter groans and starts to shake.

"Shit!" I say, scrambling down as fast as I can. Looking back up, I see that Paris has hardly moved, quite obviously struggling to get a decent foothold with his heels.

As I jump to the ground, I see Gerald climbing out, eyes as wide as dinner plates. He's muttering to himself but pushing himself forward nonetheless.

"No, no, Gerald, stay back," I say loudly, more afraid now of them all falling than of being heard.

He reaches out and grabs onto the gutter. As soon as his left foot is on it, it lurches off the wall by about a foot, making Paris shriek, Vero growl, Beatrice say, 'whoopie!' and Gerald gasp like a fish out of water.

"Down, down," says Vero, glaring at Paris.

"I can't. I'm stuck," replies Paris, and I see that one of his heels is stuck in an attachments that was holding the gutter onto the wall.

In an almost surreal manner, the gutter slowly moves away from the wall before accelerating, causing Paris to scream. A light turns on inside before the gutter falls a few feet from the ground, slowing for the last few seconds and ejecting its clandestine passengers. As Beatrice falls off, her gown gets caught, and she is left hanging there, suspended in mid air, her mature, naked body revealed for us all to see. Vero and I avert our gazes as we grab her legs. Paris fans himself dramatically, and Gerald stares at Beatrice in awe as if angel Gabriel just descended from heaven. Beatrice lifts her arms in slow motion, allowing the gown to release her, and we lift her to the ground.

As loud voices draw nearer, we all look at each other and run at full speed towards the Downs. After trying to run in his shoes, Paris quickly kicks them off and runs at an impressive speed down the hill. Vero grunts as she gradually picks up speed. Beatrice waves her arms, running like the free spirit that she is, and Gerald lies down and rolls down the hill in an attempt to keep up with the rest of us.

The shouts are far behind us, and as we pick up speed, I revel in the thrill of the run, whatever the consequences may be.

We reach a hedge at the bottom of the hill and search frantically for a way through. Gerald is the first to find an opening and, undeterred by its small size, proceeds to crawl through. We all wait in line, fidgeting impatiently as we begin to see torch lights searching the grounds. I wince as Beatrice crawls through, her naked body unprotected, but she seems unfazed. After Paris, it's my turn, and I push through, feeling the hedge around me resisting my attempts but moving forward regardless. I forget all else and just focus on getting out, pushing through, being free. I feel arms pulling at me, dragging me forward, and in a final surge, I find myself lying on the other side, curled up in a ball.

Vero is close behind me, muttering. "What ze FUCK did I let myself into? Why did I follow ze crazies?" And then she's out, too.

Once again, we're running through woodland, having no idea where we're going, but tasting freedom and exhilaration.

We arrive at a clearing that borders a small lake.

I look around, wondering whether we should regroup to decide what to do next, but before I can say anything, Paris has undressed and is running into the lake, quickly joined by Beatrice. Gerald looks at me uncertainly, but Vero picks him up as if he were a small child and carries him, as he protests loudly about chemicals, into the water. I shrug and start undressing. The water cradles me like a mother's embrace, and I close my eyes, savoring the sensation of floating effortlessly. It's as if all my worries and fears have been left behind. For a moment, I am weightless, suspended between the sky above and the depths below.

"Emiliah, look," Paris exclaims, his voice tinged with mischief as he splashes water at me. "I'm a mermaid!"

Vero dives beneath the surface and reemerges with a triumphant grin. "Look at me, I'm a submarine!" she declares, and I realize it's the first time I've seen her smile.

Gerald lies back and gazes up at the endless night sky. "Looks safe for now," he murmurs with a contented sigh.

Beatrice sends ripples through the water as she swims in circles, her laughter infectious. "Even goldfish need a break from their bowls," she says.

For a short while, we are no longer psychiatric patients; we're children re-discovering the magic of play. Then we hear shouting and turn around to see Rav and the other nurses flashing their torches at us, and we know the adventure is over.

67

"That was damn stupid! Just before your trial! What were you thinking?" I've never seen Rav angry before. He's the most patient of all the nurses.

Last night, when we returned to the ward, cold and shivering, he'd ordered us to bed. I'd expected not to see him this morning as he doesn't usually work on Thursdays, but here he is, livid. "Do you realize how much you've jeopardized your chances?"

I do feel bad, but in way, I'm so detached from it all that I don't care.

His expression hardens. "Do you realize what the consequences could be for us, the staff on duty?"

I feel cold. I hadn't thought about the staff. *Selfish. So selfish.*

I bow my head in shame.

He's pacing back and forth angrily. "You're lucky James intervened and that he's so respected here."

"James?" I ask, blushing.

Rav stares at me in disbelief and rolls his eyes. "Oh for God's sake, not you too."

I look down, shame flooding over me. "I'm so sorry... I wasn't thinking, I just needed to feel free, even for a little while."

He sighs, his expression softening. "I understand that, but you have to be more careful. The stakes are high for you right now. That kind of impulsiveness could have had serious consequences."

I nod, tears stinging my eyes.

"Anyway," Rav continues. "James told the director that what you and the others did last night, while impulsive, was a cry for freedom. He said it showed a desire to break free from the mental and emotional confines you've all been living under. He really believes that sometimes, a taste of freedom, even if it's taken impulsively, can do more for a person's spirit than weeks of structured therapy."

I feel a surge of gratitude and affection for James. "What did the director say?"

Rav's expression softens. "James convinced him not to take any disciplinary action against any of you. He argued that punitive measures would only set back your progress and would be extremely detrimental to your case. The clinic has decided to handle this internally. No formal reports will be filed, and the police won't be informed. This will remain between you and the clinic."

I PeakSleek a sigh of relief.

68

The early morning sun lights up the crumbling facade of Saint George's Resting Clinic, where I've spent the past nine months. Today is the first day of my murder trial at the Old Bailey, and the prospect of leaving the safety of Purgatory sends shivers down my spine.

David Shaw is standing by my side, offering a reassuring presence. He's been supportive throughout this ordeal, and I hope he can guide me through the tumultuous days ahead.

The journey to the Old Bailey is a blur of anxiety and uncertainty. When we finally reach London, the sights and sounds of the city rush past me in a disorienting whirlwind.

As we approach the historic courthouse that has witnessed countless trials over the centuries, my heart's pace quickens. The weight of my situation bears down on me, and I feel like a small, insignificant figure in the grand tapestry of justice.

David Shaw's encouragement provides a semblance of

reassurance, but the unease lingers. I can't escape the feeling that I'm entering a battleground where my past and my future will collide.

This is nothing like the initial hearing which took place in a nondescript Crown Court.

Inside the Old Bailey's hallowed halls, with a policemen on either side of me, the journey takes on a profound significance. The weight of my actions, the legacy of Ben's life, and the world's relentless gaze bear upon me.

Just before entering the courtroom, David looks straight into my eyes. "Okay?"

I nod.

Inside, the air is thick with the gravity of countless judgments passed. I walk to the dock, the space reserved for the accused, and take my place. The dock is a small, enclosed area with wooden panels that rise just above my waist, making me feel both exposed and confined.

The room is grand and imposing. High ceilings soar above, adorned with intricate moldings and decorative plasterwork that speak of a rich history. Tall, narrow windows line the walls, allowing slivers of light to filter through.

Directly in front of me is the judge's bench, elevated and commanding, reminding everyone of the authority it represents. The judge sits on a high-backed chair, robed in traditional garb. His expression is stern, his eyes scanning the room with a keen, discerning gaze. To his right and left are clerks and legal advisors, their desks cluttered with papers and thick law books.

To my right, the jury box is filled with twelve men and women, their faces a mix of curiosity, apprehension and solemnity. They sit in silence, eyes occasionally flicking towards me, their expressions inscrutable. My fate lies in their hands, their collective judgment hanging over me like a dark cloud.

To my left, the prosecution and defense tables are occupied by barristers in their wigs and gowns, surrounded by stacks of documents, legal pads, and laptops. They speak in hushed tones, occasionally glancing in my direction. My own defense team is a comforting presence, their determined expressions giving me a small measure of reassurance amidst my overwhelming anxiety.

The atmosphere is thick with tension. *This is real. It's happening.*

My gaze sweeps across the room, to the public gallery. My eyes lock with Augusta's. Her face is a mask of hatred, her eyes boring into mine.

Meloda, Flit and Vince, old friends so different from my crowd in Purgatory, so sane, sit among the spectators. Seeing Vince here, in this courtroom, feels surreal, as if two disparate worlds are being forced together.

The judge presiding over the proceedings looks around with a stern countenance. "Good morning, ladies and gentlemen. We are gathered here today to preside over the trial of Mrs. Emiliah Bent Goodwall, who stands accused of homicide. It is the duty of this court to ensure that justice is served impartially and fairly. As we embark upon these proceedings, I remind all present of the solemn responsibility that rests upon us. We must carefully consider the evidence presented to us. I urge both the prosecution and the defense to conduct themselves with professionalism and respect for the legal process. Let us proceed with diligence and integrity, mindful of the profound importance of the task at hand. May justice prevail. The court is now in session."

69

"Mrs. Augusta Goodwall, how would you describe the defendant's and your son's marriage?"

Augusta, on the witness stand, is a shell of her former self. She stares at me, her hatred visible. "My son was an extremely kind and generous man," she says.

An image of Ben screaming at me flashes before my eyes.

"Miss Bent seduced him by pretending to be an innocent, sweet girl, but I always knew it was a façade. She manipulated him, took advantage of his good nature." She paused. "And his money."

The prosecutor, a formidable middle-aged man with a grey beard, paces slowly, letting Augusta's words hang in the air. "Mrs. Goodall, can you provide any specific examples of such manipulation?"

Augusta's eyes narrow. "She was always so demanding, always needing his attention, his time. Ben was a busy man, but she didn't care. She acted as if she was the center of the universe, expecting him to drop everything for her."

Another memory surfaces—Ben ignoring me for days.

"Can you recall any specific incidents where you believe the defendant's behaviour was particularly manipulative or deceitful?" the prosecutor asks, his voice measured.

Augusta pauses, a look of triumph flashing across her face. "There was the time she claimed to be sick, just to keep him from attending an important business trip. She wanted him all to herself, and she didn't care how it affected his career. She even faked an illness, making him stay home to take care of her."

I had ruptured my ligaments when he let go of me, skiing. The memory brings with it a fresh torrent of injustice.

"Mrs. Goodwall," the prosecutor steps forward. "Was your son ever violent?"

Augusta's face flushes with anger. "My son was the most gentle, loving person any of us have ever known. He would NEVER have been violent, to ANYONE, especially not HER."

Ben kicking me while I'm lying on the kitchen floor.

She inhales deeply a few times, calming herself down. She stares at me. "She's the one who was never satisfied, always pushing, always complaining, always provoking him, pushing his buttons."

Me skirting around him, staying silent, so as not to set him off.

The prosecutor presses on. "And did you ever see your son

verbally or emotionally abuse Miss Bent?"

Augusta's eyes flicker with something like fear. "I've already told you, she was always the instigator. Ben would just try to defend himself, to make her see reason."

Another flash—Ben's face twisted in rage, his words cutting deep. "You're so obsessed with your image, aren't you Emiliah? Fixated on what people think. D'you want to know what people think of you? That you're worthless. They make fun of you behind your back. Your friends? They're not friends. They're jealous of our lifestyle. They hate you. You're so fucking naïve, so stupid."

The prosecutor turns to the judge. "No further questions at this time, my Lord."

As Augusta steps down, she casts me one last, hateful glance. I look away, feeling the weight of her words pressing down on me. The courtroom is silent, the air heavy with tension. This is just the beginning, and already I feel exhausted, but I know I must endure. I must find the strength to face whatever comes next.

70

The prosecutor frames his questions with calculated precision. He starts by casting doubt upon the reality of the domestic abuse, as if the scars have not been photographed, as if they are not etched deep into my memory.

"Mrs. Goodwall," he begins, his tone cold, "can you provide any concrete evidence of the alleged abuse you suffered at the hands of the deceased?"

"I believe there are hospital reports. Injuries," I reply.

"But when the hospital staff questioned you, you never said it was abuse. Yes, we've seen the photos, your bruises, the cuts. But why not be honest with the hospital staff? We have a witness statement from a doctor, saying he questioned you when your husband was out of the room."

I look into the eyes of the pompous prick questioning me. "I believe I am not the first abused wife to lie about the cause of her injuries. Just as I am not the first to stay in the relationship well after the first signs of violence."

He straightens his tie. "I believe, Mrs. Goodall, that you

are interested in BDSM."

I blush.

"We have a statement from Peter Decourt, your ex-boyfriend, who, apart from stating that you stalked him, says you enjoy 'rough, aggressive sex'. Is that true?"

I think back to James, explaining that people who suffer abuse as children often engage in rougher sex, unconsciously equating abuse with intimacy. Well, I'm definitely not going to tell him that. I lift my chin. "Yes, sir, I have engaged in rough sex, including with my husband. And yes, he often took it too far, ignoring my safe words, enjoying my pain."

"LIAR!" comes a shriek from the public gallery. Augusta is standing, spitting her rage at me. "SHE'S LYING! MY SON IS DEAD," she screams. "ISN'T THAT ENOUGH FOR YOU? YOU HAVE TO DRAG HIS NAME THROUGH THE MUD AS WELL?"

There are disapproving sounds all around the courtroom, and the judge makes a sign for Augusta to be escorted outside. As she's dragged out, her words echo around the courtroom. "SHE MURDERED HIM!"

I pause, pondering her words, before turning back to the prosecutor. "Most of my injuries didn't occur during sex. They happened mostly in the evening when he returned home from work."

He stares at me coldly. "Did you provoke him?"

A feeling of shame flushes through me. After the bubble

of safety and support at Purgatory, I'm not fully prepared for the accusation. Deep down, I know that I provoked him to some extent. And maybe I could have avoided the escalation of violence. I inhale deeply and hold my head high. "Erm, no, not really," I answer sarcastically.

I hear David hissing behind me.

"No, I never provoked him," I correct myself. "I was terrified of setting him off."

The prosecutor looks at me for a while, nodding. "Where's the money, Emiliah?"

"I- I- what money?" I ask.

"Are you aware that your husband embezzled funds from Breathe, Inc., Mrs. Goodall?"

I inhale. "My lawyer informed me of that, yes."

"He set up a company in Luxemburg, which invoiced PeakSleek for marketing work." He paused. "The company is in your name."

There's a collective gasp.

I look at him levelly. "Yes. I heard that he set up the company in my name."

He hands files to the jurors. "Please look at page one. You will see Luxemburg incorporation papers signed by the accused. On page two, a graphologist's report stating that the signature is, in fact, the accused's signature. Now, please take a look at pages three, four, five, six, seven, eight, and nine." You will see a marketing campaign sent by the Luxemburg company to Breathe. On pages ten, eleven, twelve, thirteen, fourteen, and fifteen, the invoices sent by the company to PeakSleek for a total amount of three point two million, five hundred and fifty euros. Now, please turn to page sixteen. You will find an email from Rhona Wells, Managing Director of Gant & Ballaster, the accused's former employee, stating that the proposal is in the "distinct style" of Mrs. Goodwall and even that it contains some creative elements that belong to Gant & Ballaster, as Mrs. Goodwall developed the ideas during her time at Gant & Ballaster."

I realize, as I answer, that my response is weak, even if it is true. "Yes, Ben asked me to create a campaign for Breathe. I did it as his wife, for free. I did not steal the PR tactics. I took inspiration from them, as the campaign Ben asked me to create was the internal communications counterpart of the PR campaign we created at G&B. I had absolutely no idea that my husband would then invoice PeakSleek millions of pounds based on my proposal. Yes, I also signed the paperwork. I signed a lot of paperwork for Ben and learned not to ask too many questions. He had complete control over my life. I wasn't even allowed a debit card to use the money I'd made before we married. So yes, I know how it looks, but I can promise you that I had absolutely nothing to do with the embezzlement." I stare straight into his eyes, and his gaze wavers for a second.

"Where's the money, Mrs. Goodall?"

I feel the weight of his accusation, but this time, I'm prepared. "I have no idea where the money is," I say, my voice unwavering. "I didn't even know the money existed."

I can't tell whether or not he believes me, maybe because it's not entirely true.

He turns to the jury. "You have the evidence in front of you. This case is actually very simple. Mr. and Mrs. Goodwall set up an elaborate scheme to embezzle funds from the very successful company, Breathe, Inc., which Mr. Goodwall was running. When the money was in the bank, Mrs. Goodwall moved it before killing her husband, ensuring she wouldn't have to split it. She is a cold-blooded killer, and her motive is one of the two most common motives: money."

I look at the jury, and they seem pretty convinced. *Shit.*

71

It's day eight of the trial. Eight full days with hardly any sunlight, and I'm beginning to feel depressed. David presents the photographic evidence of the domestic abuse taken on the night I was taken to hospital after stabbing Ben. I feel a lump forming in my throat. The images of that night flash before my eyes, stark and unrelenting. Once youthful and unblemished, my face is marred with bruises and cuts on the photos. Two broken ribs. He shows the pool of blood from my miscarriage.

"Emiliah," David says gently, "can you confirm that these photographs depict the injuries you sustained on the day of the incident?"

My voice trembles as I reply, "Yes, Mr. Shaw, they do."

Then, the signs of previous abuse are shown to the court: a scar on my shoulder, a burn from a hot pan that Ben shoved at me, an x-ray of an unhealed broken finger. I'm pretty sure the broken finger is from much earlier in my life, but I'm not going to mention that.

David continues, his voice resolute, as he presents

medical records detailing the miscarriage. The guilt is overwhelming, the weight of my choices and their devastating consequences pressing down on me. I start weeping. Even here, where weeping might help me, I feel weak and useless for giving in to tears yet again.

"Emiliah," David asks, his voice softer now, "can you tell the court about the evening Ben died, starting with him arriving home?"

I take a deep breath, feeling the weight of everyone's eyes on me. My hands tremble slightly as I grip the edges of the dock. "It was the day of PeakSleek's board meeting, and he had been worked up about it for weeks," I begin. "He arrived home earlier than usual, and he'd been drinking. He was furious—angrier than I had ever seen him. He asked me to pour him a glass of wine." I paused. "I was shaking so much that I spilt it on his shirt."

David stared at me. "What happened then?" he asked, gently.

I remained strangely calm and matter of fact as the memories flood back. "He grabbed me by the arm, so hard that I could feel the bruises forming. He pushed me against the wall, screaming in my face. I was terrified. I kept telling him to stop, but he wouldn't listen."

I want to look at the jury, but I force myself to stay focused on David. "He punched me in the face. I fell over. Then he kicked me in the thigh. Then in the stomach, several times."

The courtroom is silent, everyone hanging onto my every

word.

"I tried to get up, but I kept slipping. He pulled me and I knew he was going to kill me. I managed to grab the kitchen knife and when he pulled me towards him, I stabbed him in the chest. Then I stabbed him a second time." I pause. "Then a third."

David stays silent for a while. "I would like us to look at exhibit 62."

An image of my face appears on the large screen, this time a close up with my mouth open, my face covered in dark red marks, a swollen, split lip and a missing a front tooth.

A collective murmur crosses the courtroom.

"Now exhibit 71"

An image of my legs, covered in bruises and one deep gash, appears.

I steal a look up to the gallery, glimpsing Flit and Vince comforting Meloda.

David turns back to me. "Can you tell me what happened next?"

I nodded. "I felt a sharp pain in my abdomen. I knew something was wrong. I started bleeding, and the pain was unbearable. The medics did what they could, but there was too much blood. I lost the baby."

David steps closer, his expression compassionate. "Emiliah, can you tell the court how far along you were?"

I swallow hard. "I was four months pregnant. I had just found out it was a girl."

As I finish, my voice breaks, and for a moment, the courtroom falls silent, the stark reality of my suffering hanging heavy in the air. I want to explain my guilt, the overwhelming guilt, but there's no way to make them understand without telling them the entire truth, and that's not something I can do.

David marks a pause before addressing the court. "Emiliah Goodwall acted in self-defense under extreme duress, trying to protect herself and her unborn child. Her actions, though tragic, were not premeditated but a desperate response to a life-threatening situation."

As he steps back, I feel a glimmer of hope.

72

The courtroom holds its breath as the jury files in, its members' faces etched with the weight of the decision they are about to deliver. I stand there, heart pounding, breathing shallow breaths, waiting for the verdict. Every second feels like an eternity.

The foreperson, a middle-aged woman with a determined look, steps forward.

The judge looks at her and asks, "Members of the jury, have you reached a verdict?"

She nods and clears her throat. "We, the jury, find the defendant, Mrs. Emiliah Goodall, not guilty."

A storm of emotion washes over me, but I can't really register the words. *Did she really say 'not guilty?'*

The words echo in the courtroom, lifting the heavy cloud of uncertainty looming over me for so long. Not guilty.

I turn to David, and he hugs me. Then he holds my arms and looks at me without saying a word, and I understand how thrilled he is. I now know he believed my story.

We fought tirelessly, presented evidence, and endured the court's scrutiny to secure this outcome.

Augusta is sitting in the gallery, weeping silently. Her gaze meets mine for a brief moment, and I feel the anguish in her eyes. In that moment, I can't help but feel a pang of empathy for the loss she's suffered, despite what she did to me.

I can finally begin to focus on rebuilding my life, free from the shadow of the past.

73

The sun is setting, lighting up the cherry, pear and peach trees behind Meloda. Tiny cherry flower petals are floating to the ground, some landing on her hair as she begins her vows. "Flit, I fell in lust with you when you came up to me at that New Year's party and asked me if I knew how to open a bottle of beer with a shoe."

There are chuckles amongst the guests and a few whoops from Flit's reporter friends. "I fell in *love* with you when you adopted my cats without hesitation, even though they piss in your sports bag."

More laughter.

"But when my best friend was suffering and you supported me, and her, without hesitation, *that* was when I knew you were the person with whom I wanted to grow old. I'll never forget your warmth, the way you opened up to me, your patience, and all the hot chocolates with marshmallows you made." She smiles as she wipes her eyes. "I love you, Flit."

We're all blubbing, even Vince, and he's really not the type.

"I love you too, Meloda." Flit kisses her on the cheek. "I already love the mother you'll become and the friend you've been since we met." She pauses, catching my eye. I smile back encouragingly. "But most of all, I love your spirit, feistiness, passion, and fierce loyalty."

There are cheers and laughter as Flit pulls Meloda into a passionate embrace.

This is my only social visit before my flight. Strange how you can live in a country for years and end up with such a small social circle. It's small but wonderful, and these few people will be my friends for life, just like Paris, Vero, Beatrice and Gerald. As for James, well, I'm getting over my massive crush and accepting it for the great therapeutic connection that it was.

The clapping dies down, and people start moving towards the array of food laid out on bales of hay covered with rough white linen throws.

I steer clear of the photographer, snapping away with his Mamiya 645, taking pictures that I know will be fabulous.

I wait until the happy couple has been freed from family members before hugging them fiercely. "I'm so happy for you two." Meloda stares straight into my eyes before hugging me back. "And I'm so happy for you, Sweetie."

One of Meloda's university friends, Alisha, approaches us with a question about the table setting, and as Meloda guides her to her seat, I turn to Flit. "I've left you a second wedding gift, for your eyes only. It's in your room in the cottage. It contains a ledger. Everything you'll need is in that book. Please just wait for my text message before publishing anything."

She stares at me, incredulous. "Are you sure?"

I nod.

She puts a strong hand on my shoulder, showing me I've made the right decision, and this gesture, for some reason, makes me even more emotional than the vows, so I quickly excuse myself.

I locate Vince, who I know will keep the conversation light and fun.

The evening flies by in a whir as we eat wonderful Creole food, drink wine, and eventually follow the happy couple into the barn, lit up with hundreds of fairy lights, for the first dance. I smile to myself. I have no idea what lies ahead, and right now, I just want to enjoy the moment. I'll savour it and make sure I live plenty more moments like this one.

74

The morning light cascades in a gentle, golden wave, spilling across the pristine white tablecloth before me.

The plate in front of me is a testament to the simplicity of Cayman island food: fresh mango, watermelon, papaya and pineapple, their flavors sweet and nuanced.

Lifting my gaze, the breathtaking view of the Caribbean sea greets me, gentle waves lazily licking the white beach in front of the hotel. The scene is so vivid and vibrant, it feels almost surreal, like a painting come to life.

As I continue to eat, each bite reminds me of the world's simple pleasures, of the beauty that resides in the details. The soft hum of conversation around me, the gentle clinking of cutlery, the warmth of the sun as it begins to climb higher in the sky—all of it combines into a mosaic of sensory experiences, grounding me in the here and now.

I finish my coffee and wipe my mouth. Right. *Time for business.*

75

As I walk into the bank, wearing a Gucci suit, carrying a Birkin handbag and holding my passport, my hands tremble and my armpits sweat, despite the cool rush of air conditioning. I stare at the elaborate stone paneling behind the receptionist as I murmur the words I've rehearsed, trying to seem nonchalant. He checks my identity against the records. A senior manager comes to greet me. "Mrs. Straight, lovely to meet you in person."

"Hello", I reply simply, shaking his hand.

"We have just a few details to check, considering the amount you're withdrawing."

"Of course," I reply, trying to look bored.

It takes five minutes for a young assistant to bring me the bag of cash. The three of them watch closely as I sit and count the money. Three million dollars. I am leaving the change, five hundred thousand, nine hundred and fifty-two dollars and twenty-one cents, in the bank. I shake the manager's hand, ignoring the assistant. "Thank you."

I have a large Vuitton suitcase into which I pack the cash.

As I walk out, I realized I'm shaking. *Walk slowly.*

The taxi is waiting patiently twenty meters down the road.

As planned, he drops me off at the Grand Harbor shopping mall. I head to the locker section and fumble with the code until it is aligned: 6812. I pull out a large rucksack.

I hurry to the loos, trying to look natural but terrified that the police will appear at any moment. I change into used jeans, a white T-shirt, trainers and a baseball cap. Then I transfer all the cash from the suitcase to the rucksack, carefully wrapping it in towels, and leave the empty suitcase in the stall, confident that someone will take it.

I check myself in the mirror, assured that no one will recognize the elegant woman who came in.

I walk to the bus stop and wait.

76

As the bus arrives at Owen Roberts International Airport, I am acutely aware that this is the most critical part.

I walk up to the desk and hand over my passport. I act as nonchalantly as possible. Using a fake passport to carry millions in cash to Panama City is definitely not without risk. The lady behind the desk barely looks at me before handing me my boarding pass.

I FaraWave deeply, walking over to the security queue. *Thank you, Vero. I must admit, doubted you for a second there.*

I'm sweating profusely as I place my rucksack onto the x-ray belt. I hand my boarding pass and passport to the security guy and he looks at the passport, then sharply at me. He gestures to his female colleague to frisk me and watches carefully.

The woman checking me is thorough, but she finds nothing. I turn around to see the male security guard checking the X-ray screen. I keep my head down, pull my rucksack off the belt, and walk away.

I think I can hear someone talking into a walkie-talkie, but I don't dare turn around.

The plane is already waiting, and boarding begins within seconds of my arrival at the gate. I get in line.

Progress into the plane is painfully slow, and the wait for take-off even slower.

I breathe a sigh of relief when we're in the air, although I'm not safe yet. When I arrive in Panama and settle somewhere remote, then I'll feel safe.

I order a glass of sauvignon Blanc to calm my nerves and think back to the beginning of my plan.

<h1 style="text-align:center">77</h1>

Ben had just slapped me for the first time. That slap had awoken me from a stupor. I was shaken. I may have been naïve, but I knew enough to recognize that slapping your wife was a form of abuse. In my research at the library on couple problems, both online and in books, I'd read several paragraphs about domestic violence, but I'd chosen to ignore them.

What was I going to do? I was pregnant. I had burnt the Gant & Ballaster bridge I had spent so many years building. I had no connections, and he had so many. It was such an unfair fight. I could gather proof of the abuse, I could record his rages, and I could face the custody battle with all my might. I had my tiny flat, and I had willpower and resilience.

Don't be ridiculous. You'll never make it on your own. Look at you.

I tried to ignore the voice in my head while researching on my phone. I started by asking good old Google whether a slap was considered domestic violence. Even as I read 'yes' after 'yes' and 'leave, now', I still couldn't quite believe it.

It's not abuse, don't be pathetic.

My fingers hovered over the keyboard. "Why can't I trust my instincts?" "Why do I never feel good enough?" I typed.

Scrolling through various answers, I came across a book title, *Will I ever be good enough?* By Dr. Karyl McBride.

I erased the search history and went to sit on the long, cream sofa that overlooked the premium view of London that I had been so impressed with, and that now felt like a beautiful, glass cage.

After sitting for a few minutes, staring absently at the City skyline, I walked to the front door, slipped on my sneakers, and took the lift down to the building entrance. Stepping outside, I realized how suffocated I felt in the flat. I walked briskly to John Harvard public library and located the psychology section. Pulling out, *Will I ever be good enough?*, I sat down in a corner chair and started reading. As I read page after page, I felt the ground shift beneath me. The proverbial pennies came crashing to the floor in an incessant clatter, shattering the fragile reality I had constructed over the span of my life.

Shaking, I went back to sit at one of the library computers and continued my search online. Website after website, forum after forum, video after video confirmed my discovery. One guy, Richard Grannon, said that 'becoming a detective', looking for answers online, was one of the first signs. Every line I read, every and sentence I heard gave me a different perspective on my life.

Then I read parts of *Escape* by HG Tudor, and a shiver ran down my spine.

It was time to leave. I didn't want to raise suspicion, but there was so much more to know. HG Tudor had written many more books, which I desperately wanted to read, but I didn't have time.

Walking back to the flat, everything was alien. The people, the streets I'd walked so many times, the sounds and smells of the city. Everything off kilter. The whole world had flipped. I had been so wrong. Every exchange, every conversation had been a lie. How could I have been so blind?

I'd never really felt safe. For several years, when I was younger, I'd slept with a knife under my pillow. But this was a thousand times worse. I had no idea who I could trust. Even Meloda. What were her motives in our friendship? Was it all a game? I didn't know what to believe or who to trust. I walked desperately for hours. I was unhinged.

My phone rang, making me jump. I answered, breathing deeply. Ben.

"Darling, where are you?" he sounded normal, loving.

I tried my best to sound natural. "I was just on a walk. I didn't see the time."

"Well, I'm home. Come back."

"Okay. I'll be right there."

When I opened the front door, he came over to hug me. I tried hugging him back. I felt a drop of sweat slide down my back. *Don't let him feel your fear.*

He stared into my eyes. "I love you, my Emiliah." The words hit me like a punch. He took my hand and led me into the dining room, where a candle-lit dinner was set up. He'd never done that before. Was it a sign he was on to me?

He looked down at me. "Are you okay, Babe?"

He knows. He's going to kill you.

I smiled at him. "No, I- I'm just a bit tired. Let's eat."

I felt his stare as I put forkful after forkful of mushrooms into my mouth, forcing the slippery texture down with tiny sips of sparkling water. *Has he spiked my drink?*

All I knew was that I had to get out somehow. Without him being able to find me. *Could I fake my own death?*

When he finished his meal, he stared at me. "Let's go to bed."

Previously, any invitation to go to bed would have been seized as an opportunity to recapture the perfection of the early days. Now, I felt like an allied spy having to sleep with a high-ranking Nazi. I smiled as he undressed me slowly, kissing me lightly on the forehead, eyelids, cheeks, and mouth. When I felt his tongue pushing into my mouth, I felt a familiar lurch in my stomach. Lust or sickness? Heaven or hell?

Just keep going. Don't let him see what you're thinking.

I responded as best I could, and he groaned with desire. He kissed me hungrily, pushing me backwards towards the bed.

He unbuckled his trousers, pulling off his shirt. He walked to the bedside table and pulled out his four pairs of handcuffs, and proceeded to attach me to the bedrails. I felt sick. I stared at the ceiling, noticing a tiny corner of wallpaper that had come away from the wall. My body floated up, and I touched the sharp little corner of paper. I reached out with both hands and pulled myself behind it.

78

The following day was my second trip to the library. More information, more terror.

An idea was forming in my mind, and I tried to push it away. *Too risky.*

I continued to devour books, some of them by self-proclaimed psychopaths and narcissists. Each book confirmed the truth of the abuse, highlighting my ignorance and naivety. But still, I was the one who felt crazy, fragile, paranoid. Then, the answer struck me. The idea I'd pushed down came back to the surface with the strength of a buoy. *I'm deranged, paranoid. I could be psychotic.* Ben had already convinced several people, including a psychiatrist, that I had severe psychological problems. Maybe I did. If there was evidence that I was crazy, I could get away with anything. Even murder.

I delved into different sections of the library and sifted through various titles: Criminology, forensic science, forensic psychology, and murder trials. There were no cameras, and no search history.

The desperation that had enveloped me since the slap dissipated slightly, giving way to new feelings: anger, rage, revenge, hope, excitement. *Would I be able to do it, though?*

79

Ben was fully controlling our finances, and I no longer had the keys to my flat in Shoreditch. He'd told me months earlier that he'd let it out, but I hadn't been able to find any paperwork. There was very little in the flat, so I supposed he kept the paperwork at the office, at FaraWave.

I decided to find out for myself whether or not my flat had really been let out.

Before reaching the library on the first Tuesday in May, I detoured, crossing Tower Bridge and heading North. My step quickened as I entered my familiar turf, and I wondered how I could ever have favored glamourous city living over the authenticity of Shoreditch. I had tears in my eyes by the time I reached the door of the building. I decided to ring all the bells except my own and, as if by magic, the door opened.

I climbed the stairs two at a time, desperate to touch my front door. On the third floor, Mr. Hull was waiting on the landing. "Oh, 'ello, Miss Bent."

"Hello, Mr. Hull," I said.

He peered at me. "Was it you 'oo rang the bell?"

I looked at him sheepishly. "It was. I'm sorry. I couldn't get hold of the tenant."

He looked at me uncomprehendingly. "The tenant?"

Suddenly, I knew. Ben had sold my flat. "Yes," I continued hesitantly. "The tenant who's renting my flat."

Mr. Hull's face softened. "The man living there bought it. From your 'usband. E's not a tenant. E's on the landlord committee."

I took a moment. "Thank you, Mr. Hull. Of course, it must have slipped my mind."

I turned around before he could see the tears well in my eyes. I ran down the steps as fast as I could.

80

I was chopping leaks vigorously when he came home that night. As soon as I heard the door click, I knew I would kill him. Not tonight, though. *Be patient.*

He stomped over to me and whacked the pan off the hob. "I told you to have dinner ready when I get home!"

Instead of bending down to pick up the mess, I stared at him levelly. He looked surprised for a split second.

He walked around the mess to the drinks cabinet, pulling out a bottle of Armagnac and pouring himself a large measure.

He stared at me. I stared back. *Go on, do it, punch me, Fucker.*

But he didn't. 'Those PRICKS think they can pressure ME? Who the FUCK do they think they are?' He paced across the living room. When he was on the other side of the room, I squatted to pick up the pan and leeks, keeping an eye on him.

He marched back and forth. "Those cocksuckers think

they're so much cleverer than I am. But they know NOTHING. They know shit."

He'd criticized the board before, but not like this. Something bad must have happened.

He stared at me, breathing through his nose like a bull. "What they don't know is that I saw this coming ages ago. They think they're so clever that they can push me out. But guess what? I screwed them first."

I looked up from the mess on the floor but avoided eye contact.

He smiled. 'I set up a company in your name, *Darling*. In Luxemburg. And it's been invoicing PeakSleek every month for the past year. Internal communications, that's what your company does.'

I looked at him in shock.

'Well, you're quite happy taking advantage of all this, aren't you?' He gestured at the panoramic windows.

I could feel him daring me to challenge what he'd done. He stopped marching and stared at me. 'Well, are you happy I set up a company for you? It's already worth three mil.' He strode towards me, and I flinched.

I was expecting another slap, but he pushed me against the wall.

I froze as he pulled up my skirt.

'Come on, woman. Show some goddamn appreciation.

You're all fucking the same, aren't you?'

I did everything I could to show him my appreciation that night.

81

The next morning, I stuck my fingers down my throat.

This was a twist I hadn't expected. It complicated things, but it also had the potential to give the baby and me the freedom we needed.

After extensive research at the library, I realized I would need help.

It was a long shot, but I remembered this one guy I'd met a few years earlier. One of my smaller clients was an IT startup which had developed innovative new penetration software and was in the process of looking for acquiring companies. When I started asking specific questions about the software, the CEO suggested I talk to the software developer, Alex. Alex was incredibly intelligent but also very shy and withdrawn. He opened up, however, and told me how the software worked, hacking computer systems and generating reports for clients that pointed out the flaws in their IT systems. He'd told me how he'd had the idea when taking part in a hackathon during his summer holiday, having had to overcome a complex series of obstacles, giving him the idea of an algorithm that dynamically assessed and assigned risk scores to identify vulnerabilities based on their severity, potential impact, and exploitability. He had spent the rest of his holiday developing the software and demoed it to the CEO on his return. I'd wondered at the time why he hadn't kept the idea to himself and sold it, but it soon became clear that he possessed no business sense. He was passionate about development but uninterested in money or any kind of business-related activities.

When I visited the startup offices, I noticed some of his colleagues making fun of him, and it quickly became clear that he was being bullied by both his colleagues and the CEO. I decided to do a little research. I soon realized that he was in a position to claim the intellectual property as his own, and I offered to help him. I was taking a huge risk, as the startup was a promising new client, and Rhona would have killed me if she'd found out I'd been sabotaging our client's acquisition attempts.

When I explained my plan and introduced Alex to a patent attorney I'd found on Google, Alex looked dubious, but gradually began to see the benefits of claiming and selling the IP. The patent attorney explained everything clearly and brought in a business consultant to reassure Alex that he wouldn't have anything to do. Alex ended up a multi-millionaire, and neither the company CEO nor Rhona ever found out about my role in the disastrous crash of our security software client.

Alex had offered me some money at the time, but I'd turned it down. From then on, he'd always sent me a strange gift at Christmas, such as an unsolvable Chinese puzzle or a box that I couldn't open.

I remembered where he'd lived at the time, and decided to try there first. When I rang the door of his Farringdon flat, he opened the door, stared at me for a few seconds, turned around, and walked inside. I followed him and explained my problem as he made tea.

I'd known he would never tell on me, but I'd expected him to turn me away. However, he had no qualms about helping me; he was even happy to have the opportunity to return the favor. He got to work right away, explaining that he'd need to set up a company in my name in the Cayman Islands and would have about a week of work to do. He would, however, need me to gain access to Ben's computer.

82

I had met up with Alex one other time at a bus stop, and he had told me he needed a seven-digit code to avoid leaving any traces of the hacking and make it look as if Ben had moved the money himself.

There was only one way to get hold of the code: Ben needed to give it to me. I decided to coax it out of him. I stole a twenty-pound note from his wallet and bought a pair of coded handcuffs in a sex shop in Whitechapel. One evening, I mixed two crushed sleeping tablets from the box Dr. Mitchell had given me, and slipped them into Ben's wine glass before handing it to him. I then changed into the La Perla ensemble he'd bought me for my birthday. After dinner, I handcuffed myself to the railing above his bed. I cringed inwardly as he grinned hungrily, but I smiled sweetly.

When he was done, I asked him to unlock my handcuffs, giving him the wrong code. As he twisted my arm in frustration, I cried, saying I'd used the same code for years: 768 892. "I don't understand. I'm sure that's the code. I've had it for years. I don't see how I got it wrong. Maybe it's a three at the end and not a two?."

He stared at me in disbelief. "You're so fucking stupid. I've had a code since childhood, and I'd never forget a number."

"Well, maybe your code's simpler than mine," I moaned.

He looked at me in disgust. "Mine's 333 6812. How much fucking simpler does that sound?" He yawned. "You'll just have to sleep like that. I'm too damn tired to do anything about it now."

Once he was snoring, I twisted my hands and painstakingly rolled the correct code until I was free.

I resisted the urge to run to the computer that very night. But the next day, I knew I'd have to.

83

I'm finally sipping a beer on a remote beach in Panama. I live in a simple hut a few hundred meters from the beach, and I'm living my best life.

Three days ago, I sent Flit a text message giving her the green light to publish the story. I have no interest in following the unfolding of the drama. When I pressed 'send', I felt a vague pang of guilt for my estranged family, who will have to face the shit show, but to be honest, my need to be free comes first. And I feel far more compassion for the children of Biffière sur Garonne.

I suppose it's time, now that I'm safe in a foreign country, living under a different name, to provide the final piece of the puzzle and explain the sudden deaths of Maître and Monsieur.

Most children are curious, but I was a snooper. Unable to understand my family's dynamics, I learned at a very young age to search for answers and unveil every secret I could. My insatiable appetite for exploring hidden corners led me to a secret compartment under the kitchen sink of Whimsy, our narrowboat. On one unassuming evening, as the setting sun cast long shadows across the interior of our modest dwelling, when everyone else was outside, huddled around the firepit, I stumbled upon a leather-bound notebook tucked away in the hidden compartment in the under-sink cabinet.

The notebook, its pages worn with time and use, held an aura of mystery that drew me in like a moth to a flame. Its columns, meticulously inscribed in my mother's hand, revealed a chilling truth to which I had been oblivious until that very moment.

As I perused the pages, my heart quickened with each revelation. The notebook contained a ledger, a sinister chronicle of names and amounts that sent a shiver down my spine. The columns included the names of visitors—judges, lawyers from my father's chambers, politicians, businessmen, university professors—all those who had crossed the threshold of our corner of paradise in the South-West of France. Alongside their names, like damning evidence, were the amounts, each one a symbol of a sinister transaction.

The ledger continued with another set of names—children's names. It was a list of the foster children in the village. Their innocence transformed into a commodity that could be bought and sold. The amounts beside their names spoke of a heartless commerce that treated their destinies as mere transactions.

My young mind struggled to comprehend the depths of depravity that the notebook revealed. It was a ledger of exploitation, a dark secret that had remained hidden within the confines of the boat. The truth washed over me like a chilling wave, and having been subjected to Monsieur's needs, I realized with disgusted clarity the meaning of the dark machinations occurring in the place we called home.

I closed the notebook with trembling hands and replaced it, my young heart heavy with the weight of the uncovered secret. The darkness of the boat, once a sanctuary of secrets, had become a chamber of horrors that I could no longer ignore.

As I reflected on the ledger's chilling revelations, the innocence of my childhood faded into the harsh light of a brutal reality. The sinister truth had been laid bare before me, and I knew I could no longer remain a silent witness to the malevolence that had tainted my family.

At about the same time, Ralph made an earth-shaking discovery that would change our lives forever. During one of our secret forays into the nearby woods, he unveiled a discovery that left us both breathless with astonishment.

As we roamed into the forest, the oppressive silence of the woods enveloping us and the tall trees projecting eerie shadows that danced with secrets, Ralph beckoned me to a particularly gnarled and ancient oak.

With a conspiratorial grin, Ralph pushed aside a curtain of ivy that concealed a hidden cavity within the tree trunk. My eyes widened as he revealed a metal case, its surface tarnished with age and weathered by time.

The metal case, heavy in my hands, seemed to pulse with

an enigmatic energy. As I carefully opened it, my breath caught in my throat. Inside, nestled amidst a bed of dried leaves and twigs, lay a fortune in currency—mostly pound notes but also a collection of euros.

Ralph and I exchanged stunned glances, our young minds struggling to comprehend the enormity of our discovery.

Ralph understood, just as I did, and in that moment, I knew he had experienced the terrible thing I had, maybe several times, maybe many times.

In that secluded corner of the forest, as we marveled at the hidden riches before us, a growing feeling rumbled within me. Ralph and I shared a silent pact.

84

The moon was rising when Maître and Monsieur arrived at the weathered barn on the outskirts of the village. Their presence sent a shiver through the still night air as if a dark cloud had descended upon this remote corner of the world. Earlier in the day, I had plucked up the courage to approach Maître and tell him that my parents wanted to meet him and Monsieur in our barn at eight o'clock that evening, as they wanted to thank them. He'd smiled warmly and patted me gently on the head.

Maître, a tall and imposing figure, cut a sinister silhouette against the fading light. He moved with a predatory grace, each step echoing with a foreboding rhythm.

Beside him, Monsieur, a man of smaller stature, followed in lockstep. His features were shrouded in darkness, his presence like a shadowy specter that mirrored the headmaster's aura of menace.

They both stamped out their cigarettes before reaching the building.

As Maître and Monsieur opened the massive door to the

barn, the ancient timbers groaned in protest as though the very structure itself recoiled at their arrival.

Their footsteps echoed ominously as they ventured deeper into the cavernous space.

As I watched from my concealed vantage point, I sensed the weight of their presence.

I had become adept at navigating the space, even in the darkness. With each passing day, my fear had transformed into determination, and I had begun to devise a way to secure the barn door from the outside despite my small frame.

From the day of our arrival, I had noticed that the outside beam serving to lock the door was difficult to fix in place, leaving the door permanently open. Years of wear and neglect had caused it to become slightly dislodged from its designated slot in the barn door frame. I saw this vulnerability as an opportunity.

With a determined spirit and a youthful strength that belied my age, I had devised a way to use a makeshift lever fashioned from a discarded piece of wood to lift the heavy beam just enough to free it from its resting place and shift it into the metal frame designed to hold it. It was a daunting task requiring careful calculation and unflinching resolve.

Every day for three weeks, I had practiced my technique, perfecting my ability to manipulate the beam. I knew that the success of my plan hinged on precision and timing. The weight of the beam, combined with the risk of making noise that might alert Maître and Monsieur, added to the urgency of my mission.

Finally, after weeks of painstaking practice and heart-pounding attempts, I felt confident enough to execute my plan. The night was shrouded in darkness, the barn silent and still as I positioned myself before the heavy beam.

With a surge of adrenaline and a strength born of desperation, I applied pressure to the makeshift lever, slowly and steadily lifting the beam from its resting place and shifting it into the slot in the metal frame. The wood creaked and groaned in protest, but I persevered, my small frame straining with effort.

A sense of triumph and liberation washed over me as the beam finally became stuck in the frame. The barn door was now secured from the outside.

I then heard the two men inside try to dislodge it. I could hear their confusion and frustration as they pounded on the door, demanding to be set free. Their protests grew increasingly desperate, their voices echoing through the barn as they realized they were trapped.

My heart pounded like a drum in my chest. I ran as fast as I could, ascending the narrow outdoor, rusty staircase that led to the upstairs door, as my fear and determination battled for control.

As I reached the top, the door loomed before me—a rusted sentinel guarding the unknown. The hornet's nest, attached ominously to the corner of the hayloft, covered the door's entrance, its buzzing inhabitants floating around it.

My fingers, slick with sweat, trembled as I extended them toward the door. The rusted handle felt icy, sending a chill up my spine.

With a deep breath and a sense of trepidation, I turned the handle, the door groaning in protest as it budged by a few centimeters. That was all I needed, as the hornet's nest was lodged against the door. Already, a few of the bloated wasps were flying around outside.

Before me, I could see a slice of the nest, its papery exterior quivering with the restless movements of its occupants. The door had opened just a fraction, but the increased activity of the hornets and their proximity sent a surge of adrenaline coursing through my veins.

With my heart still pounding and my resolve unshaken, I carefully retrieved the long, rusty, serrated knife waiting for me on the top step. As the men began to bang on the door and shout, my heart still raced with trepidation. We were quite a way away from the canal and even further from the neighboring farms, but all they needed was one person wandering nearby, to compromise my plan.

With a trembling hand, I slid the serrated blade through the narrow slit between the door and its frame, the faint scrape of metal against metal sending shivers down my spine. I needed to be precise, for one wrong move could spell disaster.

As the blade made contact with the papery exterior of

the nest, I felt the tension in the air. The hornets within stirred, their buzzing growing more agitated.

With unwavering focus and a sense of urgency, I began to cut away at the hornet's nest. The serrated blade moved with a delicate precision.

The pain in my arm seemed to merge with my determination, becoming a driving force propelling me forward. With each cut, I could feel the nest's grip on the door frame loosening, inch by agonizing inch.

Finally, with one last, excruciating cut, the hornet's nest fell free from its perch, landing with a soft thud on the hay-strewn loft floor. My right arm throbbed with agony, the price of my defiance.

I felt a piercing pain in my chest. It was pain like I'd never felt before, but I managed not to scream, gasping silently. Then I heard the screams of the men within. It was too loud. I hadn't realized that that kind of pain could make grown men scream with such force.

Without hesitating, I pulled out the packet of Gitanes and matches I'd bought in the local épicerie weeks earlier, claiming they were for one of my parents' visitors. I struggled to light the match despite having practiced many times. I held the revolting-tasting fag between my lips and prepared to suck in the foul air as soon as I managed to light up, hands shaking. Finally, the match caught fire, and I lit the cigarette. I threw it through the slit in the door. Then I lit a second one and threw it inside. I did this until there were no more Gitanes left in the packet, and smoke was billowing from the building.

The screams began to subside as I hid in the bushes, waiting to see enough flames to ensure both men were dead. I would then lift the beam from the door again. But in what seemed like seconds, the entire building was ablaze, and it was impossible to reach the door without getting burnt, let alone remove the beam that locked the bodies inside.

I watched the barn burn in fear and fascination, an observer of a chilling tableau of justice that would remain etched in my brain for the rest of my life.

85

When my parents were taken in for questioning by the Toulouse police, another form of justice occurred to me. I remember that evening as if it were yesterday, even though it's been years. It was dusk, the kind that felt like it was holding its breath, as though the world was waiting for something to happen. The leaves underfoot whispered secrets with every step I took, as if they were telling me to turn back and abandon my audacious plan.

I moved through the forest like a shadow, heart pounding. I was even more nervous then, as the investigation was underway. We were under the care of a social worker and a gendarme for twenty-four hours. But they were drinking beer at the fire pit, content to keep an eye on Fergus, who was too young to be left alone, until it was time for us all to go to bed.

Every twig that snapped and every rustle of leaves felt like a betrayal, a reminder that I was a child navigating a world that was far too grown-up for me.

The hollow tree was my destination. It stood there like a grim sentinel, guarding the secrets Ralph had already unearthed. As I approached, the cold, metallic scent of fear hung in the air, and I felt a shiver run down my spine.

The money from the tree trunk, bundled in bin bags, was a weight I could barely carry. Each sack was filled with crumpled banknotes, a heavy reminder of the lies and deception that had torn my world apart. But I was determined and believed that by moving that chest, I could change my destiny.

With each step I took, the sacks grew heavier, their ties cutting into my small hands. The evening stretched endlessly, and I could feel the sweat on my brow mingled with dirt and grime. But I didn't stop; I couldn't stop. I was driven by a determination that defied my age once again.

As I reached the hole left by a fallen tree, I lowered the bags to the ground. I dropped to my knees. The earth felt cool and damp under my fingertips as I filled it in with loose earth.

Just as I heard the adults shouting for us to return, I saw Ralph hiding behind a large tree. In the moonlight's gentle embrace, he looked shocked and betrayed. I gasped. Then I beckoned him over, and we worked together. Working side by side, we toiled relentlessly, our fingers a blur of motion as they plunged into the earth. The earth surrendered reluctantly, but we were unyielding in our quest to conceal our burden.

Working together silently, we maneuvered some heavy logs above the grave. We shared a look, an unspoken understanding that we were no longer just children. And as we walked away, I knew my older brother wouldn't say a word. There was no one more loyal to me than Ralph.

As we made our way back to Whimsy, our clothes stained with dirt and sweat, I couldn't help but feel a sense of liberation. We had taken control of our destiny, defying the forces that had sought to imprison us, and the taste of revenge was sweet.

86

In my parents' desperation to find the culprit, they had turned to the villagers with accusing eyes, and the tension in our once-peaceful village grew palpable, forcing us to leave.

As the accusations and suspicions against Ralph emerged, I navigated a delicate dance of deceit and guilt. I knew he was holding onto the truth, guarding its secret, hoping that our actions would one day set us free, and knowing, deep down, that revealing the truth to my parents would result in severe punishment, and maybe even prison.

Years passed, and I couldn't know whether or not the money had been found. One day, Ralph disappeared, leaving no trace, and I assumed he had taken the money we'd stashed away that night. It seemed only fair, as he had been the family scapegoat, the one who had suffered the most, and been unfairly accused because of me.

Curiosity got the better of me, however, and when I was eighteen, working as a waitress to sustain myself, I decided to see if I could find the money.

When I arrived in Biffière-sur-Garonne, I felt an old nostalgia mixed with unease. I looked completely different, athletic and short-haired, so I was confident no one would recognize me. But I was careful nonetheless, and after locating the mossy pile of logs beneath the fallen tree during a daytime hike, I returned at dusk, performing a reversal of the operation I'd completed seven years earlier.

The cash was all there. All of it. Hundreds of thousands of euros and pounds.

I'd worked out how much I would need to get through university and pay a downpayment on a small flat in London. I put aside a slightly larger amount for Ralph. The rest, the bulk of the money, I put into envelopes and proceeded to locate the eleven foster children whose souls had been crushed by my family. I found all but one child, now adults, survivors, and ensured they received the money individually.

The one child I could not compensate was Ludovic, who had died of cancer at the age of twenty. The knowledge that his short life had known no respite was what relieved me of most of the guilt I felt for my family.

Now, here, on this empty seaweed-strewn beach, I am becoming aware that the weight of the secrets I have kept for so long have become an ever-present burden, a heavy anchor that has held me back from living a life unencumbered by the past. With each passing year, the need to tell my story, to unburden myself, has grown stronger and stronger.

The secrets have gnawed at me from within like a relentless storm that refused to abate. They have haunted my dreams and tainted my waking hours.

The need to speak my truth, to reveal the darkness that once defined our lives, has become a constant presence in my thoughts.

I have yearned to tell my story, to share the pain and the secrets that have shaped my life. I know that only by shedding light on the hidden truths can I hope to find some semblance of redemption and healing.

The years have not dulled the urgency of my need to speak out. If anything, they have sharpened it, honed it into a relentless determination to confront the past and the consequences of my actions.

Ben believed I was weak, and that got him killed. I am no victim. I'm a survivor. Of course, officially, I'll have to stick to the self-defense story, which may not be easy. But maybe I'll find some other way of telling the full story of Emiliah Bent. And who knows, maybe one day you'll read it?

ACKNOWLEDGMENTS

I would first like to thank my brother Dominic, not just for his contributions to this novel, but for being such a decent human being, despite everything he's been through. I love you, *Frérot*. I wouldn't know the meaning of bravery without you.

I extend my heartfelt thanks to Claire Blin, an old friend and true warrior, whose contributions to The Story of Emiliah Bent were invaluable.

To my friend Gillian, who generously dedicated her personal time to edit the (terrible) first draft and provided crucial feedback—thank you for your patience and insight.

I am forever grateful to my editor, Paige Lawson, whose meticulous eye and unwavering commitment elevated this work beyond my wildest expectations.

A big merci to Alexis Saez, who skillfully transformed my rough sketches into a stunning cover design. Your patience in making every change until it perfectly matched my vision is deeply appreciated.

To Noëlle: everything changed when you came into my

life, and I hope our journey together continues for a long time to come.

I must also thank the wonderful people who inspired or supported me along the way. First and foremost, Betty Crowther, who changed my life. Sandrine, my oldest and dearest friend, has always supported me unconditionally, even when I lost my way. Frances, thank you for helping me understand what it means to be a mother. To Ruth, Keith, and Ian, thank you for your love.

I am also grateful to all the friends I've had over the years—some of whom I neglected while focusing on my writing—but whose friendship I will always cherish, even from afar: Lydia, Eulalie-Emilie, Evan, Lara, Christophe, Deborah, Lee, Sylvaine, Josiane, Nelly, Sylvie A, Myriam, Elodie, Sylvie C, Léa, Sophie, Elidger, Valéry, Walter, Romuald, Christian, Léonore, the Choupachups, the Rebelles, Antoine, Hervé and Anja.

Thank you to Max and Chloé for your love and patience.

I will be eternally grateful to Emile, who shared his extensive experience of psychiatric institutions, providing key insights that were critical to this work.

To my writing partner and dear friend Florence, whose writing is so much better than mine: merci!

A special thanks to Stéphane and Irina Lavallée, whose support during my darkest days meant the world to me.

I am also deeply grateful to my parents for instilling in me a love of the written word.

Finally, to all the difficult people I've encountered over the years: thank you for providing me with such precise content for my writing.

The following sources were invaluable to me in researching domestic and child abuse. While there are many more out there, these titles were particularly helpful:

All of HG Tudor's books.

Complex PTSD, from surviving to thriving, by Pete Walker

Will I Ever Be Good Enough? (English Edition), by Karyl McBride

Bringing your shadow out of the dark, by Robert Augustus Masters

Malignant Self-love: Narcissism Revisited (10th edition, 2015) (English Edition), by Sam Vaknin

The Body Never Lies (English Edition), by Alice Miller

The Truth Will Set You Free: Overcoming Emotional Blindness and Finding Your True Adult Self (English Edition), by Alice Miller